MW01131154

Margie Walker

Stolen Moments

by

Margie R. Walker

ISBN-13

978-1492167990

An Images & Expressions Novel Production

DEDICATION

This work is dedicated to the women and men who aspire and work toward ending the cycles of physical, sexual and emotional abuse to create strong individuals and loving families.

Prologue

May 27ᵗʰ

The sounds of electronic saxophone and trumpets opened the final number in the set and filled the night air with song.

A repertoire of lively, up-tempo music had been selected for this occasion, a gala reception, for an audience composed of business, art and museum representatives from Houston to Galveston, dressed in after-five finery.

Even after an hour of playing, Helen retained the sense of foreboding that struck her the instant she boarded the *Henrietta Marie*.

Perhaps she could blame an over active imagination; after all, the refurbished slave ship that had been raised almost thirty years ago held many destitute lives even though she only survived two trips as a slave-trading vessel.

Helen tried to lose herself in the last number the band played, "Shining Star," by Earth, Wind & Fire.

Covering the track in a jazzy version were Mike Holstrum on keyboards, Eddie Gonzales on bass, Arthur Taylor on drums, while she played lead guitar.

Known as the Advocates - - although none of them would quit their day jobs –the four band members were all practicing attorneys who supported the arts. Their philanthropy extended to playing gigs such as this one.

As her fingers glided over the nylon strings of her instrument, Helen sang the chorus line with the group. "Shining star for you to see ..." they chorused before Eddie took the first solo, leading the ensemble. Each of them would solo before the end of the song.

The number was a tribute to the *Henrietta Marie*, which had been completely renovated to her original 17th century appearance. New wood stained to look decades old, flashy white sails that suggested her sailing prowess, with an added touch of grand lighting strung along the rafters that lit the night like day were in perpetual evidence.

Still, the *Henrietta Marie* was a slave ship, and her new face and body didn't change her insidious history.

The finale, "Shining star for you to see ..." accompanied the last notes each musician played. They received by no means a thunderous response, but an appreciative one. Between handshakes and hugs, they congratulated each other. Helen hugged each one of them separately.

"Thanks so much," she repeated to each member because she solicited his support for this fund-raising reception.

"You know you're welcome," the drummer said. "Now, point me in the direction of the food."

"That way," she replied, pointing to a far corner of the room.

Teasing the drummer good-naturedly, the rest of the band followed the direction of her finger, ambling off to the elaborate banquet.

With her hands on her hips, Helen scouted the crowd, looking for her cousin, Marcellus Cavanaugh among the 300 guests. A barrel-chested man, standing well over six-feet, towering over most; hence, he wasn't usually difficult to spot. His company, CavWell Space Industries, (CSI) along with several others, was responsible for bringing the *Henrietta Marie* to Galveston. The traveling exhibit was costly for the month it was in town, May 27th to June 27th.

Thinking Marcellus could have gone below, a knot of reluctance formed in her throat. She gave up on finding him, deciding instead to grab a little to eat before she drove back to Houston to pick up her daughter, Elaina from her godmother's, and then head home and get ready for her court appearance in the morning.

"Hello, Helen. It's good seeing you."

Helen froze, startled by the familiar, cantabile voice, and then turned facing the tall, good-looking man in her path. Six feet on a slim, muscular frame, she stared into a face she hadn't seen in person for years, a man she deliberately avoided. Her heart ran away with her breath. "Ray," she replied, swallowing.

Photos of him appeared in the newspapers as he was an active and sometimes combative politician, but she never lingered over them. Now, her gaze scouted his countenance, noting that he looked tired around the eyes, and older than the 43 years she knew him to be.

"It's been a long time."

No one would guess by the formality between her and Houston City Councilman Ray Butler that they even knew each other, when they were once engaged to be married. But that was years ago, ten in fact, Helen reminded herself as if to retard the quake coursing through her.

He looked at her with a dark, sensual stare full of appreciation that roved her body. "You're looking as lovely as ever," he said in that same ceremonial tone that belied the way he was eyeballing her.

"I'm glad to see that hasn't changed, with all of the other changes I'm sure you've made in your life."

Helen swallowed the bile emotions she felt that replaced her earlier anxiety and merely looked at him with a placid smile pasted on her face.

She knew she looked good in the black leather ensemble with four-inch heels that she only wore when performing. "I hear you're running for mayor in the next election."

He tilted his head to the side. "I hope I can count on your vote," he replied, grinning at her.

Before Helen could utter a non-committal reply, a young woman in a red, chiffon dress, burst upon them, her thin voice full of chatter. "Hi," she gushed, her expression a profusion of teeth. "You must be Helen. I've heard so much about you.

"I'm Joann, Ray's wife."

Helen looked at Ray, who looked at her with his politician's smile, a hint of pride in his eyes. No doubt for his young wife, she thought, guessing the woman was in her mid twenties. Although overly made up, she had a cute, heart-shaped face, and the complexion that wore red well.

"Joann," she said as she shook hands. "It's nice meeting you." She eased her hands behind her back.

"My daughter, Taylor …"

"Hey, Helen …"

The male voice calling her name effectively cut off whatever Joann intended to say. Helen looked around and spotted Marcellus, who was beckoning her to where he stood next to a couple near the bow of the ship. "Excuse me," she said to Ray and his wife.

"We're going to have to get together sometimes," Joann said.

"Sure thing," Helen lied as she sauntered away.

Thanks to the technology that provided Caller ID, she had no intention of taking a call from Joann Butler, she thought, respiring a long sigh of gratitude to her cousin. She didn't even care who he wanted her to meet, she chuckled, noticing the tall, light skinned balding man and a sister in a purple and gold African ensemble.

"Helen Parker," Marcellus said as he draped an arm around her shoulder and pulled her next to him. " I want you to meet Dr. Jules Jolivet and his sister, Baderinwa Jolivet.

"Jules is an archeologist and one of the black divers who worked with the Mel Fisher society to create the Henrietta Marie exhibition. Baderinwa was instrumental in securing funds to bring it here."

"It's a pleasure, Dr. Jolivet," Helen said graciously as she shook each of their hands. "The work you and others have done in excavation and research is invaluable," she directed to him. "Congratulations." To Baderinwa, she added, "We're indebted for all your help."

"Congratulations to you, too," Baderinwa chimed. "You and the others are very accomplished musicians. We enjoyed the music very much."

Helen noted she had a soft, eloquent voice, with a Louisiana French accent and a calming demeanor. "Thank you," she replied with a brief obsequious bow, thinking that she liked this woman.

"I hate Sean couldn't make it," Marcellus said conversationally to the brother and sister. Explaining to Helen, "Sean King is the third of the company's trio of owners."

"Sean is stuck in Africa," Jules said. He had a commanding voice, with a tiny trace of accent like that of his sister's. "He doesn't know how much longer it's going to take before he can wrap up this project."

Helen nodded, although she didn't have a clue about whom they spoke.

"Hopefully, he'll make it back by the Juneteenth celebration," Marcellus said.

"When have you ever known Sean to miss a party?" Jules replied teasingly.

"I know he's going to hate that he missed tonight," Baderinwa said, looking directly at Helen. "Are you planning to attend?"

"She better be there," Marcellus threatened her playfully, tapping the tip of her nose.

Helen couldn't help but wonder if her cousin was up to his matchmaking tricks again. "Marcellus," she said looking at him with a squinted gaze and a warning growl in her throat.

Chapter One

June 18th

The peculiar scent of death bulletined the solemn march to the second bedroom.

Dr. Sean King led the parade of a three-member team of Houston Police Department (HPD) homicide investigators. Actually, he was assigned to them. Each carrying his particular paraphernalia, with feet and hands gloved in plastic, they were on their way to the second body.

Neither an exceptionally big man, nor small, the street-clothes wearing cops -- who carried two hundred pounds or more apiece -- dwarfed his muscled, six feet, 180 pound medium frame. Further setting him apart was his company's uniform, a nylon khaki jumpsuit, with Artifacts, Inc. emblem emblazoned in black, gold and maroon on his left breast pocket, outfitted with many more pockets of all sizes to contain small forensic tools. A small can of Vicks resided in one on his right thigh.

Although June had arrived, it was already hotter than July. While cooler downstairs, the upstairs temperature hovered in the nineties: the heat magnified the fetid stench.

Sean however eschewed suppressing the incredibly rancid smell by any number of tricks used by law enforcement personnel: it was part of the scenery of death. His mind hoarded the data collected, and his senses reached out to amass more as he captured fresh images with his digital video camera to review later.

The Butlers were remodeling their modern, two-story home where they were also in residence. A colonial built in the 50's, it was one of the few homes on the block that survived the duplex craze.

Several closed doors lined the spacious hallway, topped by a brown-beaded, threadbare beige carpet. It was where he and the team now tread, carefully scrutinizing form and substance in search of evidence.

Someone had vacuumed. Not for the first time, Sean wondered by whom and when.

Layers of different decor tastes showed on the stripped walls, leaving traces of a burgundy wisteria wallpaper of velvet and paint the color of lemon. There were demarcations of pictures that hanged no more. A string, indicating access to the attic fell from the ceiling's peeling, textured white paint.

No perpetrator hid over their heads it had been previously confirmed; only insulation and wiring for the air conditioner, which was as silent as it was ineffective, remained.

It was late Friday afternoon, and Sean couldn't help

thinking the situation he found himself in ironic. There had been no time to think upon his arrival earlier hours ago now. He had simply fallen into routine, examining the first gruesome scene of death.

He only returned to Houston this morning following five months in Africa, of which two of them were spent in the same country. He was looking forward to a long, overdue rest, while contributing to his company's co-sponsoring of a cultural project that was more therapy than work.

He was just about to settle down for the evening when he received a call from his dear friend and former college professor who was currently the county's medical examiner. She needed his help. For him that could only mean one thing. Or so, he'd thought.

The victims he normally served were but remains and their identity unknown until he unraveled the mystery of their bones. While this was not a typical assignment, it was not out of line of what he did for a living as a forensic anthropologist who specialized in cultural crimes.

With the influx of foreigners who brought their own unique brands of killing to American soil, the police often needed the expertise he possessed. But this crime seemed the basic garden-variety style, even though the lives taken here were African American, the operative word was American.

Discerning from what he'd been told, as soon as the police realized the identities of the victims - - Joann and Taylor Butler, the wife and daughter of City Councilman Ray Butler - - a decision was made to call in an outside expert to oversee the initial forensic aspects of the case.

Ray Butler, also the Mayor Pro Tem, had been a thorn in the police department's side, and had had a number of run-ins with both the police chief and the medical examiner. Although all parties were African American, Butler had publicly called them "Oreos."

Sean felt them terribly foolish, for it was quite obvious they were more concerned with covering their asses - - fearing possible accusations of impropriety or incompetence from Butler - - than solving the crime.

It was nothing more than politics, which had a way of creating disharmony in police work. Maybe because it shared a thing or two in common with murder: all too often, no one could explain why.

At least he had detected no animosity from Sgt. Diamond or any of the HPD team of investigators. Even though all the good guys wanted the same thing, such a situation was not unheard of when an outsider was brought in to work on a case where the local police possessed clear jurisdiction.

Still, he realized each had a turf, real or imagined, to protect, and his awareness of ego went a long way to keep tensions down in the ranks.

He knew all too well what happened when his efforts didn't work: the bad guys won the advantage by default.

Reaching their destination, Sean halted on the threshold of a young girl's bedroom, and his followers pulled up in a dead stop behind him. While there were no wreaths of fruit or garlic, no clay dolls or cow's heart, or any of the condiments of a ritual killing in sight, looking in and spotting her, his whole body tightened. His breath locked in his chest.

The expression on Taylor Butler's cute baby face was contorted in such agony he could only imagine. She died crying, for even from this distance, he thought he could detect the track of tears that stained her bloodless cheeks.

Sean shook the image from his head as sadness seized his expression. Desire for revenge impinged upon his subconscious.

If he ever got his hands on the murderous bastard who did this, he would gladly save the state - - infamously known as the execution capitol of the world - - the expense of lethal injection.

"Doc . . .?"

Goaded into action, Sean lifted the portable video camera and spoke into the microphone attached to the recorder in one of his pockets. "Taylor Butler; Age, 11; Sex, Female; Ethnicity, African American; Stature, Small."

He still spoke with the lilting, lyrical traces of his Creole heritage in his voice. Born into a lineage that married Crillos and

Africanos, enslaved Africans from the colonies with those directly from Africa, he had been raised to value life and accept death. Sometimes the latter was hard on the soul, making the former appear out of reach. But with a job to do, he put the matter out of his mind and resumed recording, all the while speaking into the microphone.

"No signs of a struggle. Probably no indentations of value," he said, squatting for a closer perusal of the carpet. "Looks like someone has vacuumed. When? Check to see if the Butlers have a maid."

The pictures of the room done, Sean aimed the camera onto the bed and its lifeless occupant. "Déshonorer sur vous, la Mort. Déshonorer sur moi si je vous permettez d'obtiens loin impuni," he whispered, *Shame on you, Monsieur Death. Shame on me if I let you get away unpunished*, still staring at the little girl, his jaw chiseled in determination.

"Dr. King . . . ?"

Sean looked over his shoulder to see Sgt. Paul Diamond who headed up the investigation team still standing outside the room. He'd forgotten all about their presence, waiting to do their parts to catch a killer, or killers. Wordless, he nodded permission for them to enter and returned his attention to little Taylor Butler.

With clinical detachment, he placed the camera in his pocket and exchanged his gloves for a fresh pair. Approaching the bed, he softly said, "I'm going to take care of you now, bébé."

His French inaudible, he promised silently, *"Vieux Sean est soin de prise de gonna bon de vous."*

Chapter Two

Water flowed continuously from the high arc swivel spout of the pewter faucet, blocking the din of pitiful sobs in the fashionable bathroom.

This was not how she intended to start her busman's holiday, Helen mused, as she splashed water from her cupped hands onto her face.

She had been looking forward to today all week long when she could put the Susan Westermans and Claire Jacksons, past and present clients, out of her mind.

This Friday was reserved for drinks and fun and family and friends. Not death and murder.

Those insidious elements of life were for people whose stories made the evening news, people who were so far removed from her life that she could sympathize comfortably.

Joann Butler made damn sure that she would attend her death like an audience member with a front row seat, she thought, staring at her teary eyed reflection in the mirror above the sink. On the drive to her cousin's home, she heard about the horrible deaths on the radio. Joann and her young daughter, Taylor, were found murdered in their home.

Pulling a towel from the rack, Helen recalled that she

just made it to the bathroom in time before the guilt overwhelmed her. Drying her face, she had to consider that she was exhausted even before the news, for such an outburst was wholly uncharacteristic of her. Typically, she maintained a firm control over her emotions.

While she was not a friend of the dead women or her child, she knew them. Still, the tears she shed were not so much for them as they were her own guilt, a fact, which compounded her culpability. Joann Butler left several urgent messages at her office. Calls she deliberately had not returned.

As a sigh of regret respired across her bosom, Helen removed the ensemble she had worn to work earlier today. Stripped to panties and bra, she then traipsed to the closet in the adjoining bedroom where the lush, thick aqua carpet caressed her bare feet.

Dropping brown pumps onto the floor, she tossed pantyhose and the burnt orange business suit over a hanger, hoping to discard her doleful feelings as easily.

Quiet, cool, and dark, the room was one of several lavish guest rooms of the Cavanaugh's' mansion-size home in Clear Lake, roughly 20 miles south of Houston near NASA.

Over the next couple of days, she and Elaina would

live like royalty in the wonderfully dramatic room, with its rich aqua walls and curtains to match that blocked out the light at will.

Complementing the queen bed were a curvaceous rosewood headboard and a West African strip-woven spread of geometric patterns. On the side of the bed nearest the door, sat a round decorative table that held a slim, brass lamp and small black square clock. An old time rocking chair with a footstool rested on the other side of the bed.

Discontentment and self-castigation aside, Helen moved with the grace instilled by etiquette lessons from childhood. One of the advantages of being raised by parents with money to spend on frivolities; although her adoptive parents weren't, and neither was the child they raised. Quite the opposite, she was a determined woman, bent on achieving a perfect posture in all aspects of her life.

It wasn't always as easy as keeping her chin up, she grumbled silently, as she began transferring the contents of her overnight bag to a drawer in the waist-high dresser and half-moon mirror. With her expression steeped in a frown of determination to ignore her unexpected discomfort, she grabbed her makeup kit and headed back for the bathroom to restore her makeup.

Someone knocked on the door, and she froze. "Yes?"

"It's me."

Hearing her hostess' voice, Helen dropped the kit on the bed and patted her cheeks, which she knew had lost their luster, making way for bright contentment in her expression, and pulled a robe from the dresser drawer. "Come in," she said, slipping into the robe.

Looking every bit the elegant lady of the house in a silk caftan pant set in brown and white, Pauline Cavanaugh sauntered in, carrying a tall glass, garnished with a maraschino cherry and pineapple wedge. "Here's a little something to help you unwind."

"Oh, bless you," Helen said enthusiastically. She freed Pauline of the glass to drink her first sip. A pina colada with a kick. She licked her lips, sighing, "Hmm. This is delicious." And exactly what she needed.

Her cousin, Marcellus married a beauty, both inside and out, in Pauline. They were regrettably not as close as Helen would have liked, but it wasn't Pauline's fault.

A nurse by training, Pauline possessed a warm, genuine aura, with keen, sensitive eyes that missed nothing. It made for guarded moments between them, even though Helen genuinely liked Pauline.

"You look a little pale," Pauline said, eyeing her critically. "Are you all right?"

"Sinuses, that's all," Helen replied, sniffing. "A couple more swallows of this," she added, holding up her glass, "and I won't feel a thing, and you'll know where my red eyes come from."

"The pollen count is unusually high now, so let me know if you need anything," Pauline replied, obviously satisfied with Helen's response as she sat on the side of the bed. "Your daughter is with Brittany and Julie at the Winters' home, by the way."

"Aw, the neighbors around the corner," Helen said, bobbing her head with recollection as she swallowed another sip.

For once she was grateful that her daughter had been self-absorbed and talking to a friend on the cell when the news bulletin about Joann and Taylor Butler came on. Once they arrived, Elaina hadn't even bothered to unpack; her overnight case was still in a corner on the floor.

"Where are the boys? I haven't heard them? Is it nap time?" Helen asked as she set her drink on the dresser to shove her overnight under the bed. Five and three, respectively, Marc and Paul were a pair of handsome young devils, magnets to trouble.

Chuckling, Pauline replied, "Grandma and Granddaddy are probably wishing it were. They'll bring them home tonight, or tomorrow."

"And where is my crazy cousin?" Helen asked, opening her kit on the dresser. "I expected him to be locked away in his chef's hut barbecuing."

"Marcellus had to run to Galveston," Pauline answered, crossing her legs in a yoga style. "Some last minute minor crisis came up with the *Henrietta Marie* exhibit."

While Pauline prattled on about the minor problems Marcellus encountered getting the exhibit to Texas, his high expectations for its success, Helen perched before the mirror to restore her make-up, occasionally stopping to take a sip of her drink.

"Enough about that," Pauline said with a airy wave of her hand. "How are you? How's your blood pressure?" Pauline asked, changing the subject as she examined Helen from head to toe with her gaze.

"Aww, don't start on me," Helen moaned as she chuckled. She eased into the rocking chair, careful with her drink. She propped her feet on the footstool.

"A little more weight wouldn't hurt you, either," Pauline said.

Pauline was coke-bottle fine compared to her model slim body. "Hell, we all can't be a brick-house like you."

"Stop being a smart-mouth. I'm serious, Helen. You've got to start taking better care of yourself."

"Damn, Pauline, I'm doing the best I can. As soon as I find a partner, I'm going to take a **real** vacation, moderate my schedule, and live a life of hope," she added dramatically. "In fact, I'm planning a short vacation in two weeks."

Helen did envy the pampered look of Pauline's smooth, golden brown complexion, and the graceful ease in which she carried herself. She strove to achieve a similar balance in her life. A *but* hung at the end of her wish.

"Bring me up to date, but I don't need to hear about your practice. I can tell business is booming by your tale tell marks of exhaustion."

Next to Elaina, work was the best thing in her life. Her music followed, but she enjoyed the law better than she had teaching. "It is, I'm happy to report."

She spoke animatedly about her practice, her plans for moving to another office, enticing a criminal attorney to join her practice, and her recent new hire of a computer expert. It was more than work; it was her salvation, where she could see the proof of her achievement, feel a sense of pride.

It was only in her dreams where her life was different, but that was her secret to keep.

When she finished, she felt as if Pauline issued a straight-no-chaser, asking, "What about your personal life that doesn't have anything to do with work or Elaina?"

"I'm fine," Helen said, shrugging her shoulders. Pauline's concern for her welfare mirrored those of her parents', Candace and James Parker, who lived in Virginia. They too had a solid, loving marriage. Despite the distance, they dropped the occasional hint that she should think about getting back on the dating horse. She let them think it was possible.

Pauline sighed, feinting exasperation. "Is there a man you're taking your sweet time telling me about?"

Helen flashed a secretively smile, a teasing prevarication. Her love life was composed of composites of men drawn from her imagination or borrowed from tales told by other women she knew.

Her lies hurt no one, she thought flippantly. "Malik Yoba has been appearing in my dreams lately."

They both burst out laughing.

"Oh my, you have been falling asleep while watching reruns," Pauline teased.

Helen replied with an uttering of humor. "That about sums it up. I haven't had the time to even think about it." Nor the inclination, she thought as she spoke with a facile conviction that was not true.

"And quite frankly," she continued, "I really don't

miss the hassles of getting involved in a relationship." Honestly speaking, the thought of a relationship scared her to death.

Still, she hoped that would put an end to the subject, for she hated lying to Pauline about the men in her life. Experience taught her, however, that a lie was better than the truth.

"Hell, if he comes easy . . ." Pauline was saying.

Helen cut her off, stating, "I know."

"He's probably not worth it," they chorused together, chuckling.

Everybody knew a good man was hard to find. It was a safe excuse. Helen only wondered how much longer she could keep the false bubble of contentment in her countenance from bursting.

"What happened to that stock broker you were dating earlier in the year? What was his name? You said he had rabbit ears."

"Richard," Helen said, plucking a name from her memory. "Richard Davis."

Pauline frowned. "I thought Richard was last year's bad news," she said puzzled.

Helen squirmed inwardly. She felt like a criminal caught in her own lie. "Oh yeah," she said, snapping her fingers. "You're right. Mark. His name was Mark Stone." Hell, she'd made up so many names, even she was getting them confused. "So now you know what happened to him."

"Don't give up hope," Pauline said. "There's somebody out there for you."

"I'm fine, really," Helen said assuredly, backing up her tone with a look. "Elaina is all I need. And neither of us needs a man in our life."

"Elaina is too young for a man," Pauline retorted.

"Please tell me that Marcellus is not trying to hook me up," she said.

"I've warned him about that," Pauline replied laughing. "But I don't know of any plan he concocted."

Helen nodded, pleased to hear that. General girl talk was safe, and she decided to become a victim to the alcohol in her drink. She began to rock gently in the chair, and slowly, her head began to clear.

"I know you've heard about Ray Butler. Isn't it incredible about his family?"

Helen stopped the chair, then resumed rocking, not as gently as before. "It's the talk of the town," she said somberly.

Helen's expression darkened with memory that she had not returned Joann Butler's calls to her office. That she could have somehow prevented the deaths was a muse she'd struggled to suppress ever since she learned of the murders. Unconsciously gnawing her bottom lip, she knew it was only a matter of time before the police contacted her, eager to know the answer to a question she had no answer for.

"Did you know his wife?"

"I met her once, but I didn't know her," she said, hoping to end all queries in that direction.

"Weren't you engaged to her husband, the councilman, at one time?"

Here we go, Helen thought, her body taut as a tightrope. She chided herself for not anticipating the subject's rebirth beforehand. It was inevitable that Ray Butler would crop up in the conversation. "A lifetime ago," she replied as much for herself as Pauline.

Pauline raised a curious brow at Helen. "Don't tell me the flame flickers on."

Denial wouldn't exonerate her, and agreement would be met with scorn. Regardless her answer, Helen knew she faced a no-win situation. "I don't want to talk about it, Pauline." Even her neutral tone would be suspect.

In the extra beat of silence that lingered, Helen felt a twitch of anxiety ripple across her bosom. The talk about murder awakened another concern. While there had been no reports of domestic violence implicated in the deaths of Joann Butler and her daughter, she knew it could be a real problem for her most recent client.

She hoped she wouldn't live to regret not getting a restraining order for Howard Jackson, although Claire assured her one wouldn't be needed.

"All right, enough seriousness," Pauline interjected, unfolding her legs. "This is supposed to be a pleasant, restful weekend, remember?"

Helen remembered all right; she just wasn't so sure any longer about the pleasant, restful part.

Chapter Three

It was a near perfect evening.

Stars twinkled high in the dark, purple muted sky, dancing to the sounds of contemporary jazz playing from inside the Cavanaugh house. The delicious aroma of barbecue smoking in hickory wood, which Marcellus was preparing for tomorrow's meal, added to the excitement of the pre-holiday commemoration. Lanterns surrounding the patio provided more than ample light for Donald Wellsing, Marcellus' business partner and a non-drinker, to keep a close eye on the children playing in the pool.

The content of the alcohol multiplied by several drinks massaged Helen's central nervous system, loosening tensed muscles and pushing heavy thoughts away. Stretched out in a lounge chair, another drink at her fingertips, she listened with half a mind attending the cheerful squeals of the children playing in the pool and less than that to the adult conversation around her.

"The *Henrietta Marie* never made it to Galveston. It sank off the coast of Florida in 1700, almost a hundred years before slavery began in Texas."

"And that pisses you off . . . that the *Henrietta Marie* didn't drop any of her precious cargo in Galveston?" another guest said, emphasizing "precious cargo" snidely.

Laughter followed from the dozen or so of swimsuit clad adults, friends and co-workers of Pauline and Marcellus, part of their personal guests for tomorrow's jaunt to the *Henrietta Marie*. Helen sat among them, clustered in lounge chairs at the far end of the pool, closest to the waterfall that made the heat bearable. Or maybe, the bearable part was attributable to the potent pina coladas she had been consuming ever since she arrived.

"As far as I'm concerned, General Granger showed up a hundred years too late," another said sarcastically.

"His time in history hadn't come yet," Helen reminded the guest, her voice lazy with her rum based cocktail.

"Even when it did," the most talkative among them said, "he was still two years and six months too late with the news."

On the eve of Juneteenth - - as the state holiday was known - - the *Henrietta Marie* exhibit and slavery dominated the conversation as they celebrated the history of freedom granted enslaved Africans via the Emancipation Proclamation.

Signed by then President Lincoln, January 1, 1863, the news that was delivered by Gen. Granger didn't reach Texas until June 19, 1865. Galveston, then known as the "Queen City of the Gulf" was pivotal in both events, past and present.

"I read somewhere that some Africans were in partnership with the European slave traders, " Donald's wife, Sarah added hesitantly.

The remark provided the perfect opening for the gregarious aficionado of all things, Leonard Scott. "That made them equally culpable in its perpetuation. And for the same almighty dollar. Only they traded us off for some damn beads.

"Since we didn't have any brotherly love back then, I guess it's too much to expect us to have it now," he concluded, his tone suddenly diffident with shame and sorrow.

"What do you mean by that?"

It was the first time since the conversation veered toward slavery that one of the Asian guests spoke. Introduced as Karen Kwan to Helen, she was a biochemist, who worked at Marcellus and Donald's space technology company, CSI.

"I'm talking about black-on-black crime. Look at what happened to that sister and her daughter."

"You're talking about the Butlers," another guest added. "Ray Butler's wife and daughter."

"The little girl wasn't his child."

"It doesn't matter," Leonard piped hastily with anger in his voice. "A brother, a black man killed that woman and that little girl."

Helen sighed at length. She had no interest in discussing the deaths of Ray Butler's family or hearing pseudo-criminologists, hypothesizing the identity of the killer.

Even though she covered her face with the sombrero she'd borrowed from Pauline, she couldn't hide from her culpability.

"I'd bank on him myself."

"Who? Ray Butler? Come on."

"It only stands to reason . . ."

She would have preferred continuing their previous topic of conversation. Murder, however, was news; slavery, old history. While easier on the emotional palate, murder was no less sinister than slavery.

"Normally, I would agree, but remember he's a politician. He wouldn't do anything so stupid as to jeopardize his career."

"That never stopped a fool before."

Unfortunately, Helen thought, her lounge chair was right in the middle of their conversation as she lifted her hat to take a sip of her drink. She felt as if she was paying penance for some unknown crime: maybe she could have been more sympathetic toward Susan Westerman, or more persistent with Claire Jackson. Or, returned Joann Butler's call.

"Wow! That sounds personal."

"Well, I admit, I don't like Ray Butler."

"Why? Because his eyes are too close together?"

The retort brought laughter from the group, and a quiet snort from Helen. She knew Ray Butler better than any of them.

Well, that wasn't entirely true. When a man practically abandons you at the altar, it means you don't know him as well as you thought.

Helen wondered how could she have been so blind about him; she closed her eyes as if it would black out the memory.

The persistent talk about Ray acted like a key, unlocking the past she had worked so hard to bury, forcing her to remember 10 years ago.

Ray had been an energetic community activist when they met. In her first year of law school then, she was attracted by his drive and ambition. He had a plan for his future, with an interest for and in the African American community. Within two months of dating, they both believed that she would have a role in it.

She was a 23-year old virgin at the time, which he found intriguing: he had seemed quite proud actually. It must have worn off, because the pressure began about a few weeks before the wedding, after invitations were mailed, her gown made, and the church rented. Her parents spent a mint.

Ray got it in his head that they should sleep together. Since they were getting married, it didn't matter, he had argued. She countered that since they had waited that long, what could a few more days hurt? But he was charming if nothing else, and …

"Mama, can I get my hair cut?"

The hat was lifted from Helen's face. She was actually relieved by the intrusion from her 12-year-old daughter. Two other girls, neighbor's kids of the same age, accompanied Elaina, called 'Butterscotch' in private, for it was both her favorite candy and the color of her skin.

Wearing bathing suits that scared fathers to death, they looked like little wet sirens. Not exactly little as in small, for Elaina was almost as tall as she, already 5'3" and still growing, but guileless.

Helen flashed a mock glare at Elaina. "May I?" she corrected.

"Mom!"

Helen identified the cry as the *"don't correct me wail."* She smiled to herself.

"Ple . . . ease."

"All those syllables," Helen said, shaking her head with a tsk-tsk. She gazed sidelong up into Elaina's perfectly oval face, brown eyes shining like diamonds with her eagerness.

A pinhead of joy burst in her bosom, spreading motherly pride through her. Elaina normally wore her long, wavy black hair braided and twisted in a ball at the top of her head, seldom down as it was now, hanging to her waist. Pretending to be annoyed, she asked, "Do we have to do this now?"

"Mom!" Elaina whined as she usually did when she couldn't get her way. "Please."

No. Helen refrained issuing the impetuous thought on her tongue. Instead, she replied, "Let me think about it."

"You got five minutes," Elaina replied, before she and friends ran off and dived in the pool.

Helen replaced her sombrero and crossed her ankles. She adopted Elaina, who was born to a Hispanic mother and African American father, when Elaina was seven five years ago. It felt as if they'd been mother and daughter forever as their relationship was quite typical.

"Don't sweat the small stuff."

That had been her mother's philosophy, Helen recalled fondly, and she tried daily to make it hers.

She remembered that her parents once feared she wanted to adopt a child for the wrong reasons when she announced her intentions to them, for it happened after she and Ray had broken up.

They didn't attempt to stop her, guessing and no doubt hoping she would change her mind during the lengthy process from application to actual adoption.

They should have known better. The only mind changing came in her initial request to the adoption agency for a black male child.

It was practically love at first sight when she and Elaina saw each other during the picnic-like open house. After shadowing Helen for hours, they shared lunch, and then the chubby little darling climbed into her lap and promptly fell asleep.

"Have you decided, yet?" Elaina asked, lifting the hat from Helen's face.

"You're back already?" she pouted, recalling her mother's words: *"Don't sweat the small stuff. Wait until she starts her period, falls in love and gets her heart broken, or simply decides she wants a car, her own apartment, and freedom, whatever the hell that is."*

Since Elaina had started her cycle, Helen knew the rest wasn't far off. She was looking forward to it. "Be my guest," she replied, a pleasant secret alight in her smile.

"I'm not. I just wanted to see what you were going to say," Elaina giggled impishly, before scampering off to rejoin her friends in the pool.

Helen chuckled softly, replaced the hat over her face, and squired into the lounge chair, seeking the comfortable position she had before the interruption. She noticed the conversation had steered to punishment. Having convicted Ray Butler, the jury of public sentiment was now deliberating whether or not he deserved the death penalty. They seemed to have forgotten they were still in America, where one was presumed innocent until proven guilty.

"What do you think, Helen? You're a lawyer?" one of the guests asked.

***

Sean watched the adults arguing the pros and cons of the death penalty. Most sounded like a busy advertisement, protesting nausea, the amoral, abusive, and subjective application of the death penalty.

A couple supported it, most were against it, and one person remained silent, a sombrero covering her face.

As the patio was lit up like a light show, while close up features weren't clearly distinguishable from where he stood, slim, trim and slender, described her build. He wondered who she was.

Since his arrival a half hour ago, he'd been hiding out in the shed where his host, Marcellus, was barbecuing.

The so-called shed, however, was an architect's fancy, a chef's dream. It was a brick enclave in the shape of an adobe, with a pull down door, glass windows and small chimney to release the smoke.

It was fully equipped for outdoor cooking, with a stack of woods and racks of fancy utensils above and on both sides of the huge pit.

Nursing a can of ice-cold beer, Sean stood adjacent to the opening, half in and half out, listening to the other invitees who sat huddled poolside. He wasn't quite ready to socialize yet.

He chuckled with the irony that he had gone all the way to Africa, Ghana specifically, to meet his host, who was also a business neighbor. Artifacts, Inc. was within walking distance from CavWell Space Industries (CSI), which Marcellus owned with Donald Wellsing. Invited by the Ghanaian government, they had been panelists at an international symposium to promote business opportunities in the African country.

That was four years ago, but work and a bit of disaster experienced by CSI, coupled with his work schedule, prevented them from socializing more often than they did.

Just as he was about to join his host inside the shed, he heard . . .

"Justice shouldn't operate on your best guess, Mr. Scott. That's what evidence is for. ..."

Sean swung around to see who had spoken with such authority in her voice, but he was too late.

Still, that voice lingered in his mind, like a whole note coaxed into longevity by a master musician with alluring appeal. He sought the source of the melodious tone, his eyes plotting the various speakers, waiting to hear her speak again. She didn't disappoint him, quipping to one of the guests, "The death penalty is nothing more than legalized murder."

Deception was very much a part of the siren's song, he reminded himself as his gaze landed on one in particular. Slim, trim, and slender. *Amincissez, equilibrez, et mince*, he thought, looking in her direction with an unconscious grin warming his expression.

He used to think that, too, staring at the woman who covered her face with a sombrero, her piece spoken. If she would have seen what his eyes had, would it change her mind, he wondered, her rich sable voice lingering in his ear.

Sean exhaled a hearty, disheartening sigh. Just once he would like nothing better than to cheat unnatural death, steal a life from its vicious grasp.

"He made an appearance at the breakfast reception," Marcellus said.

"Who?" Sean asked, turning to face his host. "What reception?"

"I'm talking about the event that your company helped sponsor for the local bigwigs to have a private showing of the *Henrietta Marie* exhibit. They didn't come through with as much as we'd hoped," Marcellus said with a shrug, "but it'll help defray some of the costs."

"My flight got in late," he said, recalling even then he had only been home long enough to shower and change before he got the call from Dr. Clemens. "I picked up an unexpected case," he added inadvertently as it was still on his mind. He didn't discuss his cases with those outside the business. Even though they often meant no harm, people had a morbid curiosity that he could control by merely saying next to nothing about his line of work. "Who made an appearance that I should know about?"

"Ray Butler," Marcellus replied, as if the name were a foregone conclusion. "A name that I imagine is on a lot of tongues."

"He showed up at the breakfast?" Sean asked. He was thinking that Butler's wife and daughter were dead by then, had been for quite some time. When the politician did arrive home at the crime scene, minutes after the bodies had been removed, he claimed to be too emotionally distraught to give a statement to the police.

"Live and in person," Marcellus replied, placing another slab of meat on the grill. "He didn't stay long, but frankly, I couldn't have done it if my wife and child had just been murdered."

Where had Ray Butler been? Sean wondered. He remembered Sgt. Diamond had posed that same question. "I'm having a hard time believing it myself," he replied absently.

He shook his head as if to rid the tangent of thoughts that came from the news. He wet his throat, gulping a long swallow of beer, then belched quietly and directed his attention to the gathering. Leisurely, as this was to be a leisure time for him, his eyes scanned the children playing. A race among the youngest was about to start from the other end of the pool; they were jockeying for members.

Seeing them well cared for, safe and happy, he again thought of Taylor Butler. *Du Petit Taylor* as he had begun to think of her.

What secrets did she hold? What was it about du petit Taylor that made her a threat?

The questions had begun to consume his thoughts even before the bodies had been removed. He knew Sgt. Diamond believed that the mother, Joann Butler, held the clues that would lead to the killer. The supposition was based on a lead Sgt. Diamond had gotten from a Ruby Poindexter who notified the police when Joann didn't show up for work.

And he'd believed it, too, initially, Sean mused. But not anymore. Not since *du petite Taylor* had begun haunting his thoughts. He felt as if she was trying to tell him something.

There was no resemblance between the girl who seized his gaze and the one in his thoughts. She was closer to womanhood than *du petit Taylor*, if she hadn't already crossed the threshold.

She was taller, a year or two older, and she was alive.

"Elaina."

He heard the other children call her name and watched them flock to her like moths to a flame, seeking attention, or approval, as was the case with Paul and Marc, his host's sons. In addition to her aquatic prowess, she was the natural leader of the children. Like them, he, too, was drawn to her, staring, but with curiosity, not deviance.

He wondered if *du petit Taylor's* killer had stood off to the side of a building, or a field adjacent to a playground, one day, or many, watching her, admiring the magic of her youth and innocence, planning the time he would steal them from her.

That individual had not been deterred by the threat of the death penalty, he thought grimacing. Il a mérité de payer avec sa vie.

"What you thinking about so hard over there?"

"You have a pair of handsome sons," Sean replied, facing his host.

He knew with uncharacteristic certainty--only death was certain--that he was not going to be able to walk away so easily as a professional consultant. The Butler case wasn't over for him.

"Thank you. I think so myself. My wife, too. Although she's threatening to kick me from our bed unless I promise the next one will be a girl."

"Tell Pauline she should take comfort in knowing that in some societies she would be as valuable as the hen that laid the golden egg because she produces male children.

"They're still in high demand."

"Now you're trying to get me kicked out of the house," Marcellus laughed in reply. "My wife is great in a lot of respects, but her sense of humor doesn't stretch that far."

"You seem happy. I mean, with the married life and all."

He'd come close once, but she called it off to pursue her career. It was a twist, he smiled to himself.

Now, he was too used to his freedom, too set in his ways for a permanent relationship; although he enjoyed a fling or an affair occasionally.

"Man, I love it. I know it's not for everybody, but I wouldn't have it any other way."

Sean returned to the opening to look out toward the patio. His eyes found her; she was standing at the buffet table, talking to Pauline.

Animated, she had a lovely smile and talked with her hands. She could help take his mind off of death, he thought. At least, for a little while.

Tilting his can in her direction, he asked, "Who's that woman?"

They probably didn't have anything in common. Then again, he wasn't looking for a permanent relationship, just companionship for as long as it was good for the both of them.

Wiping his hands on his apron, as he stepped from the pit, Marcellus asked, "Who?"

"That attractive sister wearing a see-through jacket over the violet bathing suit talking to your wife."

Chapter Four

"Her name is Helen Parker. I've known her for quite some time, and I can vouch for her character."

He had a name for the lovely, sable-voiced woman, Sean thought, as he matched Marcellus stride for stride on his way to meet Helen Parker. Mindful of her mythological and legendary namesakes, he wondered if she were all the woman her name implied. Feminine strength, he thought conceptually, supplanting her image with his definition.

"How about giving me a run down on Helen's vital statistics?"

"Aren't you looking at them?"

Sean was momentarily nonplussed by the retort. Heaven forbid he didn't achieve his goal, he thought, noting Marcellus correctly assumed his interest was purely . . . physical. Still, he detected something else in his host's manner that suggested tact was the better part of valor.

"Well, the more I know going into a situation, the better prepared I am for what could happen."

"With Helen, you won't have to wonder long, unless you don't ask," Marcellus quipped, chuckling. "But if you think it helps, she's an attorney and single mom."

"Never married?"

"That's her daughter over there, Elaina, the one in the rainbow colored swimsuit."

Sean noticed things hadn't changed much from when he first spotted Elaina: the youngsters were still vying for her attention. He also noted Marcellus ignored his previous question. Deliberately? "Is the father Hispanic?"

"That's a question for Helen."

Sean nodded, finding Marcellus' evasive replies quite intriguing. No problem: ferreting information was what he did for a living, and when it came to his personal life, he enjoyed discovering a woman's secrets on his own even more, he thought with serendipitous delight.

Particularly as Attorney Helen Parker was 'belle femme', a lovely woman, a real honey.

The more he saw, the more he liked what he saw as they got closer to where she was standing, looking over the buffet, with a plate in her hand.

Though none of it mattered significantly, her face was well modeled and feminine, with a temptingly curved mouth. Long auburn hair fell from a ponytail clasped at the nape of her neck. Her nutmeg complexion was as vibrant as her amber eyes, unique bright and dark shades of brown. Her jacket open, he considered her an incredibly desirable woman, with a pert bosom and slim hips that flared into slender thighs.

"Is there a significant other lurking around somewhere?" Sean asked. He felt eagerness, like hunger pains, roar in his stomach. He couldn't remember when he was last excited by the thought of a chase. He'd be disappointed if he didn't get one.

"Would it matter?"

Chuckling, Sean replied with smooth confidence, "I'd say he couldn't be too significant."

"Well, the most important thing you need to know," Marcellus said, pulling up to a stop, "is that Helen's my baby cousin."

So that explained the protectiveness he sensed from Marcellus about her. He returned his host's intense stare with one of his own. "Is that going to be a problem for you?"

Marcellus grinned broadly. "No. She's a big girl. I believe she's more than capable of handling a little pip squeak like you." He bellowed a hearty laugh as he walked off.

Sean nodded, pleased by the warning as he skipped into step alongside Marcellus. "I got your message loud and clear."

"Helen, stop stuffing your face a moment, there's someone I want you to meet," Marcellus called out as they neared the table.

Helen was casually going about her business of trying to decide which among the buffet of seafood delicacies and fresh fruit to put on her plate.

When they were an arm's length away, she didn't look at him directly; he got a corner of her eye as she debated whether or not he was worthy enough to prolong her priority. Sean wondered if he actually licked his lips.

"Sean King, Helen Parker," Marcellus said.

He must have merited some interest, for she set her plate on the edge of the table, then gave him a long measured look. Absolutely delightful! His insides tingled with relish, and he was tempted to rub his hands together. Already he could tell this was going to be fun.

"Helen, Sean."

***

Helen struggled to subdue the quake that burgeoned inside her. She was almost certain it was not a manifestation of lust, or even awareness, although she was more aware of him than she could recall feeling towards any man. Nerves, she decided.

"Hello, Ms. Parker. It's a pleasure to meet you."

Marshaling her game, Helen performed some quick internal adjustment in her head as she stared at Sean King who bore out his Creole heritage in appearance.

He wasn't as broad in the shoulders, or as tall as Marcellus, but he was endowed with a well-defined physique and a smooth, velvet-edged voice.

"I couldn't help overhear someone refer to you as an attorney," he both asked and stated.

"Yes," she replied softly, under his intrigued interest. She wondered where her breath had gone.

A head full of thick, black hair, he topped out at six feet; a dynamic energy trumpeted his lean, sinewy build. Determination flashed from every chiseled feature on his face; heavy eyebrows, thin mustache over a firm mouth, and a stubborn chin to match. And rather than detract from it, the sparkling diamond stud in his left ear, added a unique eminence to his masculinity. Inexplicably, her heart flip-flopped in her bosom.

"Criminal?"

She wouldn't go so far as to consider him handsome, for his deep penetrating eyes gave him a swarthy, sinister look. Her insides scattered as if seeking safety, but she couldn't take her eyes off of him. "No." And what happened to her strong voice?!

"May I call you Helen?"

Smooth and confident, too. Helen eyed his proffered

hand, wondering if he were always so sure of himself? Or, was he simply, sure of her? Nice hands, though. She accepted his handshake and watched hers disappear in his. Not clammy, but cool and dry, and big to boot. Her heart turned over again.

Easing her hand from his warm possession, she replied, "I'll think about it, Mr. King."

At least she sounded cooler this time than she felt. All the things she knew about herself seemed, strikingly and suddenly, a contradiction. She shuddered and unconsciously, licked her top lip to taste the salty residue anxiety left there.

"Doctor," he emphasized, with a haughtily, raised brow and crooked smile, "King."

So he liked to play. Well, she knew how the game was played, too. "What kind of doctor are you?" If he said shrink, then the conversation was over, she thought, unconsciously holding her breath.

"I pay homage to the dead," he replied. "I'm a forensic anthropologist."

That should have bothered her as well, she thought. Instead, it tickled her fancy. Maybe it was because she now had a face to go with the name she'd heard before. And what a beautifully sculptured face. With an imperceptible shiver coursing through her, she forced disapproval to her countenance as she turned her attention to Marcellus.

"I should tell Pauline on you," she threatened good-naturedly, wagging a finger at him.

Marcellus gave her his sad, hopeful expression that made him look like the impish boy he once was, and she forgave his meddling with a chuckle and nod of her head.

Ever since she had been brought into the family, Marcellus had looked out for her. Age hadn't changed that, at all, she thought, pleased.

"Well," Marcellus said, rubbing his hands together, "I'll leave you two alone to do whatever it is that two peas in a pod do together."

"I hope I won't have to seek restitution from you for this, Cuz," Helen said amusingly to Marcellus. With a tweak of her nose, she doubted seriously there would be a battle: after-all, Dr. Sean King was just a man.

Marcellus rolled his shoulders. "My back is strong."

With the phrase *Just a man* echoing in her mind, Helen thought it a meager classification that defied its cynical intention, and shivered as Marcellus walked off laughing.

"Well, Ms. Parker," Sean said, staring at her intently from head to toe, "would you care to choose your weapon?"

"What do you want from me . . . Dr. King?"

She realized that she had worn Pauline's sombrero to prohibit small talk or any attention whatsoever, removing it only to sip her drink and to eat. Lingering at the buffet table accomplished the same thing. She feared ever wanting to hide again, or that it was no longer even possible.

"Oh, I'll have a bite of everything you'd like to share," he replied guilelessly, although his look wasn't. With his black gaze firmly locked in hers, he plucked a shrimp from her plate, popped it into his mouth, and chewed as he intoned a savory mutter.

Helen quivered, as if a warm touch caressed her flesh. The distinctive hardening of her breasts and the fluttering in her stomach seemed to cry out for adult intimacy. It was utterly uncharacteristic, this bevy of feelings untainted by images of enslavement to man's power over her. Her innards never did that for a man. Not even Ray Butler.

Why did she think of him now?

Chapter Five

Every light in the modest, seven-room house was on, obscuring the secret mission that was being carried out.

The atmosphere was fraught with tension as a sense of passive resistance clashed with one of panic, despite the seemed openness under the glare of lights.

The panic belonged to Claire Jackson. She was already anxious about the divorce, already scared that Howard was going to surprise them by returning before they finished. But she was determined to move out of his house tonight. Her teenage daughter, Toni, short for Antonia was not cooperating.

"You should have told me!"

Toni, 15, was a Caribbean-brown wisp of a girl, who looked as if a good breeze would blow her away. She was as tall as Claire, and swimming made her stronger than she looked.

"Get out of my way," Claire snapped impatiently.

They were in Toni's bedroom where Claire indiscriminately tossed clothes into one of the four packing boxes on the floor.

Toni huffily parked her slim hips against a corner of the dresser. She folded her arms across her small-breasted bosom and cast evil looks at her mother as she blew hot air through her nostrils in an expression of her displeasure.

"Don't do my Tommy shirt like that," the teenager yelled, springing into action. She snatched the shirt from the box and refolded it.

"I don't even know where we're going," Toni said disgruntled.

"I told you that, too," Claire replied, thinking about the small rent house where they were moving to.

Located in Third Ward – practically under Howard's nose from the *Café*, though she hoped he wouldn't think to look- - the house was nestled on a cul de sac between a set of apartments and single-family dwellings.

Easy to overlook, the place was owned by Honey who was giving her a break on the rent: she wouldn't need it long.

Of the three interviews last month, one had paid off. She started her new position as manager of *The Cook's Chamber*, located in the Artifacts, Inc. office building, Monday morning. It was in Clear Lake near NASA and just a couple of miles from Kemah, Texas near the Galveston Bay where she could buy fresh seafood daily. It was a long drive from where they were moving, but the pay was worth it.

"You only said it was a nice place, not where," Toni

replied. "You think everything's nice. For all I know, we're moving to the chimpanzee cage at the zoo."

"If that's where I tell you we're going, then that's where we're going," Claire replied steely. Standing over the bed, she began stripping it of its covers.

"I bet you don't even have a place for us," Toni said. "I bet you've arranged for us to stay with her." The pronoun *her* was full of innuendo.

"What's wrong with you, girl?" Claire asked puzzled by her daughter's attitude toward Honey. If it hadn't been for Honey … Well, she didn't want to think about how they would have survived all those years before Howard.

"That's it, isn't it?' Toni asked, her hands dropping to her sides indignantly. "You're moving us to Honey's. I'd rather be homeless."

Before either of them realized it, Toni was holding the side of her face. Both froze, shocked, staring at the other.

With eyes wide open and incredulous, as tears pooled in their depths, Toni cried, "You hit me."

"Are you about done now?"

Claire looked up to see Honey standing in the doorway and smiled unconsciously. Honey was a black woman the color of her name. Of average height, sporting a reddish, flat-top, Afro hairstyle and as buffed as Angela Bassett was in *How Stella Got Her Groove Back*, she didn't look a day over 25, when actually, she was 41, ten years older than Claire.

"Just about," Claire replied.

Honey used to be a prostitute known as Miss Honeybee. But that was many years ago. She was proud of what she'd become, claiming she always was. No longer in what she called *'in denial'*, she'd given up her female identity, but not her sense of style. Tonight, she wore a fashionable fatigue ensemble in navy, complete with black boots. *Easy to wear, ready to work*, Honey had said of her attire when she arrived.

"Here," Honey said, walking to the bed where Claire stood, "let me get that."

"I don't want her touching my stuff," Toni snapped.

Claire exchanged a look with Honey, her expression was one of utter mortification.

Honey raised her hands in the air. "Fine," she said, backing out of the room.

Claire felt Honey's hurt. Standing there fuming, hands on her hips and head bowed as she blew air from her cheeks, she accepted her share of the blame for her daughter's behavior toward Honey who was Howard's cousin.

Ironically, Howard expressly forbade her from allowing Honey in his house when they married five years ago. After working on her feet all day, six days a week, she was too tired to meet Honey somewhere.

Then with Toni's busy schedule of school activities, swim meets, and practices, even going to Honey's home for a visit seemed like more work.

Before long, all contact between them ceased until recently, when desperation had taken hold of her. Still, she believed she had raised Toni better than the way she'd been acting.

"Do you want me to take the computer, too?" Toni asked.

Claire faced Toni, frowning, wondering what the hell was wrong with her child. She remembered Toni begged and cried for that computer last Xmas. Howard had said it costs too much, that Toni could type her papers on a typewriter - - which was much cheaper, although he didn't offer to buy one - - and refused to buy it.

"Why wouldn't you?" she asked baffled.

"Because Howard bought it," Toni replied. "You said to only take what was ours."

Howard only bought Toni useless things, expensive

Polo tennis and Tommy shirts, Claire thought, her jaw twitching. He never bought, said, or did anything that would aid her in becoming an independent young woman.

Howard wanted them dependent on him because it made him feel like a big man.

"You've got Honey to thank for that computer," Claire said tightly. "If you want to leave it, that's up to you."

In hot despair, she picked up a box near the door and headed out, praying silently to the Lord to give her strength to endure her child's stupidity.

She followed the trail of light from inside the house out to the driveway where a van was parked. Closing in on midnight, it was good and dark. The street was quiet, and all the neighbors tucked in.

Except for the nosy neighbor that lived across the street. Claire was very much aware of Ms. Bea Hamilton peeking out her picture window from the behind the curtains.

Knowing that lifted her mood as she slid the box across the floor of the van alongside the others, thinking Howard would hear all about their midnight escape when he returned from his fishing trip Sunday afternoon.

Chapter Six

His lead was easy to follow.

Sean's left hand in the small of her back, and her left hand securely in his right, Helen thought of nothing but the music, Steve Wonder's "Always," playing on the speakers that were mounted over the patio area.

When the song began, every adult - - and more had since joined the pre-Juneteenth celebration at her cousins' home - - took to the floor. Instead of refreshing her drink, which she was doing at the time, Sean commandingly without being overbearing, set her glass on the buffet table. For a reason she couldn't fathom, the indignation signaling her very first response to his bold move vanished like a puff of smoke, and she put her hand in his proffered one.

While the rest of the adults formed a Soul Train line, which she thought they would join as well, Sean whispered in her ear, "Je vous veux tout à me."

She didn't know what he had said, but it proved that sometimes *what* was said wasn't as important as *how* it was said. While Steve Wonder provided the beat, she matched the rhythm of Sean's moves.

"Somebody's showing their age. Can't remember the last time I've seen a couple on the dance floor actually touch."

Helen smiled, undaunted by the teasing from her cousin, Marcellus whose rhythm was limited to rocking from side-to-side and clapping his hand as he strolled through the line.

"And a two-step, no less!" someone else teased.

Laughter floated across the patio and then faded into the melodic beat. The stars, winking sparklers way up high in the hot, black night possessed more rhythm than some of the dancers that concentrated on their movement, she noticed absently. There was no comparison to Sean.

He continued to hold her firmly, possessively almost, yet gently as he spun her around, and then just as gently, pulled her against him.

It was obvious he enjoyed dancing, and just as obvious that he was good at it. His moves were deft, smooth, requiring no thought. For a fleeting instant, she wondered if he were the same in bed, and a shudder coursed through her.

"Vous vous sentez gentil à côté de moi ; vous vous êtes adapté admirablement dans des mes bras," Sean whispered as he held her near.

Helen shivered imperceptibly. She considered that she had had one too many drinks, and even though the children had been sent inside to bed, she knew that in all likelihood, they were still up. That included her child, as well.

Still, she felt beautiful, wanted, without a care in the world.

"l'amour vrai demande rien," Sean chanted melodiously for her ears alone, and this time, she understood that he was reciting the words of the song, *True love asks for nothing.* "Je serai affectueux vous toujours," he intoned rhythmically with the chorus as he spun her around. *I'll be loving you always.* "Toujours," he added, his melodious voice a whisper. *Always.*

Helen forgot about her daughter. Caressed against his thick, wide chest, bared since he'd gone swimming, the temptation of running her fingers through the silky hairs there was great. She folded her bottom lip in her mouth in some kind of unconscious suppression from acting out the wistful want that created ripples of desire in her and simply enjoyed the manly feel of him.

As the song ended, he crooned softly, "Soyez mon amoureux tant qu'il nous est bon tous les deux."

Helen didn't have to ask for a translation. She saw meaning in his gaze, heard it in his tone, and felt it in the shiver that coursed down her spine.

But he took no chance that she misunderstood. "Be my lover, I said, for as long as it is good for us both."

Parliament's "Atomic Dog" boomed from the speakers, and even the dancers who were headed for seats returned to dance to the up-tempo, funky beat.

Neither Helen nor Sean seemed aware that they were crowded by dancers all around them, still standing in the spot when the last song ended.

"But you don't even know me," she protested in a breathless whisper. If only that were the only reason, she thought. She reminded herself that she was mother to a teenager and all the circumspection that came with the role was expected of her. She tried to take her hand away, but he held on.

"I know what I need to know," he replied. "I more than like what I see."

"That's lust," she said harsher than she intended as she successfully reclaimed her hand. As if sobered by a bucket of cold water, she became aware of a number of things that time held irrelevant moments ago. She spun, returning to retrieve her glass, her insides trembling uncontrollably.

Sean took her glass as she reached the drink table. There, he filled it with the alcoholic mixture that was in the blender on ice.

"You make desire sound like a dirty word," he said, handing the glass to her.

Even though the patio was well lit, she wondered if what she saw in his eyes was real or pretense. So dark they looked as black as the night sky, bedroom eyes. She cursed herself for wanting to experience the emotions promised in his gaze - - the plain as day desire he was offering. She swallowed thickly.

"Thank you." As emotions waged a war inside her, dodging the dancers still moving wildly to the funky beat of the music, she returned to her lounge chair, with her fresh drink.

Sean pulled a lounge chair next to hers. She stretched out, and then aware that he was watching her, she sat upright, planted her feet on the patio floor, legs together primly.

Their knees almost touched, and she almost pulled away as if he were crowding her spot, but defiantly stayed put.

"Lust, yearning, desire, call it what you what, but none is a dirty word, ma belle dame. Is it not the fist sign of attraction?" he asked with naked candor, his head cocked at an angle as he looked at her with a smile on his mouth.

Her heart reacted immediately, a timbale playing in her chest, to that smile, at once both sweet and wicked, the sultry tone of his voice … corporal foreplay performed so easily on his handsome face. She liked it, and she didn't. "Are you laughing at me?"

"Non," he replied softly, his accent heavy as he shook his head from side to side. "Never that. I'm attracted to you, and I believe, dear counselor, the feeling is reciprocated."

Helen couldn't find her voice. She looked into her glass, for what, she didn't know. This man had a power over her she wasn't sure she liked. More potent than her drink, for sure, she thought, setting her glass on the patio floor.

"Am I wrong? Are you not attracted to me as I am to you?"

"It's too soon," she blurted, feeling dense all of a sudden, as if the subject of wanting was difficult to assimilate and understand.

He had correctly read her response to him. She wanted him, but she was also afraid. So very afraid.

"I'm not sure I understand what you mean by that," he replied. "I admit, I may be more decisive than others, but when I see what I want …" He let the splay of his hands, the shameless expression on his face complete the thought.

Helen picked up her drink this time because returning his look was emotionally dangerous. It seemed his every provocative gaze evoked feelings that scared her. She stared into the milky substance in her glass, the bottom cloudy, hiding the bits of pineapple from view. She was at the bottom of that glass, she thought. "But you don't know me," she said with melancholy mirroring in her voice, her expression.

"You've said that before," he smiled.

The resounding hard beat of Parliament faded, segueing into a slow ballad, and within seconds, the voice of Pattie LaBelle began to croon, "If Only You Knew."

Sean extended his hand to Helen, and against her better judgment . . .

Chapter Seven

Juneteenth fell on an absolutely gorgeous day.

Although the temperature hovered in the nineties, the occasion, the *Henrietta Marie* exhibit drew a crowd that numbered in the thousands to Galveston. Helen, with Elaina on one side of her and Sean on the other, were in a long line of people who plowed up the plank to board the slave ship.

The feature star in the mild wind blowing off the Galveston Bay was a bright yellow sun flaring from high in the mosaic blue sky. Exotic scents and the more common aroma of smoked barbeque wafted over the wide boulevard that ran parallel to the dock. It was a festive vista, a carnival of colors, a bazaar of excitement.

Several thousand people celebrating this June 19th made walkways where there were none, moving from any number of stalls set up to sell Black arts and crafts, food and books, or milled at the end of the partitioned area where poets, singers and musicians performed from a portable stage.

"She's a beauty."

A look of appealing provocation shone in Sean's dark gaze as he made the bold declaration. Helen shivered even as she denied that he was referring to her directly. Still, his eyes were trained on her, and warmth that didn't come from nature's sun streamed like liquid butter through her.

"Yes, she is," a male voice concurred with awe in his tone.

Even though the original slave ship lay miles under the ocean off the Florida coast for hundreds of years, the replica evoked no less powerful emotions. Her new face of high polished wood and Tide-white canvases, she glistened in the sun like a brazen woman out to catch.

She was 80 feet long and fit on a flatbed raised about 40 to 50 feet off the ground. Like the mast schooners of her time, she was built for speed to out race pirates who might steal the priceless cargo she carried from her homeport to Africa, through the Middle Passage and back again.

Her hair . . . one, four, seven . . . Helen counted 10 sails in all, attached to masts located at the stern, middle and bow of the ship billowed in the mildly blowing wind. How could something so beautiful have been used for so ugly a purpose as slavery?

"The *Henrietta Marie* was a London based vessel, registered as 120 tons burden with eight guns," Sean said, gracing them with his knowledge on the exhibit they were about to see.

Helen smiled unconsciously. Listening to him, she felt proud to know him. Even as talkative as he had been, he didn't strike her as a conceited, egotistical man.

Regarding the *Henrietta Marie*, he had been uncannily unpretentious, saying nothing about his company's involvement in the sponsorship of the exhibit. She only learned of it on the trek to Galveston with the twenty some odd people who departed from her cousin's home.

Mimicking an English accent, Sean said dramatically, "Do not waste time and energy caring for the sick, dying, and those who wished they were dead." On his Creole tongue, the imitation earned laughter from those around them.

Sean resumed speaking in his natural voice, laced with residual humor. "That was the advice given slave ship captains because time was crucial to their valuable and fragile cargo of enslaved Africans.

"Estimates run in the millions of Africans who were stolen from the coasts of Africa at New Calabar in the second leg of the infamous triangular trade route known as the Middle Passage. It is interesting to note that African males were valued at seventeen dollars, women and children less than that."

"That doesn't seem to have changed much."

That, from the highly opinionated Leonard Scott who wouldn't let the Butler murders rest last night.

Helen wanted to lash out at him, but Sean's brooding look, his brows knitted in a frown stole her attention. In that instant, she wondered what he was thinking, and then he looked at her and winked, a smile spreading across his handsome face. Something swelled inside her, and she couldn't help smiling back.

"The *Henrietta Marie's* involvement in slavery began in 1697," Sean continued. "She enjoyed three years as a slave ship from 1697 until her final delivery in Jamaica on May 18, 1700, when she mysteriously sank in the summer of that year."

"Good riddance," Elaina mumbled.

"I second that," another among them chimed.

"We owe a debt of gratitude to Mel Fisher and his team who made the initial discovery while searching for *Nuestra Senora de Atocha*, a sunken Spanish galleon.

"They brought up an ivory tusk and immediately assumed the ship had been to Africa. But when they found iron shackles, a history many of us would like to forget surfaced all over again."

Helen felt as if Sean spoke to her personally as "Ooos" and "Aahhs" rang across the deck where they could see down into the belly of the ship. Dummies positioned like bodies, lay stacked and packed like sardines in a can, just as the captured Africans once uncomfortably lay on the long journey from their homes.

The staged scene made a poignant showing of abuse, torture, and degradation, and it elicited every repulsive image of slavery Helen read, heard about or saw on screen.

Likewise, it reawakened a vile sensation, a vague nightmare of a time in her life akin to the abominable sufferings ever imposed on a human being. She felt her entire being under siege by a hot flash of humiliation, and her heart pounded in an off-rhythm beat.

"Ouch! Mom!" Elaina cried, jerking her hand from Helen's shackle-tight grasp.

"Sorry," Helen mumbled embarrassed and shaken.

"Here. Take mine," Sean offered, extending his hand.

***

The beach was crowded with people who'd come out to enjoy this holiday, or just because it was the kind of day for it.

Some had even brought their dogs that chased and barked after the seagulls trying to rest from flight over the muddy brown waters of Galveston Bay.

A cacophony of music - - rock, Mexican, blues, and soul - - boomed from one reveler's party to the next. Soul music, with some zydeco thrown in between dominated the type of the Cavanaugh group.

Sean attended none of the cheerful revelry as he stared curiously, and with longing into the distance where the object of his puzzlement stood about ten feet from the sandy shoreline.

There, Helen seemed almost giddy with excitement, very much alive, and playful.

The picnic was well underway behind him on a staked out section of West Beach.

Under a huge green canopy, their party sat on lawn chairs, coolers, or pallets, eating the traditional Juneteenth meal of barbeque, potato salad, and beans, with red sodas and watermelon that had been sliced in advance for the occasion.

Those children willing to withstand the intensity of the sun's rays were playing in the water. Helen was among them. The Cavanaugh youngsters, Marc and Paul, claimed her undivided attention with joyous delight as she pulled and twirled them on their orange and blue float.

Sean sighed enviously. He was stripped to his trunks, and could join her in a flash, but he wasn't sure he'd be invited. He doubted his attention would receive the relishing welcome the young boys enjoyed from her.

Ever since they left the *Henrietta Marie*, he noticed the change in her behavior. She had become quiet, and distant, and unwilling to talk about what could be troubling her.

Her remote demeanor was noticeable even before they left the ship, he corrected, recalling that she didn't take his hand.

He absently flipped it now, palm up and then down again before fanning the air in a disgusted gesture of frustration.

"Hey, Sean!"

He turned when he heard his name. Strolling toward him were his cousins, brother and sister, Jules and Baderinwa Jolivet. Even before they founded Artifacts, Inc., they were closer than cousins, more like brothers and sister as their mothers were close sisters.

Jules was a big bear of a man, and although only 42, had resorted to combing his fine, curly hair sideways where he was balding at the top. He used to tease that Baderinwa and Sean were the cause. Baderinwa, born Chantal, looked every bit a queen of the woman she was, stunning in looks and even more so on the inside. Her limp no longer angered him as it did eight years ago when a possessive, jealous husband tried to kill her. It was when she took the name, Baderinwa, meaning worthy of respect.

"We haven't had a chance to talk. How was it?" Jules asked.

Jules was an archeologist, who also taught the subject at Texas A&M. Sean was partly influenced by his career choice. Baderinwa was their business manager and financial consultant. She made sure they, and the company, stayed in the black.

"Don't ever let me do that again," he replied, with a chuckle in his voice.

"I know what you mean. Valerie FedExed a copy of the crime scene video you shot."

Sean muttered surprised that the ME was able to get the tape in the first place, and so soon.

"The cops nearly removed the tape from the camera for me. I didn't think she'd get a copy before next week."

Jules laughed. "She wouldn't have if she had not gone to the police station and demanded a copy immediately. I never would have believed it that a day would come when the badass Houston police allowed political fear to change the usual methods of operations."

"Butler sells good wolf tickets," Baderinwa said. "It is unfortunate that self-interest has become his prime motivation."

"You know him?" Sean asked.

"I met him at the breakfast. He thinks he's invincible. At least, he did before someone murdered his family."

Sean stared at his cousin, wondering if she knew more than she was telling. Baderinwa sensed things, and when in her presence, the world seemed a better place. It was as if she injected a sweet halo into the spaces she walked, which everyone in the family found surprising. She hadn't always been that way. Not until her near-fatal incident did they notice, and feel the changes in her.

"Vous êtes frappé par elle." Baderinwa said.

"Ne le niez pas," Jules warned him.

Sean blushed. He wouldn't dare deny Baderinwa's comment that he was taken with Helen, he thought. His gaze followed those of his cousins who looked toward the water where Helen and the boys were mimicking the dives of the porpoise that swam in these waters.

"Je pas." *I won't,* Sean said absently. "There's something about her."

"Je le prends que la chasse est passionnante," Jules teased.

"Oh, yes," Sean chuckled in reply. "There's no fun without the chase. I do believe that she is going to give me a run for my money."

"Vous ne pouvez pas être celui qu'elle exécute de," Baderinwa proclaimed with oblique solemnity, staring out toward Helen.

Sean shivered, and averted his gaze back on Helen, too.

"Those little girls have gone too far," Jules pointed out.

Sean tore his gaze from Helen. Shielding his eyes from the sun's glare, he followed the direction Jules pointed. Elaina and two other girls were a good 25 yards out, beyond the 15-yard safety zone for these waters. He cupped his hands over his mouth, yelling, "Elaina, come back!"

Baderinwa noted the obvious. "They can't hear you."

Sean made no announcement as he walked deeper into the water that climbed up to his knees, when he dived in, swimming for the girls.

***

"Mama, wake up!"

Very late that night, Elaina shook Helen who was twisting and turning frantically in the bed they shared at their cousin's home.

She had never seen her mother like this, and it made her heart beat faster with fear. She wondered if she should run and get Aunt Pauline.

The cacophony of chaos assaulted Helen from all directions. Babies were crying and women were moaning; men mumbled words in languages she couldn't speak. Yet comprehension was clear. She understood their fear, for it was hers to share.

Pulled, dragged, teased with her helplessness and her cries ignored, she struggled in vain against the iron rope cutting into her wrists, the end of it in her tormentor's hands.

And then all of a sudden, she was free and running indiscriminately, not knowing where she was going.

She came upon a river and was shocked still for there on the edge of the bank kneeled a woman holding a long, sharp knife in one hand, her baby girl in the other.

"Mom!"

"Nooo!" Helen screamed.

"You're having a bad dream, wake up!" Elaina cried.

Another sound intruded her subconscious; it was light against the loud din of confusion and fear; it was familiar and warm. She reached for it, and finally, managed to open her eyes.

"It's all right, Mama," Elaina said comforting her, rubbing her arm gently. "You were having a nightmare."

Helen couldn't speak right away for her ragged breathing as she scooted to an upright position. She surveyed the familiar guest bedroom where she and Elaina shared the bed, drawing fresh air into her lungs. A nightmare for sure, she thought, as her pulse calmed considerably, the fear in her dreams slowly abating.

Until recently, it had been ages since she had a nightmare; definitely not since she became a mother. She would awaken from them with a sad feeling, sometimes crying, but never any details.

She blew out her cheeks, her hands clutching the front of her gown as she realized that her subconscious had cast her into that world of the *Henrietta Marie's* slave running period.

She was one of its *precious* cargoes, an unwilling passenger, imported on foreign soil to be auctioned and sold.

Only, the Slave Master in her nightmare wasn't some faceless white man.

And the woman to whom she raced toward wore her face.

"You all right now?" Elaina asked.

Helen's heart skipped a beat, and then fell into an uneasy rhythm. She swallowed, nodded her head woodenly as she schooled a neutral expression on her face. "Yeah, baby. I'm sorry I woke you." She flashed a smile into the worried look on her daughter's face. "I'm fine now."

"Shall I leave the light on?"

"No. You can turn it off."

Elaina turned off the light, and then plopped back into her comfortable sleeping position. Helen feared closing her eyes.

Although her breathing returned to normal, she trembled ever so lightly from the residuals of anxiety. She stared up at the dark ceiling, pondering her nightmare, the bits and pieces of reality interwoven with a surrealistic fantasy. She recalled the haunting dream seemed to have started the night she performed on the Henrietta Marie.

Tony Morrison's **Beloved** crossed her mind. She couldn't read the book, and at the time, wished she hadn't seen the movie, she recalled with a shudder. The similarity of her dream to the story about a mother who was haunted by her murdered child's ghost was uncanny, not to mention, painfully horrible. The story was understandable; her nightmare wasn't.

For certain, her nightmare held a fear that was very real in her life. She wondered if it were an omen, warning her against Sean, or to him? But this wasn't the first time she'd had the dream. And it preceded Sean, she thought, shaking her head. She felt literally and figuratively in the dark.

She glanced sidelong at her daughter who had drifted back to sleep and was snoring lightly next to her. She was comforted by the sound, and felt a pleasant sparkle of warmth balloon in her bosom.

Elaina had been right, she thought. It was nothing more than a bad dream. Comfortable with her rationalization, she turned on her side and closed her eyes.

***

Taylor held her breath.

Sean knew she wouldn't be able to hold it for longer, maybe 45 seconds. With no time to spare, he couldn't afford to be late. He'd been late before.

The reminder quickened his pace, but it seemed he wasn't moving at all, couldn't propel up those steps fast enough. He struggled harder to run faster than he'd ever run before in his life. He knew the process, the respiratory system, the help it needed to sustain life. Time was running out.

Her small diaphragm moved as she exchanged carbon dioxide for the air that she inhaled through her nostrils. Her lungs stretched like a balloon. Her lips were sealed tight as not to let any air escape.

He saw her in his mind. Winded himself, he felt her fighting for life with every ounce of drawn breath and intelligence she possessed.

He couldn't get up those damn steps! They kept moving away!

She held the air in her lungs -- supplying oxygen to her blood and brain, replacing CO_2, circulating, nourishing tissues -- until her chest hurt.

The need for fresh oxygen mushroomed. She strained so hard to keep the air in that pain crept into her baby face. Finally, her air sacs collapsed, betraying her effort to fool the thief.

He ran as hard as a four-legged animal to get there on time.

The moment he heard - - "Sean, help me!"- - he knew. His dead heat run slowed into a canter. "I couldn't hold it any longer, Sean."

Sean popped straight up in bed. Breathing hard, as if the wind had been knocked out of him. He felt like someone who'd just exhaled an exceedingly long held breath, and it hurt. Taylor felt the same pain.

He dreamed about her again, when ironically, he had fallen asleep with lusty thoughts of Helen. Even more strange was that it had been Elaina's voice calling to him in his dream turned nightmare. It was Elaina's lifeless face he saw when he finally arrived, too late.

He blew out his cheeks, and tried consoling himself that the dream had no basis in reality. Nevertheless, he doubted his thoughts would allow sleep to return. After all, *du petit Taylor* and her mother would dream no more, and he felt guilty for trying.

He wondered if Helen were getting any sleep tonight?

Chapter Eight

Monday morning arrived with a clean emotional slate for Helen.

Almost, Helen amended, attending bumper-to-bumper traffic as she drove Elaina to school. While Sean made no demands for an explanation of her inexplicable cool and distant behavior Saturday after leaving the *Henrietta Marie,* she recalled, he propositioned her over the phone last night.

"I want to have an affair with an intelligent woman, and I'd like for that woman to be you. You definitely fit an important criterion, and you're attractive. Not necessarily a criteria, but I consider it a bonus for me that you are."

"I don't like him."

Helen leisurely allowed herself to be drawn from the past, as the strident whine of her daughter's voice replaced Sean's compelling one. She smiled to herself, still amazed that he actually said those words to her.

"Mama, usted no está escuchando," Elaina huffed in Spanish.

Anger and embarrassment were the two emotional states that brought out the Spanish on Elaina's tongue.

Groaning inwardly, Helen almost wished she hadn't insisted that she learn the language, for it required a search of college Spanish from her memory in order to reply.

She tried to remember the simplest reply to *"Mom, you're not listening to me."*

Elaina resumed the point she started last night, Sunday, on the drive home from Pauline and Marcellus's. Still not done, she renewed it upon waking this morning at 7. Which was amusing, for she, too, had awakened with Sean King on her mind and the fuddled longing that came with her thoughts of him. Last night he even replaced the *Henrietta Marie* sans slavery nightmare that haunted her sleep. Helen shook her head to get her naughty muse under control.

"Sí, soy," she replied at last. *I can't help but to hear you,* she thought.

Elaina was busy finishing her toiletries, applying lotion to her arms and legs, which she should have done at home. It was an annoying habit, but Helen was used to it.

Just about the time the clock on the dashboard flipped to 8:50 AM, the radio announcer declared, *"You've got the morning show, and if you're not up and out, you're late."*

They were stuck in Hermann Park traffic, five minutes from the entrance to Rice University where Elaina was enrolled in the summer enrichment program. Music and private piano lessons started her morning, followed by swimming for fun, and then lunch before American History that she was taking for credit.

"Bien, qué dije?" Elaina persisted in Spanish, knowing the language demanded her attention.

The radio announcer seemed just as insistent. *"What about the guy they brought in? Have you gotten a line on him?"*

"Well, Bob, we know his name, Dr. Sean King, and he's a forensic anthropologist with a company called Artifacts, Inc. But he's been quieter than a mummy about the case. He won't even say 'No comment'."

Elaina clicked off the radio and glowered at Helen.

"Believe me, I heard you, Elaina," she said ardently. The light up ahead turned green, traffic moved, and she inched along with it.

"Are you going to see him again?" Elaina demanded.

Helen knew a "why?" would follow, no matter her reply, yes or no. "No sé," she said wisely.

The response duplicated the one she gave Sean last night when they talked on the phone like teenagers. To Elaina, she stammered, "Tendré que pensar de él." She almost wished she could say she didn't remember what they talked about, recalling her responses, *"I don't know,"* and *"I'll have to think about it."* She sounded like a broken record.

"But I don't want you to see him anymore," Elaina said, brushing her hair.

Helen cast a sidelong, neutral glance at her daughter. *'No kidding,'* stayed unvoiced in her thoughts.

Elaina stopped brushing her hair long enough to demand, "Mom, did you hear me? I don't want you to see him. I don't like him."

"I got that last night," Helen replied, just because a response was demanded of her. Little did Elaina know, she didn't have anything to worry about, she thought with a feeling akin to fatalism. The jury was still out on whether she would see Sean again. "How many more times do I have to hear it?" she asked, inching along with the traffic.

"You heard it, but you're not paying attention," Elaina replied. "Don't you want to know why I don't like him?"

I already know, Helen thought. *You're jealous, even though you don't need to be.* An obstacle far bigger than Elaina's jealousy stood in her way.

"I could tell he didn't want me around," Elaina replied. With the arrogant confidence of youth, she added, "He doesn't like kids. We sense things like that."

"I see," Helen muttered as she bobbed her head as if giving credence to her daughter's assertion. Except the possibility of being angered when Sean made her and her friends return closer to shore, she hadn't the foggiest idea from where her child got that impression.

"And he works with dead people."

"He's a forensic scientist, not a mortician," Helen

chuckled in reply. Unaccustomed to seeing her mother in a social context with a man largely explained why Elaina felt ill at ease about Sean. In the times they'd spent together this past weekend, his behavior had been above reproach. But of course, she could feel safe in the company of others. Speculating her reaction around him without the protection provided by safety in numbers, she shuddered. "Look it up while you're in school."

"I don't want to look it up," Elaina said, pouting. "I don't want to know anything else about him."

"Suit yourself," Helen replied, issuing a silent thanks to the traffic that sped up once they passed the construction.

"He wears a stud in his ear." Elaina added to her list of complaints against Sean. "He's almost 40 years old. That's too old for a man to be wearing a stud."

Helen's lips twitched with humor. Apparently Elaina didn't object to his thin mustache. "So only young people can be stylish? And for your information, he's only 38."

Elaina misinterpreted Helen's response and attempted to clean up the age reference hastily. "But you're only 33. He's too old for you."

"How's your history class?" Helen asked. She was well aware that history was not her daughter's favorite subject. It was the only way to divert Elaina's and her attention from the subject of Dr. Sean King.

Elaina groaned. "I hate it even more than before," she spat out.

"If you don't know history, then your future is up for grabs," Helen replied with a variation of the proverb black leaders had cited for centuries about the importance of knowing one's history toward mapping the future.

"Well, white people ought to pay better attention," Elaina quipped. "That's all we talk about …it's either how white people reacted to some law or bill, or how great or stupid some white person was. It's just like in regular school."

"All you need to remember is that if you pass American History this summer …"

Elaina cut her off, replying in a snide tone, "Then there'll be World History, so I still won't be done with the boring subject."

The chuckle in Helen's voice faded into folded lips as a look of consternation flitted across her expression. More than white people needed to attend the axiom, she mused, realizing that despite the years of knowing and even
agreeing with the philosophical instruction, she had not internalized it for herself. For sure, she was a little more knowledgeable of black history than many, but she couldn't say the same about her personal history.

Wasn't what was good for the goose, good for the gander? Even before she could give Sean's request serious thought, there were things about herself that she needed to know. She squirmed slightly, uncomfortable with the exposure of her own shortsightedness, absently telling her daughter, "Do the best you can, Butterscotch."

With their destination in sight, Elaina began gathering her things, tossing her hairbrush and tube of lotion inside her backpack. "Don't be late today."

Pulled from her muse, Helen replied, "Why not today?"

"The movie, remember? There's no swim practice, and you promised we could see a movie and then have dinner at a restaurant."

"Alright," she agreed, bobbing her head. A promise was a promise.

"Be on time. Please," Elaina added as an afterthought, tugging her gym bag from the back seat. "The movie starts at 3:30, and you know how it's always so hard to find a parking space, so we need to get there a little early."

Her daughter could be such a little general sometimes.

"Yes, ma'am," she said, suppressing the sarcasm in her tone. "I'll be here at three, on the dot."

The light turned green, and Helen sped off and straight onto the university grounds. There were several other cars, with parents dropping off kids, heading for the same drop-off point. She amused herself wondering if they were as anxious as she was to unload their children this morning. Her turn came, and she pulled to a stop in front of the gothic building.

"Here you go," she said, trying not to sound too eager. "Have a good day," she added, as Elaina leaned over the seat to kiss her on the cheek.

"I will," Elaina replied, opening the door to get out. "Don't forget, three o'clock." She waited for Helen to nod an assurance before she got out and slammed the door shut.

Helen didn't drive off until she saw Elaina join a group of kids going in her direction. Her sigh of relief was almost as long as the driveway that took her back onto the main thoroughfare. Feeling the semblance of control again, she turned the radio back on.

"Well, what else do you know about this guy, Sean King?"

***

There was no dress code for the people who worked for, or out of Artifacts, Inc. Many looked like the college student some of them were, but most already had earned two degrees in anthropology, archeology, or a related field.

Regardless, they all possessed a card key and all had business at Artifacts, Inc.

The lobby reflected a professional office building with chrome furnishings, and decorative touches in gold, black and maroon, the company's color scheme. Pictures depicting archeological finds from around the world lined the grey stoned walls.

Sean absently observed them march or meander into the lobby of Artifacts, Inc., the premier forensic center of the southwest from his perch on a black leather couch in front of an oblong-shaped glass-topped coffee table where he reviewed the contents of a black portfolio.

Those who meandered in this early had projects going on on one of the four floors upstairs. Twelve years ago, ever since he studied at the Forensic Center of Tennessee with the famous Dr. Bass, he dreamed of establishing a similar institution.

Convincing Jules to share his dream had been easy, he mused. The anthropology of African Americans would be ignored, if not for companies like Artifacts, Inc. The Henrietta Marie was one such project.

And while they did quite a bit of foreign work in forensics, DNA testing was a large part of the company's success.

With more and more African Americans interested in learning where they came from before slavery, he had no doubt in the company's growth. Half of the third floor was donated to processing the requests and analyzing DNA samples the clients sent.

Additionally, they performed joint projects with four universities in Texas, locally with University of Houston and Texas Southern University, regionally with Texas A & M and UT-San Antonio, offering a place for academicians to conduct field studies, while benefiting from their research.

Sean scrawled his signature on several pages, and then moved the portfolio aside to pull the binder-size checkbook onto his lap. He went to work signing checks, thinking that he and Jules had been especially fortunate to have Badarinwa on their team, for it was she who helped bring their dreams to fruition.

In actuality, he was waiting for Badarinwa, who was conferring with Jules across the way near the entrance to the Cook's Chamber, the company's cafeteria.

He had learned that a new cook and manager had been hired, and the person had already made a big impression with a meal prepared as a test last week.

Before, the cafeteria had been losing money, and

Badarinwa had been charged with turning it around or they would let it go, and the hundred or so people who worked in the building would have to go elsewhere for breakfast and lunch.

Badarinwa sighed heavily as she dropped into an adjacent chair. "Where are you off to so early?" she asked.

"I'm going to the morgue."

"The Butlers?" she guessed. "You don't have to, you know. I've already submitted the invoice in triplicate."

Ignoring her advice, Sean smiled at her benignly. "You need to hire an assistant," he replied, sticking his pen inside his coat pocket. "These are for you," he added, placing the portfolio and checkbook in her lap. "Where is the nearest flower shop?"

"Right across the street," she replied, a sly smile on her lips. "Helen Parker?"

"Yep," he replied, rising. "Gotta go." He leaned to kiss her on the cheek.

"Good luck," she said. "With Helen Parker."

"I don't need luck," he quipped laughingly as he walked off.

***

"A single tulip?"

Sean looked up from the map he had been trying to make heads and tails of to the sales woman behind the counter in the flower shop. She was staring at him rather curiously.

He had been charting his expedition to track down *du petit Taylor's* killer as soon as he finished at the morgue.

"Yes. One tulip. Purple, please," he replied with the confidence of a man who knew his decision would be honored.

Having chosen his flower of choice to send Helen - - there was something about a purple tulip that reminded him of her - - he debated whether or not to get something for Elaina, too.

"That's to go at lunch to the first address." He planned to have the tulip sent to her office, and some type of bouquet sent to her home.

"I'm afraid that's going to be almost impossible, Dr. King. A tulip would have to be ordered from another state, so it won't be here in time."

"Oh," he said disappointed. "Well, something purple. And I'd like to have a floral arrangement delivered later, preferably between 5:30 and 6:30, to the address at the bottom of the page."

That would do for starters, he thought, firmly aware that Helen was not going to be easy: he would have to work hard to get her.

He believed a mercurial force, almost like a violent rage lived inside Helen under her calm exterior.

On the surface she seemed the most self-possessed woman he'd ever met and wondered how much her legal training contributed to her outward sense of serenity. Or was it his own lust he was feeling, he chuckled amused. Still, he felt there was something unique about her, and like a dog in heat, he wanted some of what she had.

He wanted her. Emotional warts, which Baderinwa assured him existed, and all.

"Do you see something on display that you like?" the clerk asked with the splay of her hand, forcing his gaze to follow. "Or do you have something particular in mind?"

Contrary to what Marcellus said about Helen, he did have to wonder, and on several occasions ask what she was thinking, he recalled, folding the map close to peruse the arrangements on display throughout the shop. Except for a few instances when she seemed to have mentally escaped to another world - - a practice he was known to indulge, as well - - he knew not much more about her than what one might find on a resume.

Spotting a refrigerator in the far corner of the single business room, he walked over to look inside the glass doors. Arrangements featuring roses dominated the shelves.

Helen spoke a little about her parents and daughter, but said nothing about her work or life's goals, either professionally or personally. Still, he felt they were important to her and sensed her passions ran deep. And she kept them to herself, he mused, shaking his head at the roses.

Sean returned to the counter and the sales clerk, whose former baffled attitude now showed amusement. "I don't have anything in particular in mind," he said, "but I can tell you that it's for someone special. A woman." Whatever Helen's story, she had him thinking hard about the kind of woman he wanted, comparing her to those he'd dated over the years. *Getting her to say yes to him was not going to be easy.* "I can only tell you that only some type of purple flower will do."

"Okay, Dr. King. If you want to trust my judgment, then I'll make something special. I'll call up to your office and let you know when it's ready so that you can have a look at it before it's sent."

"I trust your judgment, he replied, pulling his card-case from his coat pocket. Handing her the white card, he instructed, "Just send the bill here, and I'll take care of it."

Satisfied that his request would be carried out, Sean hurried from the shop, his mind already on the unpleasant matter he was determined to see through.

Chapter Nine

An affair was out of the question.

Helen had made her decision by the time she arrived at Almeda Plaza where her law practice was located in one of the city's historic wards, Third Ward, also known as the center of Houston's African American community. While the idea sounded titillating and exciting, it was simply not for her.

Elaina had nothing to worry about. And as for history, she absolved herself from its alleged significance. She decided it was nothing more than moments stolen from the present and best left where it belonged - - in the past.

As she rode up the busy elevator to the fifth floor, her encounter with Claire Jackson this past Friday invaded her thoughts. She remembered that it had been late in the evening; most of the businesses were closed. She had only returned to drop off some papers, and the building was nearly deserted, so Claire had startled her when she stepped out from a hidden corridor.

A quiet, reserved woman who still pressed her hair, Claire Jackson, was not unattractive, but for such a young woman in her thirties, she always dressed down.

She had behaved nervously, Helen recalled. She was constantly looking around as if expecting the devil to jump

)ut from any space at   any   moment,   all   the   while
:lutching her cheap handbag as if it contained everything she
)wned.

The elevator stopped, and Helen stepped off onto the
iallway, suddenly conscious that she was clutching her
)riefcase and handbag. Much the way Claire did that day, she
:hided.

Still, she felt good about the intrusion; concern for
_laire's safety was her responsibility.

Walking pass freshly painted white walls, yellow
:eiling lights and gray carpet, she recalled that Claire wanted a
livorce. Her husband, Howard Jackson was away on a
veekend fishing trip. Claire planned to be out of the house by
he time he returned.

Could Helen arrange to have the papers delivered to
iim Monday, today?

The action she took should have resulted in Howard
Jackson being served before he left his home this morning,
Helen thought, reaching the last door near the end of the
hallway.

Framed by dark wood, Helen Parker, Attorney-At-
Law, in old English black lettering was stenciled onto the
opaque white glass.

She pushed open the door into a large, rectangular waiting room whose gold and white decor bespoke a subtle elegance and dignity. Live plants, plush beaded beige carpet, and office furniture of teak wood served to relax and instill confidence in troubled clients. The works of one artist, Brenda Joy, dominated the walls with pastel paintings that depicted happy moments, lives of hope. Miriam White, her secretary, looked up from typing at her computer.

"Morning. How was your weekend? Did you and Elaina enjoy the *Henrietta Marie* exhibit?"

Helen nearly blurted, "*I met a man.*" It wasn't until that moment she realized she had not banished Sean King from her thoughts. Nor was she especially pleased by the small quake that disrupted inside her, changing the beat of her heart.

"As much as anyone can, I guess," she replied, closing the door behind her. "I would still recommend it."

Rising from her seat, Miriam replied, "I don't know if I want to confront slavery on that level. I know that makes me a coward, but it's the way I feel."

As tall as Helen, Miriam was a reed thin woman, with gray brushed, wheat colored hair, wise brown eyes, and a long pinched nose.

She was also a good guard.

Ten years Helen's senior, Miriam was more than ecretary. Helen didn't know what she would have done vithout her. She was still amazed that she almost hadn't hired Miriam two years ago.

"You are not alone, Miriam," Helen replied sincerely is her own behavior teased her conscious.

With an under her breath sigh, she felt embarrassed to idmit that she didn't handle the *Henrietta Marie* too well as she auntered past Miriam on the way to her office.

Could she expect the same of Sean in her memory - -)assing the small kitchenette and then up another corridor - - irriving like the proverbial bad penny that kept cropping up inpredictably, wreaking havoc with her senses?

Slightly smaller than the waiting area, Helen's)ersonal office had a more personal, homey feel due to the)icture window, with a view overlooking Highway 288. ihe set her briefcase atop the rosewood, kneehole desk and)ut her handbag in a drawer.

Returning to the kitchenette, Helen got her blue kente lesign mug from the overhead cabinet and filled it with :offee, still warming in the pot.

If marriage were her goal, then he wasn't the man to get nvolved with, she recalled Sean telling her. Not that she needed o know, she thought sarcastically, stirring sugar and cream into her mug.

Miriam joined her, carrying several folders.

"Doug reports that the database is up and running. Any case you ever wanted to know about is now at our fingertips. Any problems, just page him."

Helen nodded absently, and then returned to her office, with Miriam on her heels. "Did Clark & Scott send that file over?" she asked, referring to the law firm that held the will in which one of her clients was contesting. The judge had ordered the parties to work it out, or he was going to appoint an executor, whereby all would end up losing more money than they got to keep.

"I'm afraid not," Miriam replied, setting folders on top of the desk.

Helen bit off a curse as she sat in one of the two chairs facing her desk. "I guess I'll start with them. Oh, did you see the Jackson File? I think I left it on your desk."

Miriam smiled at her. "You left it on **your** desk, and yes, I got it."

"Bless you," Helen mumbled into her cup. Sean claimed he was married to his career: he enjoyed his freedom, and the variety it afforded him. She should think his absence could be viewed as a plus factor if she decided to have an affair with him.

Which she decided against, she reminded herself.

"Is Claire still going to work at the *Cafe*?" Miriam asked, walking from behind the desk to stand by the vacant chair next to Helen's.

Miriam used to frequent the *Cafe*; she loved Claire's cooking.

"No," Helen replied, both her hands around the warm cup as she drank another swallow of coffee. While marriage wasn't remotely on her mind, she did have to consider the effects of an affair on her daughter. "She didn't know where she was going to be working." Was she really talking herself into saying *yes* to Sean?

Miriam donned that austere look of hers that made her seem unapproachable. "I noticed she's not requesting temporary support."

Helen nodded absently as she dragged her wayward thoughts to the matter at hand. Because of their association, her secretary was as aware as she that the homicide rate for women murdered by husbands and boyfriends, both present and former, was epidemically high. Women were particularly at-risk when in the process of leaving a relationship. However, the period after a woman left was most risky, generally becoming a homicide victim within two months after the separation.

Helen shook her head recalling that Clair had been firm, declaring, "*I don't want anything from Howard except my freedom.*" She drank a sip of coffee. "I couldn't budge her on that. And believe me," she added, swallowing another sip of coffee, "I tried."

"Well, I guess I've got to find another place to eat. There aren't too many good places nearby."

"Hopefully," Helen said, getting up to walk behind her desk, "she'll call and let us know before you starve to death."

"I noticed you didn't get her home number."

"She doesn't have one yet," Helen replied, scanning the names labeled on the folders Miriam had placed on her desk.

"Now, wait a minute," Miriam said, hands on her hips. "What is she going to do? How will she survive?"

"Believe me, I share your outrage and concern," Helen said, sitting behind her desk. She recalled putting the same questions before Claire the other night. "She promised to call as soon as she was situated. Meanwhile, we're going to have to cross our fingers that she knows what she's doing."

"Alrighty," Miriam said mollified. "It's time to get to work."

"Yeah, and don't let the time pass on me. Miss Elaina warned me not to be late. We're going to IMAX and the show starts at 3:30. I should leave at about a quarter to three."

No, Elaina was not a problem for him, she recalled Sean saying, but that was easy for him to say. How could she prepare her daughter for Sean in their lives on a temporary basis? What would Elaina think of her for going into a relationship that she knew from the onset wouldn't be permanent?

"What would you do without the little dictator?" Miriam said laughingly on her way out the door.

If she were honest, she would admit that Elaina wasn't the problem. Her daughter merely gave her a reason to say *no*, when a cry for courage was trying to steer her in the opposite direction.

"Hell, sometimes I wonder how I've managed all these years without her," Helen quipped amused.

It wasn't a broken heart she feared, either. She would relish the opportunity to flaunt a relationship fraught with troubles, and wail with her sisters who cried over men when passion failed to fulfill.

"Oh," Miriam said as she turned abruptly to face Helen, who looked up expectantly. "I know you heard about the Butler murders," she said ruefully.

Helen was jolted by the mention of the murders. Simultaneously, the haunted, murdering mother nightmare popped into her head as if it had been standing by, waiting on its cue to remind her. Carefully swallowing a sip of coffee or risk choking, she nodded affirmatively as a nibble of guilt gnawed at her conscious.

"She called here twice last week," Miriam said. "Joann Butler. You were in court each time. You did get the messages I left for you, didn't you?"

Helen tried to interpret exactly what Miriam was asking. Could she be wondering whether she was in trouble for not double-checking to ensure Helen got the messages? Or was she blaming herself, believing that a failure to deliver those messages contributed to Joann Butler's death, and that of her daughter?

Helen absolved her secretary openly. "I got them, Miriam, thanks." Now, if only she could pardon herself.

Miriam sighed relieved and proceeded to her desk in the reception area. Helen sat behind hers. Taking sips of coffee, she perused the folders, trying to decide which case to tackle first. She picked up one, and then tossed it back on the desk and picked up another.

Before she knew it, half an hour had passed, a glance at her watch confirmed, and all she had managed to do was rearrange the file folders on her desk.

It was no use. She couldn't concentrate.

She wished Joann Butler had not called her. She pushed away from her desk and meandered to the window to stare out absently at the cars zooming east and west on the freeway. It was too late to do anything for Joann Butler, she advised herself.

And too soon to seek a restraining order on Claire Jackson's behalf.

Even if she could have helped Joann, she would not have accepted any work from her. Certainly the woman knew she had once been engaged to her husband. And for sure, Helen thought, Joann wouldn't have asked her to represent her in a divorce against Ray.

Now, she'll never know why Joann Butler called.

The intercom on her desk buzzed, ending her muse. "Yes, Miriam?"

"Ms. Parker, there are three gentlemen out here to see you. Are you available?"

Helen looked puzzled. She returned to her desk to consult her calendar. "I don't have any meetings on my schedule today. You know that."

"Mr. Ray Butler wants to talk to you."

Miriam's voice came over the intercom in an enigmatic whisper.

Helen's adrenaline level shot up and a frown sprang to her expression.

Slowly, she dropped into her seat, her expression mired in deep thought until she realized Miriam could not answer the question she unintentionally asked aloud. "What does he want?"

"He's here with his son and campaign manager. They know you're busy, but hope you can squeeze them in for an appointment," Miriam replied, her voice steeled in softness. "Are you available?"

The question was posed as to give Helen the opportunity to say no. It clouded her gaze with indecision. Quite frankly, she was much too startled to think of a suitable excuse that she wouldn't have to explain later about denying his request for a meeting.

"Give me a minute, then bring them back," she heard herself say. It was without a doubt time to put all her training to the test. "Oh, and Miriam," she added, her voice lowered with surreptitious meaning, "we're out of coffee, okay?"

Chapter Ten

"Coffee?"

"None for me, thanks," Sgt. Diamond replied.

Sean dittoed Sgt. Diamond's reply before Dr. Valeria Clemens could extend the offer to him, shaking his head. "I'm going to stop here," he said, indicating the room marked MEN off the corridor where they walked, heading to her first floor office in the administration section of the building.

In the restroom of the Joseph Jachimczyk Forensic Center, Sean turned on the faucet, scooped handfuls of water and splashed his face with the cool liquid, not once, but several times. Every time he entered the house of the dead, he wondered if he'd ever get the smell off his skin. The air refresher used to mask the scent of death did crazy things to his senses. As if he were coming down with a case of mysophobia, a fear of contamination.

They -- he, Dr. Clemens, and Sgt. Diamond who arrived just minutes before him - - had peeked in on the autopsies of Joann and Taylor Butler.

Even though he worked with the dead, he never wanted to do what pathologists did. Cutting into flesh, dead or alive, gave him the willies.

He could handle the bones, where he did his best work with the remains: bones, but no blood. He felt no such discomfort, imagining how his subjects looked from their remains, but there was no way in hell he could cut into their flesh.

The death of little Taylor, more than her mother, had inspired an atypical reaction in him. Something about her death, her abruptly shortened life undoubtedly hit a nerve. Young black murdered girls were not a professional anomaly. He'd seen worse, if one could imagine that.

Maybe he was his own victim, fed up with the insidious killings people of color inflicted on one another, he thought, snatching several cornbread hard paper towels from the bin on the wall to wipe his face. There seemed no depths to the gross savagery, and no end of it in sight. After drying his hands, he balled the towels, tossed them in the trash, and left the restroom for Dr. Clemens office.

The Harris County run morgue located within Houston's massive medical center complex was a ten-year old building that retained its pristine white and steel clean look outside and in its six floors. He took the hallway that lead to Dr. Valerie Clemens' office. Large framed studio portraits of the Harris County Commissioners, as well as that of Dr. Jachimczyk himself lined the walls.

The voices coming from an opened door off the corridor took Sean to his destination. One of the voices belonged to Dr. Clemens.

She had been one of his former forensic professors, a relationship they had to keep secret as **CYA** *(cover your ass)* showed itself to be **SOP** *(standard operating procedure)* on this particular case, the handling, of which, had more peculiarities than the murders themselves.

"I don't recall having to dot so many I's and cross so many T's in my career," she had remarked.

The paranoia was not wholly unfounded. The previous ME could attest to that.

Upon reaching the door, he saw her sitting behind her oak desk, listening with stone-faced attentiveness.

To look at her, one would guess Dr. Valerie Clemens with her soft features and berry-brown complexion was in her mid to late forties. Her credentials, however, were those of a person twice her 56 years.

Housed in a petite frame, she was a dynamo with a Classic A-type personality. Her temperament could slide from polite and charming to gruff and unyielding in jet speed.

Sgt. Paul Diamond occupied one of the two chairs in front of her desk, with his notepad on his crossed right knee, his right hand clutching a BIC ballpoint.

Sensing him at the door, Dr. Clemens whose eyes never left Sgt. Diamond, invited, "Come on in and have a seat, Sean."

The room looked more like a mini-library than an office, with three tall wooden bookcases lining the beige walls and a picture window that didn't offer much of a view: it overlooked the employee parking lot. Sean took the chair next to Sgt. Diamond.

"The grandmother picked up the little girl from summer school Thursday afternoon around three, took her to the much coveted Mickey Dees, and then dropped her off at home shortly after four. This seems their regular routine. Mrs. Butler usually got home from work by 5:30."

"A lot can happen to a child in an hour," Dr. Clemens said.

Although her tone was neutral, Sean could tell she disapproved of leaving children unattended even for a short period. In his generation the incident seemed a cultural characteristic of working parents, which became euphemistically known as the days of the " latch key kids." But even those days were gone when a child could safely be left alone at home.

"Any leads on *Claire's Kitchen*?" he asked, recalling that the police discovered meals prepared by a local caterer in the freezer and refrigerator. "Maybe this Claire person knows something."

With a thumb marking the page he'd been referring to in his notebook, Sgt. Diamond flipped several pages. "Name's Claire Jackson." He read from the page. "She works at the *Almeda Cafe*, but we haven't been able to reach her." He flipped back to his original page and resumed. "Mrs. Singleton . . ."

"Who's Mrs. Singleton?" Sean asked.

"Joann Butler's mother. She hadn't spoken to her daughter since last Wednesday when she dropped off the little girls' ballerina costume. Her daughter didn't mention anything that was troubling her. Mrs. Butler went to work Thursday morning, and possibly left early. One fellow worker said she left around noon, another thinks she saw Mrs. Butler in the parking garage around two-thirty."

Sean exchanged a silent stare with Dr. Clemens. She closed her eyes fractionally, and he knew she was trying to blot out the image of the murdered child. She had to put what she knew about her death before someone took her life into perspective in order to move on. He understood fully her anguish, yet love for the job she did.

"The co-worker of the noon sighting offered a theory we hadn't considered, but it went nowhere," Sgt. Diamond added.

Sean frowned. "What was the theory?" he asked, wondering what he could have overlooked at the crime scene. Neither he nor Artifacts, Inc. could afford a label of producing careless work.

A smirk of a smile snaked around Sgt. Diamond's lips as he replied, "She blames the murders on Chester Mason. Her name by the way is Ruby Poindexter."

Dr. Clemens saved Sean the trouble of asking. "Why does she think this Mason did it?"

Sgt. Diamond chuckled. "The woman has issues," he replied, shaking his head. "I probably ought to leave it at that. Mason was the little girl's biological father. Ex-offender; petty crimes. We checked him out. Zero."

"Do you mind if I talk to these people?"

"You'll be wasting your time, but it's your time," Sgt. Diamond replied, scribbling on a sheet in his notebook. He tore the sheet out and handed it to Sean. "If you happen to learn anything, useful or not, let me know.

"Alright, doc," he said, turning his full attention to Dr. Clemens, "let me have it."

Dr.Clemens began rifling through her desk drawer to finally locate a stick of gum. "Neither of us would stake our life on it," she said, removing the wrapper. She stuck the gum in her mouth and continued. "It looks like Joann Butler died late Friday morning," she said, chewing.

Sgt. Diamond struggled to suppress the urge to rush her along as she stopped speaking to chew more sweetness from the gum. Sean smiled to himself at the torture she doled.

"Taylor Butler," she resumed. "Well, the little girl died earlier, between Thursday night and Friday morning," she concluded, and then sat utterly still, no longer chewing.

Sgt. Diamond's face crumbled in a painful expression. He flashed a frown at Sean, then Dr. Clemens. "That's all you can tell me? You can't narrow it down anymore than that?"

"I can tell you the little girl had been bathed with Dove soap," she replied. "That the Mickey Dees burger, fries and strawberry ice cream was her last meal."

"Dr. Clemens," Sgt. Diamond said, "you don't understand. The case is getting cold, reaching freezing temperature. I wouldn't be here except I can't get anything more than superficial answers to superficial questions. Butler is still stonewalling. If we're not careful, this case will get away from us just like it did the Boulder, Colorado police department when they failed to indict someone for the murder of Jon Benet Ramsey."

Sgt. Diamond really poured it on thick, Sean thought,

smiling amused. There wasn't a medical examiner in the world that hadn't heard the blues ballad sung by a homicide investigator. The words may be different, but the cry of urgency was just the same. Dr. Clemens had already broken a record, allowing the Butler murders to skip to the head of the autopsy line.

"You saw the media vultures when you came in," she said testily as she folded her arms on the desk. "They have been camped out in the lobby since we opened at 6:30 this morning, some fool from Butler's office has called on the hour every hour, wanting to know when the bodies will be released so the funeral can be arranged, so don't come in here and make a nuisance of yourself, Diamond.

"Damn, I could use a cigarette," she bemoaned with a nicotine addict's cry, flipping the pages of a report on her desk.

"Bad habit," Sgt. Diamond warned conversationally. "Come on, stop playing with me. I know you've got more."

"Don't start nagging," she replied, opening one of the folders before her. "I don't know how much help this is going to be, but okay."

Trying not to slouch in his seat, Sean barely paid attention as Dr. Clemens detailed the initial autopsies' findings. He already knew some of the results were going to raise more questions than they answered. What they knew for certain was that homicide was the manner of death by asphyxiation due to lack of oxygen, caused by suffocation. The vessels had been occluded or closed, and the face and neck had been congested and dark red. While there was no indication of sexual assault prior to Taylor Butler's death, the autopsy confirmed chronic sexual abuse. She had been someone's sexual object long before the killer took her life.

"Butler's wife was pregnant?"

The raised tone of surprise from Sgt. Diamond slightly jolted Sean. He inhaled deeply, noting the air didn't get any fresher, and sat up straighter in his seat, realizing he'd missed whatever Dr. Clemens revealed of Joann Butler's death.

The homicide investigator was scribbling away in his notebook, as questions rolled off his tongue like a machine gun.

"How many months along was she? Is Ray Butler the father? What's the blood type? . . ."

"The autopsy is being done on the fetus by one of my assistants, as we speak," she said. "Dr. Walters, who also did the autopsy on Mrs. Butler, should be done in a couple more hours, baring no surprises. It's up to you to get a blood sample from the councilman."

A familiar lyric, the theme song from Batman played a full measure before Sgt. Diamond, annoyed by the interruption, answered his cell. "Diamond," he said gruffly with impatience. Rising, he walked out of the room, the cell at his ear as he listened intently.

"Excuse me," Dr. Clemens said, and then slipped from the room, a finger looped through the holder of her empty coffee cup.

Sean folded his arms across his chest and slouched in his chair, with the death of Joann Butler and that of *Little Taylor's* turning over in his head.

He felt envious of Sgt. Diamond, an acute need, like jealously, to trade places with the investigator.

It was Sgt. Diamond's job to find the motive that would explain the whys that would lead to a killer. Not that any sane person could comprehend why one person killed another, or, especially a child.

Still, apprehending a savage killer was in Sgt. Diamond's hands. The homicide investigator, by far, faced the toughest challenge and the most satisfying vengeance.

Save for a final report and testifying in court should the killer be caught, his role in the case was over, Sean reminded himself. Quick, easy money for Artifacts, Inc. The contract fulfilled, was now free to enjoy his vacation and the *Henrietta Marie* exhibit. He should be satisfied, however, he wasn't. He knew he felt that way because there was no resolution; the killer remained unknown.

Dr. Clemens returned, blowing over a cup of steaming coffee.

"Diamond was called away on another case, I presume," he said, sitting upright in his seat.

"I guess so," she said, sitting in the chair next to Sean. "I hated disturbing you on the first day of your vacation," she said, drinking a sip of coffee, "but I really needed you. If I forgot to say thanks, let me do so now."

"Don't worry about it. I was glad to be of help. In fact, some ..."

"How bad was Abijan?"

Sean slightly cocked his head to the side, a transitory thought that she knew what he was thinking and diverted his attention from it intentionally occurred to him. And it worked, for he instantly recalled the carnage he witnessed working to identify the charred remains of two dozen people found buried on a site where construction of a new hotel was about to get underway.

"It was pretty bad," he said at last, worrying his mustache. Before they were set on fire, their bodies had been split down the middle from sternum to crotch, representing divided loyalties, which was not tolerated. The dead had opposed the government's joint project with a US corporation. He dropped his hands to his lap. "But that's done, thank God. About the Butler case . . ."

This time Dr. Valerie Clemens was not subtle as she cut him off succinctly. "Let it go, Sean," she said, wagging a finger at him. "You've done your job, let the police do theirs. It's going to stink real bad before it's over. Go home and get drunk, or go out and get laid.

"You did fine by little Taylor and her mother."

Chapter Eleven

Helen felt ill at-ease with her present company, her senses a hotbed of discontent.

"I don't practice criminal law." She literally clamped her mouth shut. She had already advised them to see a criminal attorney. Even that innocent advice was enough to lock her into an attorney-client privilege scenario she wanted no part of. Still, she maintained her composure with a neutral expression and unaffected emotion.

"Well, I can tell you that we don't need a criminal lawyer. We just need competent representation when Ray talks to the police."

Although there were four of them in the room, the conversation for the past half hour occurred between herself and Barry Barnes.

Of average everything - - medium brown complexion and roughly two inches taller than she at 5'10" - - except his mouth, Barnes was Ray's mayoral campaign manager. In his early-thirties, his ego, arrogance, and nerve filled more of his Italian cut suit than his lean frame.

Helen unconsciously drummed the desk with her fingers before catching herself, and stopped. She should have known when they walked in, looking like those three monkeys, *Hear, See, and Speak No Evil* that they were full of nonsense, and this unscheduled and wholly unexpected meeting was going to be a waste of her time.

"A criminal lawyer would give the impression that he's guilty," Barnes repeated passionately. He stuck his hands in his pockets and strode to the picture window and looked out. "We don't want to give that impression," he added in a calmer tone as he faced Helen. "Particularly not now," his tone dramatically soft.

"He's going to file next week. Do you realize how bad it would look if he walked into the police station with a criminal attorney on his arms?"

Ray didn't seem to mind that they were talking about him as if he weren't in the room. Helen never knew him to be that quiet, nor as subdued as he'd been since they filed into her office.

After a few moments spent with condolences offered and accepted, Ray and his son, Stan sat on the couch, content to let Barry do all the talking. She guessed his behavior wasn't too out of the ordinary, considering the reason.

Regardless, she did not believe their explanation as to why they sought her out to represent Ray, who as far as she knew, was not a suspect in his wife and daughter's murders. Not that it mattered, she thought sarcastically.

"Let me see if I got this right," she said, tactfully, masking her suspicion. She rose from her seat and walked around to perch her hips on the corner of her desk. "You want me to accompany Ray to his interview with the police to protect his rights from responses that could incriminate him, even though he's not guilty of anything, so people" - - translate voting public, she thought - - "will believe that he's innocent. And that's how you will explain **your** decision **not** to use a criminal lawyer."

"Yes," Barnes replied with emphasis, an *'Amen'* attached in his tone.

She lightly passed a hand across her forehead, wondering if the word "Stupid" was written there in bold letters. She wet her lips before she replied. "I will simply say again that I don't care to be a part of this."

"Initially, you claimed you weren't competent, now you're saying you don't care to help out the councilman," Barnes said as if incredulous that she would pass on a great opportunity.

Helen wondered whether he was also trying to bait her. Taking no chances, she said, "Good day, gentleman."

"I told you she wouldn't do it!"

Stan Butler, Ray's son, who sprang from the couch and was bolting for the door, naturally seized Helen's attention. With a light brown, café au lait complexion like his father, he was thin framed and pretty for a young man, with thick brows and long curly lashes edging his deep-set eyes. Dressed in a suit with a vest like a prep student, she put his age around the late teens or early twenties. A man, yet, not quite. Impetuous and maybe hotheaded, too. She felt sorry for him.

"Stan," Barry barked, "come back here."

The young man pivoted sharply to glare at Barry, then his father who was sitting as meekly as a lamb on the couch.

Seeing Ray, a beaten man, eyes red and swollen, it was hard to believe she was once attracted to him, Helen thought. The charcoal suit was ill fitting on his slumped shoulders; grief made him small, even though he was a six-footer.

Then again, it wasn't his physical looks that had attracted her to him. He used to be a sensitive, caring man who was passionately concerned about the black community. An activist, he was always leading a demonstration against or for something that benefited his people.

"Dad, this was a waste of time," Stan said hotly. "You knew she was not going to help. I told you that. I told both of you," he added, his beady brown-eyed glare shooting daggers at Helen.

Helen nonchalantly folded her arms across her bosom as she gazed at Stan who she had only seen photographs of before.

He was living out-of-state with his mother when she dated Ray who played the proud papa in public, but she couldn't recall him including his son when they planned their lives together. At the time, she hadn't given it a second thought.

Barry, on the other hand, was blessed with a familiar last name. His grandfather was one of the first black judges appointed to a federal court, and her parents knew his parents. There had been some social contact between them, but their families were not close.

"Helen . . ."

Ray finally spoke, and she gave him her attention.

"We go back," he continued slowly as if feeling his way. "I know our history together can't be one of your fondest memories, but I was hoping you would do this for me."

"Hm," Stan snorted. "Have you forgotten the old saying? Hell hath no fury like a woman scorned, and only God can save you when you piss off a black woman."

Helen stiffened at the challenge his remark posed, but caught herself before a snide retort came out of her mouth.

Her patience nevertheless was fast running out with the lot of them.

"Oh, now don't act like you don't know what I'm talking about . . ." Stan fired at Helen.

"Stan," Ray reproached mildly. "You don't know Helen, and my history with her is none of your business."

Outraged, Stan fired back, "I don't believe how incredibly naive you are about her."

"Maybe you better leave," Barry said decisively, his eyes narrowed with his suppressed anger. "You're not helping matters at all."

Now they were talking about her as if she wasn't in the room, Helen thought annoyed, and she didn't like it. "All of you can leave," she said, standing to her full height, hands dropping to her sides. "You know where the door is."

"Helen, please," Ray said softly, a plea in his sleepy brown eyes.

He pushed himself up and walked across the room to stand directly in front of her. He intruded her space, but she refused to move. He attempted to take her hands, which she refused to give, instead, folding her arms across her chest.

"Barry, Stan," Ray said, his gaze sweeping over them, " let me talk to Helen alone. Please."

"I'll wait in the car," Stan snapped, seconds before he stormed from the room.

Barry inhaled deeply, nodded, and then left them alone.

A somber tension hovered in the air as Helen remained on her feet, standing at the corner of her desk, her arms still folded across her bosom. She didn't sit because it would give Ray an impression she didn't want him to assume, an advantage she didn't dare yield. It was bad enough just being alone in the room with him. Even her insides trembled as if blood and bone had a memory.

"Your campaign manager is an idiot," she said, her tone unlike her words neutral. "He's taking advantage of your weakness right now. If you were thinking properly, you would not have come to me for representation in a criminal matter in the first place." She wouldn't represent him even in those areas of the law on which she was qualified.

Ray sauntered away to stand in front of the picture window. His bottom lip folded in his mouth, he looked out, but she doubted he could identify anything he saw. His hands were in his pant pockets, and as his coat was still buttoned in the front, the sides and back of it flipped up unattractively with his stance.

"You only met Joann that one time, didn't you?"

Houston wasn't nicknamed the Space City for nothing. The sprawling 600 square miles meant that if you ran into someone you didn't want to see it was most likely accidental.

While Taylor Butler took swim lessons from the coaches of Elaina's swim team, the Parkers and Butler's paths never crossed. Still, she wondered if things - - life for both Joann and her daughter - - would have turned out differently had she taken that call.

"I didn't think you knew her before the night of the gala on that slave ship," he continued as if her silence corroborated his assertion. "She heard about you from her father, I think. It could have been her mother, but in either case, I imagine," he continued, bunching his shoulders with confusion on his face, "they must have held you up as some kind of role model."

Helen wondered where this was going. She saw no point to it. There was nothing Ray could say that would change her mind.

"I don't know what Joann was thinking, especially when she put Taylor in swimming …"

"Ray, I don't care to hear any of this," Helen said firmly, her hands dropping to her sides in fists. She refused to be manipulated by him, and in fact, was offended by his attempt. "I don't want to get involved."

He turned his head to look at her. "You're already involved, Helen. Every woman in this city is involved, whether they want to be or not. Who would have thought something like this could happen to the wife and daughter of a politician?"

Such an ego! Helen thought. She would have admitted that she was indeed involved, but not the way he meant. Definitely more than she ever hoped to be. Forget that his rationale reeked of self-serving machismo.

"This woman does not want anything to do with your case," she reiterated vehemently. "I will not represent you."

Ray turned to face her fully. He removed his hands from his pockets, only to rub the balls of his palms together.

"It seems you and my son are in accord about that," he said softly with a temperate chuckle. "Smart kid, don't you think?" He cracked his knuckles. "But he's too hot-headed."

Spoiled, Helen wanted to add, but she remained silent. She knew what Ray was trying to do, and she wasn't going for it.

"Do you know why?"

"Why, what?" Helen asked, and then flinched. She could kick herself. "Never mind, I don't want to know," she said hastily, throwing her hands up as she walked to stand behind her chair.

"What I want is for you to leave my office," she added, pointing to the door. "I can have my secretary compile a list of numbers for several good criminal attorneys in the city who would love to handle your case."

"His mother is the one," Ray continued, ignoring her appeals of disinterest.

He stared at her with his head slightly cocked, as if looking for a sign of awareness from her. "I know it's been a long time, but I doubt you have forgotten. Black women seem to hang onto bad memories of the past when a black man has done them wrong."

Helen trembled with outrage as she held her tongue, hid her emotions and shut down, no longer listening to Ray. The only noise she heard were thoughts of self-murder for not listening to her first mind, but those thoughts soon gave way to the memory of her one night of indiscretion.

She remembered the night chosen to prove her love to Ray . . . the panic, instead of desire that had teased her as they'd edged toward intimacy . . . the screaming fit that propelled him from the bed. She barely recognized her own voice until her throat ached from the wild cries.

"Anyway, I just wanted to clear that up. He believes that because I broke off our engagement you were still holding a grudge. I explained to him that you weren't like that. After all, that was ten years ago, pure history."

Ray left her alone with her inexplicable cries and feelings of guilt and shame, Helen recalled, with a renewal of those twin emotions coursing through her.

Sometimes during the night, drenched in confusion and fear, she realized she needed professional help.

When the sun broke though the curtains the next morning, she awakened to find him sitting in a chair on the side of the bed. She never got to pursue her argument for a second chance. He called off the wedding.

There had been no man for her since. An unconscious sigh trembled in her bosom.

She wouldn't let herself cry over him. On some level, she must have known deep down that he wasn't worth her tears. But, oh how painful the humiliation had been!

The reminder jolted her back to the present. She stared peeved at Ray, and her anger grew as he prattled on, sounding well rehearsed.

"There are some things about my wife that I can't trust with anybody. I would rather they not come out, but I'm sure the police will interpret my silence on the matter to mean that I'm hindering their investigation."

"Excuse me," Helen said, interrupting him. If he thought he was going to trick her into a confidentiality game, he was mistaken.

"Where are you going?"

Helen was halfway to the door. "Since you won't leave, I will." She considered having Miriam call up security from the first floor.

"Helen, come back."

She heard him calling after her seconds before she looked over her shoulder to see him following. She was in the hallway adjacent to the opening to the kitchen area. She didn't stop until reaching the reception area. Miriam looked up from her typing at the computer.

"What's . . .?" Miriam abruptly stopped speaking when Ray appeared.

"I was just walking Councilman Butler out," Helen said as the office phone rang.

Ray sidled next to Helen as Miriam answered the phone. "I see you haven't changed, still trying to be the perfect daughter," he whispered snidely in her ear. "You're just as immature as you were back then."

Helen returned his harsh stare with a totally bored, unimpressed look. She refused to dignify his parting shot with a response, but it still hurt.

Needing all her energy to keep the memories in check, she faked a yawn to get her message across to him.

With rage seizing his expression, Ray looked as if he wanted to strike her. Instead, he drew himself up, and with a snap of his shoulders, he brushed past her and walked out, slamming the door behind him.

With her hand covering the phone, Miriam stared after Ray puzzled. "What was that all about?"

Helen hid her unnerved innards with a forced smile. "Nothing. Who's on the phone?"

"A Dr. Sean King. He wants to speak with you."

Chapter Twelve

Helen agreed to have lunch with him.

Having just completed his second call within a ten-minute time span, Sean continued to hold his cell as if it were a precious item. There was a lopsided grin on his face, and a feeling of accomplishment in his heart. And then, as if suddenly realizing where he was, he sighed and slipped the cell into its case.

There would be plenty of time to moon over his luck later, he told himself, as he sat in the cool confines of his cranberry Jag idling across the street, in front of a two-story, red brick home.

Surrounded by a knee-high, white picket fence, and styled similarly to its contemporary companions on the street, it belonged to the Singletons.

He felt certain that they'd give up their nice, middleclass house in a suburbs of Acres Home in exchange for the lives of their daughter and granddaughter, Joann and *du petit Taylor* Butler in a heartbeat.

He readjusted the knot of his tie, killed the engine, grabbed his sports coat resting on the passenger seat under the map of Houston, and got out.

This was a courtesy he always performed when the deceased left family to grieve. Expensive shades shielded his eyes from the sun's glare, and despite the heat, he slipped on his coat. Respect and duty won out over comfort.

He noticed the emerald grounds, the labors of a talented yard person with a green thumb apparently shared by the neighbors as he sauntered up the sidewalk to the front door. Calvin Singleton owned a yard service, he recalled learning from Sgt. Diamond as he pressed the door buzzer. He was also pastor of his church where his wife, Shirley, volunteered in a kind of social worker capacity for the church's senior members.

The door cracked open and a heavy-voiced woman called out. "Yes? May I help you?"

"Mrs. Singleton?" Sean said cautiously, unable to see to whom he was speaking. "I'm Dr. Sean King. I'm working on the investigation." He didn't add his explicit role, assuming she would know that he referred to the murders of Joann and Taylor Butler.

The door opened wider. "Come in, Dr. King. I'll get the Singletons for you."

The back of a woman, with the compact build of a linebacker and sporting a short-cut Afro dressed in a fancy paramilitary ensemble walked out as Sean entered the living room. He doubted she was one of the Singleton's church members. As far as he knew, Joann was their only child, he thought, wondering who was the woman that let him in.

It was an attractive room in a rectangle shape, with light green walls, brown carpet, and a plaid couch of earth tones, with matching chairs. There was no coffee table, but against the far wall sat a waist-high bookshelf.

Displayed on top was a twelve-inch long wooden cross next to a large black bible; knickknacks lined the shelves below. He spotted an ivy limb that had snaked out from under the heavy drapes that covered the front window, and couldn't help noticing the framed charcoal sketch of a 'Black Jesus' that hung on the wall over the couch.

"Yawl find who took my girls from us, yet?"

Sean turned his attention from the picture to the Singletons as they entered.

The drawling tenor came from Calvin Singleton, a wiry, muscular man who stood only about 5'7" and wore suspenders that were now hanging at his sides. He saw Joann in her father's face. Shirley Singleton, he presumed, was shorter in height and heavy-boned, but still considered a petit woman. She wasn't ugly, but definitely not attractive or even commonplace pretty.

"I'm sorry to say that we haven't, Mr. Singleton."

Sorrow and despair had aged them beyond their mid-sixties, stealing the luster from their smooth brown skin, deepening age lines around their eyes, and souring their expressions.

"Then why are you here?" Shirley Singleton demanded harshly.

She had a deep, commanding voice. And, she was angry, and rightly so, Sean thought. He could honestly say that he'd never thought of it before . . . the conscious realization that even if he lived 900 years, he'd never internalize the grief of a mother whose child preceded her in death. In this case, two generations were lost.

"I know this is a bad time for you and your husband, Mrs. Singleton. I want you to know that I'm truly sorry for your loss and that I intend to do everything in my power to bring your daughter and granddaughter's killer to justice."

"Thank you for coming," Calvin said with sincere solemnity. "We appreciate that."

"I was wondering if you knew whether Joann had any enemies," Sean said, sensing they were about to retreat.

"We already told the police everything we know." With that, Calvin Singleton turned and left the room. Mrs. Singleton merely stared at him, with a scowl that he knew would be there a long time between her brows.

"Again, Mrs. Singleton, please accept my condolences."

A half hour later, Sean arrived at his next destination on his investigative quest to find a killer. "Good . . .." He never got "afternoon" out, as a disgruntled customer on his way out the door cut it off.

"Claire's not here today. I wouldn't try my luck on anything more complicated than a burger and fries, if I were you."

Stunned by the announcement, Sean muttered, "Thank you." His curious gaze followed the speaker, a husky, middle-aged man in a barber's jacket as he got into a green Buick and drove off the parking lot of the *Community Cafe*.

Located in midtown Houston, more popularly Third Ward, where potential for a successful black business was great, the *Cafe* was situated at the corners of Almeda and Southmore, right off Highway 288. He was roughly fifteen minutes from the forensics center within the largest medical center complex in the country, and within walking distance from Helen's office.

The eating establishment was similar in nature to the *Cook's Chamber*, the cafeteria-styled restaurant in the

Artifacts, Inc. building, only smaller and nowhere near as stylish. He found it strangely quiet; it seemed the few patrons he spied had nothing to say.

The service line divided the long rectangular room east and west. There were no patrons in line to be served, nor was anyone attending the cash register close to the front door.

Three bored-looking, male servers dressed in white stood inanimately against the wall behind the various entrees that were laid out in hot trays to his left.

Opposite, to his right, red and white booth seating ran along an L-corner, with a view of the parking lot to the south. A side door split the front section from the back.

Thinking the servers might be a little more animated, and definitely more approachable if he placed an order, Sean headed for the line, intending to order the suggested burger and fries. Suddenly, a clamorous din of crashing pots and pans and shattering glass caught the attention of everyone in the place.

The servers' netted heads all turned toward the back room from where the noise originated. It seemed as if everybody froze defensively, ready to run if trouble persisted.

One of the servers threw up his hands, snatched the hairnet off his head, and stormed out the front door. Sean, who silently named him the *Tin Man* because a hard life showed in his long, thin, dark brown face, followed.

Outside the building, the *Tin Man* was lighting a cigarette. Sean put his age in the late thirties and waited until he drew his first puff of nicotine before he sparked up conversation. "What was going on in there?"

"Howard's acting a fool. If he thinks I'm going to put up with his bullshit, he's crazy. I see why Claire left his sorry ass."

"Claire left?" he asked in hopes of ascertaining some information. Visiting the Singletons was almost fruitless; he had been hoping this trip wouldn't be. "Where did she go?"

The server shrugged, blowing a string of smoke. "Don't know. She didn't come in at all today. Howard was served divorce papers this morning, so I don't think Claire will be back just to cook."

"Ouch," Sean said, although he felt nothing about the matter. Hell, he didn't even know Claire and Howard were married. "That's got to hurt."

"Hurt?" Tin Man snorted sarcastically. "As far as Howard's concerned, her absence only hurt his cash register."

Sean waited quietly and wasn't disappointed, although as he had suspected, the information was hardly useful in the murders.

"Claire was a helluva cook. That's why this place was doing as well as it was. Several regulars came in this morning for breakfast and couldn't get none of her biscuits . . . man, they turned around and left."

Just then, a shiny black, late model Chevy truck jetted from the back lot to the front and onto the street. It cut into the path of several cars, barely missing them, and sped off, with a squeal of tires burning the hot asphalt.

"That was Howard," Tin Man said, drawing another puff from his cigarette. "Well, at least, we'll get some peace and quiet for a little while. I hope he doesn't come back." He tossed the burning cigarette, and then returned inside the *Cafe*.

Although the morning round of interviews had not been as fruitful as he'd like, Sean wasn't terribly disappointed. Striding to his car, he began to feel the euphoria of romantic enchantment as he thought about his next stop.

Chapter Thirteen

"Why did you call me?"

Helen couldn't believe she accepted Sean's invitation to lunch. Although even as he had reminded her, she did intend to eat a midday meal somewhere. While true, she knew it wouldn't have been at a place that provided such a lovely romantic ambience that not even the scorching hot sun perched in the endless stretch of blue sky could detract.

And it certainly wouldn't have been with a man so obviously comfortable with himself who knew how to wear a suit as deftly as he did leisurewear, she thought, noting the perfect fit for his fine physique, the color complementing his butterscotch complexion.

Sean flashed a speculative smile, his rich gaze as unnerving as the foolish nonchalance of his expression. *There was always a price to pay*, she thought, determined to remain undaunted. And then he smiled in earnest, and her innards erupted delightfully.

"Why did you come?"

They sat next to one another -- close enough to touch, but didn't except incidentally - - at an umbrellaed table at the patio-styled Rainbow Room, one of four couples lunching under the care of white-uniformed waiters.

"Curiosity," she replied, denying him the answer he sought. Still, she tried to convince herself that this wasn't real. The birds chirping alongside a lush and dreamy jazz rendition of *Summertime* came from a recording, and an outdoor semblance of an air conditioner starved the heat. She probably would have eaten at her desk as usual, she thought, as her gaze slid down the sloping green landscape where the pebbled patio ended, and the manmade pond below began where the ducks were doing a swan dance.

She shook concern of the fanciful surroundings from her head and looked at him headlong. With a tweak of her nose, she added, "You sounded desperate on the phone."

"Moi? Desperate?" he quipped, a hand on his chest as he feinted outrage.

"Okay," she chuckled, "not desperate, but urgent for sure. Did something happen?"

His face askew as he muttered a sound, undistinguishable except for the look of frustration that blinked across his expression, he replied, "Oui. You can say that."

"But you can't, or don't want to talk about it," she guessed.

"Both."

Helen bobbed her head pensively, sensing that she didn't want to hear it anyway. Her mental plate was already full: the guilt she assumed knowing that Joann called her before she died, and then Ray's unexpected appeal edged her subconscious like marionettes. She shook her head lightly.

"So? Are you ready to answer my question?"

Sean pulled her attention back to him, coaxing a smile from her and a streaming sense of joy inside her with his eager expression. She'd rather think of him over Ray and Joann Butler any old day.

"Which one would that be?" she asked with playful amusement.

Sean laughed, his broad shoulders in the olive sports coat writhing amused over his muscular torso. "Is it always going to be like this with you … you answer my every question with a question?"

Helen opened her mouth to reply, and then caught herself. It was the preface of his query that gave her pause, for it occurred to her that either a negative or affirmative reply meant she accepted the terms of his proposal that they have an affair. She felt coy curling the corners of her mouth. "I must say you do require full and complete attention."

"That's exactly what I want."

"And what are you willing to give?" she retorted in jest.

He stared at her a moment, levity pushed aside, his expression serious and still.

She held her breath as if afraid of the answer, or rather, that the question demanded an answer from her.

When he spoke at last, his voice lowered in a sensual whisper filled with resolution, "Anything you want," Helen shivered imperceptibly.

"Are you and Elaina safe, Helen?"

Helen shook her head as she stared puzzled at Sean. She wondered where the question came from, and why. "What do you mean?"

She recalled that he had seemed a little nervous when he came to the office to pick her up, but on the drive he reverted to the cool, super confident man she met a few days ago. She doubted driving was what soothed him, but neither would she say that her presence restored him.

Sean smiled sheepishly, and ducked his head. "Forget it."

"No," she insisted. "Tell me."

Unconscious and instinctive, she covered his hand on the table, and naturally, her heart beat a staccato ditty in her bosom. She removed her hand and folded both in her lap.

Sean inhaled deeply, and then released his breath with a mellow sigh. "You didn't have to do that that. I don't mind being touched. In fact, I like it when you touch me. It instills hope."

"My touch instills hope?" she queried with a self-depreciating chuckle.

He stared wordlessly at her, that familiar jaunty grin on his mouth. She felt trapped, seized by the intrepid look of entreaty in his eyes. Her pulse quickened, and a hearty sensation coursed through her.

"Here's your lemonade," the waiter announced as he placed two tall frosty glasses before each of them. "I'll be back with your order shortly," he said with a slight obsequious bow and a smile before he slipped away as unobtrusive as he appeared.

Grateful for the respite, Helen picked up her glass and drank several sips of lemonade. Its cool sweetness did wonders for her suddenly parched throat, but not her senses or thoughts, both running haywire inside her.

Sean swallowed from his drink, and then returned the glass to the table. "I'm willing," he said, as he crossed his knee.

"You're willing?"

"Yes. I've learned patience in my profession, although my relatives would swear differently. Answers always come," he said confidently, and then admitting with a shrug,

"Often not when we'd like." He chortled, adding, "Usually, we don't like the answer, or even expect the one we get," as if thinking out loud.

"But something tells me that trying to rush you to a decision may not be in my best interest, so I'm willing to give you a little more time." He picked up his glass. "Let me warn you now, Helen, I never give up until I've found my truth."

Helen could but stare, and wish, and wonder over what she considered a cryptic message. She had a sense that he had stolen a glimpse into the black depths of her mind where she didn't know the answers, or even the questions that haunted her soul. She changed the subject.

"Elaina and I heard your name mentioned this morning on one of the radio news programs."

"The Butler case," Sean acknowledged, a hint of displeasure in the back of his throat. He drank a sip of lemonade, and then set the glass on the table and resumed looking at her.

Wrong subject, Helen chided nervously. She took another sip of her drink. Wasn't her rational for accepting his invitation to help take her mind off the Butler's, especially Ray's visit? Beyond recognizing he had some role in the case, Sean remained silent on the subject. She was more grateful than he would ever know.

***

Sean didn't want to talk about his life with the dead to Helen. Especially with Taylor and Joann Butler's murders so fresh in his mind and his morning's failure to close the gap on a killer, he thought as the waiter wheeled their orders on a tray to the table.

"I hope you're hungry. I believe our chef outdid himself with the grilled lobster," the waiter said, placing lobsters before each of them. "And here's your pasta salad, and for you," he said to Sean as he placed a small bowl next to his plates, "cucumbers and tomatoes in vinaigrette."

Sean felt no longer sure of why he asked Helen to lunch. At first, it just seemed appropriate, SOP, part of the pursuit to win over a lovely woman.

Only now, he wasn't so sure that was all it was anymore as desire prickled his flesh, crawling just beneath the top layer of his skin.

He had joked with Jules in manly, macho fashion, he recalled, but Baderinwa sensed something else, something deeper that he was just beginning to realize.

"It looks delicious," Helen said, unfolding her napkin.

Yes, he thought, *she did*, wondering whether she would acquiesce to his request. He craved a yes from her so, that he could almost taste it in the succulent smoky scent of the lobster on his plate.

"Are you sure I can't talk you into a glass of wine?" the waiter asked. "We have a red Clos Du Bois that would really compliment your lunch."

"We're saving ourselves for dessert," Sean replied. Helen was neither commonplace pretty or gorgeous like a Halle Berry. He thought her much more beautiful, with her dreamy chocolate frosting complexion and watchful doe eyes, a soft, yellowish- brown, and vulnerable.

"I've been told that your flan is outstanding," he replied to the waiter, looking at Helen. He wondered again, as he did Saturday after the *Henrietta Marie* tour, what pain or fear she kept hidden under her professional veneer and non-effacing personality. By Sunday, she was again the woman he met Friday night, quick with a quip and high-spirited.

"You've been told the absolute truth. Do you require anything else?"

"We're fine, thank you," Sean said, dismissing the waiter who disappeared. "Grace?" he offered in question to Helen as he spread his napkin on his lap.

Without awaiting her reply, he took her hand and lowered his head. He noticed from a sidelong glance that Helen did the same, and they each prayed silently.

But a prayer of gratitude wasn't in his thoughts; rather, the Butlers, Joann and *du petit Taylor* were and inexplicitably, the similar sense of responsibility he had for them seemed to extend to Helen and her daughter. That changed things, and he wasn't sure he liked it.

"Amen," he concluded, picking up his fork and knife. "Let's see what kind of job the chef did." While Helen forked into her pasta first, he cut into the lobster.

"Mmm," he muttered pleased. "How's the pasta?"

Still, he knew he couldn't take Dr. Clemens's advice that absolved him of responsibility for their deaths. No one defended *du petit Taylor*, or her mother. And even though he didn't know the reason now, he intended to make sure that no harm came to Helen or her daughter, Elaina.

"I'm going to have to work off the butter," she replied, smiling. "It's good."

"I have the perfect exercise for such an occasion."

Helen blushed, and he laughed fully. It wasn't so much that he enjoyed her discomfort, as it was his own sense of comfort in question. All joshing aside, he felt completely baffled by his ardent interest in Helen Parker, a woman whose professional armor complimented the tight rein she held over her emotions.

***

The conversation Sean and Helen started over lunch Monday resumed Tuesday evening over a din of splashing water, creating an echo of liquid music.

What wasn't said spoke volumes in stealth glances, casual touches, and the unmistakable physical awareness that radiated between them like electricity.

They sat to themselves, side-by-side on a section of aluminum bleachers that surrounded the indoor pool where Elaina's swim team worked-out on the campus of Texas Southern University.

Sean wanted to attend practice out of curiosity to see their interaction in an environment normal to them. And, he hoped, to convince Elaina - - who met his arrival with a look of scorching dislike - - that he was not trying to steal her mother from her.

What he wanted to steal was her mother's heart from under emotional lock and key.

Helen definitely seemed more relaxed, and he wondered if it were the setting or that she felt more comfortable with him.

Still, there was an unspoken guardedness he detected before. He even sensed it in her attire - - a cute, short-sleeved, white cotton shirt with dainty flowers in orange and green on the front that buttoned in the back over a pair of off-white calf-length slacks and sleek beige sandals that revealed her pretty salmon-colored toes.

Regardless, she radiated a vitality that drew him like a magnet.

"What?" she asked, looking curiously at him.

Sean ducked his head, embarrassed that she caught him staring at her from head to toe. "If you knew how utterly enticing you look, you wouldn't have asked me that."

She smiled demurely at him, and then promptly directed her gaze on the pool. Sean reigned in his aggression, and joined her watching.

It was loud in the natatorium. Two male coaches, opposites in complexion, build, and temperament, sauntered around the pool, observing their young swimmers. One barked out instructions while the other caught a swimmer's attention and corrected his form with a silent demonstration.

There were at least forty swimmers, a rainbow of genders and complexions, ranging from preteens to high school, lapping in rounds. Over and over, one right behind the other, they swam the butterfly from one end of the 25-foot pool to the other, and back. Like Helen, several proud parents watched from the four sets of bleachers against the brick walls. A big-faced clock with a Tiger in the center showed the time: 7:59pm.

As his gaze swept the athletes, noting their technique, stamina and dedication, déjà vu eased into his conscious as he recalled the pre-Juneteenth celebration party at the Cavanaugh's.

His surrealistic dream of Little Taylor holding her breath followed naturally, and he shivered inwardly. He couldn't help thinking that swimming would have enhanced her capacity to hold her breath longer than normal.

"Elaina is quite a strong little swimmer," he commented with admiration.

"She took to the water like a fish," Helen smiled in reply, pride in her tone. "But I don't push her. If she decides to pursue other interests later on, I'll be disappointed, but it won't be the end of the world."

"My parents were pretty much like that with me and my siblings. But I bet only a handful of the parents here," he said, indicating with his chin, "would abide by that."

"You're right," Helen said lazily, "and I understand. For a few of them, swimming is a way out of poverty, or a way to a college education, like football or basketball.

Some of these kids have been swimming most of their young lives, and parents have to pay for it in time and money. It's not an inexpensive sport. The kids practice to compete, and meets are not free."

Sean leaned back, resting his hunches on the bleacher above. Elaina was the third swimmer in a line of five, head down, arms and shoulders lifted slightly out of the water, and then down again. Like a vulture on the attack, he amused himself. "I imagine she's going to be starving after practice."

"Is that a subtle invitation to dinner?" Helen asked, her amber eyes bright with amusement.

Sean quietly sucked in a breath of arousal, masking it in a chuckle. "I guess not so subtle, but yes. How about it? Your daughter was not pleased to see me showing up here. I need to do something to get in her good grace."

"I'm sure my daughter would say that being an only child has its privileges," Helen replied with amused sass in her tone.

"Just as being my woman would for you."

Her eyes instantly glazed dreamily before she lowered her thick lashes, hiding from his scrutiny. She averted her head from him to the pool, but he sensed she was not as unaffected as she pretended.

Driven from the pool area as practice neared an end and the fun began, Sean coerced Helen outside to the parking lot next to the building. Although it felt like the eight o'clock hour, a hazy blue sky lit the night. With the added bonus of security lights glowing, it was hardly dark out.

Sean took Helen's hand, leading her farther away from the building. He felt the shiver that rolled through her body, and stopped. "You're not cold, are you?" There wasn't a wind in the sky.

She shook her head vehemently, and they continued to his parked car. He leaned against the side of the Jag, and encouraged her to do the same.

Not far away, a group of athletes practiced soccer on a grass field. Students seemed to come and go from all directions, and whether walking or driving, rap music singed the night air.

But it was Helen who held his attention. The attorney, mother, and stunning woman intrigued him like no woman ever had before. And maybe it was just that ... her sensual entity posed a mystery to him, and like the puzzle of Joann Butler and her daughter's deaths, he wanted to be the one to solve it.

Curiosity killed the cat, he recited the childhood adage. *But satisfaction brought it back.*

"Do I stand a chance with you, Helen? And don't slip into legalese. Just a simple yes or no will suffice." It wasn't that he had another woman waiting in the wings, but he needed to know now where he stood with her.

A tremor touched her smooth lips. An emotion he couldn't define flickered in her bright eyes, and then vanished as quickly as it came. He was even more intrigued.

"What happened to all that patience you professed to have?" she asked, a note of jest in her tone.

He wondered if it was strain and not an attempt of forced humor he heard in her tone. But she was looking at him so beguilingly innocent, he knew it had to be a trick. "Answer the question, woman," he growled laughingly.

She folded her arms across her bosom and when his gaze dipped to appreciate the fabric's pull over her lovely bosom, she dropped them to her sides. He thought she was so unaware of how beautiful she was that he wanted to kiss her … make her his … and not just for the length of a short affair, he realized with a tad of disconcertion.

With her head cocked at an angle, and an otherwise, nonreadable expression, she prolonged her reply. He held his breath.

"Yes," she said at last.

Eureka reverberated through him, but he wanted it all. "Yes, what?" he demanded, again noticing something fragile flicker in her eyes. He wondered if he'd pushed too far too fast. Still, "I want to hear it in total."

"Yes," she said hesitantly at first. " I want to have an affair with you, but …"

"Non, non, no buts," he declared, wagging a finger, refusing to allow her an out.

Her mouth pouting, she asked, "Satisfied with yourself, are you?"

He reached for her hands, unfolded them from her bosom, and held them gently in his. "What are you protecting?" He couldn't forget that transitory look of fear that flashed in her eyes.

"Pardon me?" she replied, her brows arched under her pointed gaze.

"You have no one but yourself to blame for my curiosity," he replied, his eyes floating over her. "Is it because you've been hurt by a man before?"

"That's a presumptuous stereotype," she quipped, pulling her hands from his.

"Is it true?" he persisted.

"Is what true?" she replied.

He could tell the question annoyed her. She was gnawing her bottom lip, bemusement in her gaze as she looked off in the distance. But it occurred to him that given more time, Helen would only take more before reaching a decision.

"Are you so accustomed to loose women that one who isn't baffles you?"

Insulted, Sean froze and stared at her with an arched brow of his own. "What's a loose woman?" he asked in a softly tensed voice. He crossed his arms over his chest, his legs at the ankles.

"You know," she said cavalierly, waving her hands. "One who throws herself at you," she explained. "If that's what you need to make you feel like a man, then I'm not the one for you."

She looked at him headlong, her chin slightly elevated, her eyes sparkling like jewels. It was her one-upmanship look, and served to reign in his temper.

Chuckling, Sean uncrossed his arms and clapped his hands. He started this, didn't he? He smiled, thinking that while Helen may have secrets, she was not a pushover.

"I've made you angry," he said, retrieving her hands. "That's good."

"Happy to oblige," she quipped, a piquant smile on her face.

"You will be, Helen Parker. I promise you that," he grinned suggestively. "Vous serez."

Chapter Fourteen

The next morning, Helen felt as if last night never left her.

With her insides jangling excitedly and a smile of contentment on her face, she sauntered out of the air-conditioned Family Law Center Building in downtown Houston. There wasn't a thing about Sean she couldn't describe from memory, she thought, instantly bombarded by noise and smog that fueled the humidity of the midday's scorching heat. She slipped on her shades to begin the trek to her car in the covered parking garage across the street.

In the midst of the panoramic view of congestion, she hardly attended the constant din of heavy construction equipment tearing up the sidewalks or the honking from the steady flow of four-way traffic in the streets.

Sean's handsome face - - whether smiling, serious, or thoughtful - - played on the lens of her glasses like a movie. The fine hairs on his chest peeking from the V of his shirt teased her senses anew with emotions she had believed forever dead in her.

He awakened the woman inside her, making her feel alive.

She laughed out loud at the thought.

Even when she believed alcohol had dampened her perception the first time they met, she had thought he was a most attractive man. She didn't want to trust herself then, but over the past several days, he provided conclusive proof. If he had any warts, she certainly hadn't seen them.

But more telling than that, her numerous and varied licentious reactions to him affirmed her decision to see a psychiatrist.

Her eyes darkened fractionally behind the shades as she recalled that for an instant last night when she was alone with him and he took her hands, a chord of sensuousness connecting them, the unknown demon in her mind reared its ugly head like a snake and bit her with its poison of fear.

She inhaled deeply. Now, as then, she didn't know how to handle the dichotomous sensations - - wanting, yet afraid.

An appointment set for 1 0'clock, she had an hour to get there, a 40 mile drive to the Woodlands near Bush Intercontinental Airport. If she hurried, even with traffic being what it was, she should just make it on time.

Her cell rang as she reached the corner where the streetlight halted pedestrian traffic. She dug it out of her purse, checked the caller ID, and answered, "Hi Butterscotch," in a singsong rhythm, sincerely delighted by the interruption from her daughter.

"Some of my swim teammates are going to the wake this afternoon before practice. Can I go with them? I know I'm asking late, but I just found out about it. Why didn't you tell me?"

Helen frowned instantly, although it wasn't from disappointment by her child's instant request that skipped over a normal greeting. She wished she could deny knowledge of what Elaina referred to, but the news carried details of the funeral, taking the opportunity to rehash the murders.

And while Joann's pregnancy provided fodder for courthouse gossip, she had pushed the deaths so far in the back of her mind that she had forgotten. Additionally, she had been absorbed by her own needs that had to do with life, she reminded herself when guilt threatened to invade her good feelings.

The light turned green, and Helen turned in the opposite direction. Her heart thumped anxiously as she headed for one of the cement patios in the Center's courtyard, wondering how to respond. "Elaina," she said in a calm, rational voice, "you hardly knew that little girl."

"Her name was Taylor, Mama," Elaina replied unkindly. And then she turned the tables on Helen, adopting a calm voice, reasoning, "Even though she was on the beginner's squad, she was still a member of our team."

Helen arched a brow of surprise, and instantaneously, she remembered Ray had started telling her something about his wife putting their child in swimming.

The beginners practiced at a different time, so that would explain why she never noticed the little girl.

But Elaina confirmed she was indeed on the team, she thought with anguish. Forced to wonder again why Joann called her, she dropped onto the hard cement bench and inhaled deeply.

Elaina didn't know she had once been engaged to Ray, she thought pensively. She didn't want to take the chance that some busybody would revisit the topic, which opened a can of worms she didn't want to address. Her mind racing, she knew it was not beyond the realm of possibility.

"Sweetheart," she said hesitantly, "I don't think so."

"How come?" Elaina whined.

She steeled herself to reply, "Because I said so."

"Bye."

As abruptly as her request was made, Elaina ended the call. If motherhood were a popularity contest, Helen sighed, she would lose hands down. She closed her cell.

Mindful of her appointment, she quickly retraced her steps to the light. Since the deaths had been placed back on her mind, her spirits began to erode, squashing the happiness she felt only moments ago.

The ring of her cell still in her hand caught her off-guard, and she nearly tripped over a crack in the sidewalk. Seeing the name, a sense of relief came over her, and she answered, "Claire, I'm glad you called. Miriam and I have been concerned about you."

***

"I see here that you've seen a number of doctors in the past."

Attacked by a case of cold feet, Helen's mind raced for reasons to explain her presence. She knew everything about Sean she needed to know, she reminded herself.   Still, she recounted that he grew up in Ames, Texas, his retired parents were still alive, as were his two older sisters and brother, James, who was autistic. His successful employment was evident, and the most important thing of all - - he wanted her.

"Yes," Helen replied. She couldn't sit in the chair proffered her. She stood by the long, arched ninth floor window, absently viewing the empty jogging trail around a heavily forested area below.

"Are you here because you believed that they couldn't help you?"

Facing Dr. Greer headlong, she found the woman's gray eyes boring into her as if waiting for her to lie. There seemed an uncanny calmness about the doctor, but maybe,

Helen thought, she noticed it because she was just the opposite right now.

"No," Helen replied, shaking her head from side-to-side. "I never gave them a chance really."

Dr. Greer, an eyeglass wearing, athletic-looking, licensed psychologist, sat sideways behind her walnut desk, with her elbows resting on the arms of her swivel chair and hands lightly clasped together.

"What makes this time any different?"

According to what Helen read about her on the Internet, Dr. Greer had been in private practice for fifteen years. She specialized in the treatment of acute and chronic trauma. If the thought of intimacy with a man were not a traumatic situation, then Helen didn't know what was, she thought.

Contemplating her reply, she sat on the edge of the chair in front of the desk. That she wasn't really ready, didn't like the doctor, or was too cowardly, were just a few of the multitude of excuses she could recite. Instead, she replied summarily, "I met a man," with a somewhat awkward smile on her face.

She was referring to Sean King, but Ray Butler had become a constant in her thoughts ever since Elaina called, requesting to attend the wake.

The innocent call reawakened memory of the 10-year-old incident with him like it happened yesterday. That memory would kill her future, and make allowing Sean closer, impossible.

"I'm sure it's not the first time," the doctor replied as she removed her glasses. The wee smile on her square jaw altered her expression.

Dr. Greer looked to be in her mid to late fifties, her auburn hair peppered with gray, and a healthy tan to her peachy complexion. Her office was over an hours drive away from Helen's office or her home when three very good shrinks maintained an office in her building. She believed the great distance assured that no one would find out.

"Yes, and no," Helen replied. She knew men were attracted to her, but she never allowed anything beyond a state of casual acquaintance with them. Never alone with one, and always in a group. Until now, she thought, thinking of Sean, remembering the purple flowers he had sent to her office everyday this week. She knew one would be there when she returned, and another at her home this evening. She wanted more than a platonic relationship.

"Please explain that."

"I think this one may be worth it," Helen replied, her fingers mentally crossed. Not because she was lying, but because she desperately hoped it was true. Even more significant than that, she longed for it to be true.

Dr. Greer donned glasses and looked down to consult the questionnaire Helen had completed upon arriving. Removing her glasses, the tip in her mouth, she looked at Helen thoughtfully. "Are you sure you want to do this?"

"Yes," Helen said firmly. Still, doubt resided around the edges of her certainty.

"How long have you believed yourself frigid?"

"It's been ten years since . . . " she stopped, not wanting to mention Ray's name. "The last time I tried," she concluded, carefully abridging her reply, hoping the doctor understood. She swallowed the lump that suddenly lodged in her throat and wiped her palms together. They were perspired.

"And you've had no lovers in all that time nor tried to remember what it is that you've programmed your mind not to remember?"

Helen detected neither amazement nor judgment in Dr. Greer's voice, merely a quest for clarification. Still, she was embarrassed as she replied with a negative shake of her head.

Seeking clarification, Dr. Greer continued, "And you want to try now because you've met someone with whom you desire a full relationship?"

Helen looked directly across at her. "Yes." God, she hoped Sean was worth the risk she was taking. She trembled, mindful that it wasn't just for her sake. She had a responsibility, a daughter whose self-esteem and psyche to consider. If she were wrong, she thought, muttering a painful groan deep in her throat.

"What was that?" Dr. Greer asked.

"Just thinking out loud," Helen replied.

"Helen, I'm not going to lie to you. I strongly suspect that it might be difficult, even painful … remembering what you've managed to repress so thoroughly. Do you have someone other than me to hold your hand, so to speak, during the process?"

"No," Helen replied with a note of desperate urgency.

"I take your vehement response means that you don't want anyone to know."

"You're right." She never even told her parents the truth of why she and Ray called off the wedding.

"But if this man is worth it, as you say, shouldn't he be a part of your healing?"

"Never ask a question that you don't know the answer to," Helen replied. "It's one of the first lessons I leaned when I interned with a criminal defense attorney."

Dr. Greer bobbed her head in understanding, a respectful smile on her face. She pulled her chair closer to her desk and opened the calendar there.

Helen heard the tiny peel of her cell ringing in her handbag on the floor by the chair. She ignored it, thinking it must be a personal call, for she had asked Miriam to pick up Elaina and take her to the museum. She had planned to be done by the time the movie was over, and would pick up Elaina herself, and then take her to dinner.

"Alright, Helen," Dr. Greer said, consulting the appointment calendar on her desk, "I have an opening …" As the cell rang persistently, she stopped. "Maybe you better get that."

"I'm sorry for the interruption," Helen apologized as she retrieved the cell from her handbag. She looked at the caller ID before answering, a puzzled frown on her face, "Miriam, what's up?"

Hearing that Elaina was nowhere to be found caused the look of pure fright that burrowed over Helen's expression as she sprang from the chair, tightness in her chest. "Did you notify the authorities?" she asked hastily. "I'm on my way."

She reached down to pick up her bag as she closed her cell phone. "Dr. Greer, I'm going to have to get back to you." Heading for the door, she explained, "My daughter's missing."

***

He watched from the door, peeking into the room where silence seemed as comfortable and contented as its occupant.

Pulse throbbing in his throat, he basked in the sight of her, wanting her.

The room was Claire's small office, located off the corridor across from the kitchen where the food was prepared. It was plain white and well lit. A computer shared the teak desk with a multi-line phone; stacks of books and magazines promoting food were perched like little mountains on the floor, atop the desk, and in the extra chair in the room. Claire's head was buried in one as she wrote on the yellow pad under her right arm.

He had only known her a short time. But time was relative, Jules mused, feeling as if he had known her forever, maybe in another lifetime. The anthropologist in him appreciated the value of things ancient, and the man, in things present, like Claire, her quiet nature, her butterfly grace. Still, he couldn't believe the joy he felt just looking at her.

It was past quitting time by over an hour, as it was after three, yet, she appeared as happy as a child in a toy store, not ready to leave work. Suddenly, she snapped her finger and hopped up to peruse the books shelved on the metal bookcase. She plucked one from the shelf.

With her heart shape face locked in a studious look, she scanned its contents, her finger as a pointer, scrolling down a page as she returned to her desk.

She wasn't a stylish dresser like the women he usually gravitated toward, but he liked her simple flower print cotton twill shirtdress, the shapes of her fine calves, and functional, black soft-soled leather shoes on her feet. She wore no jewelry, and still used a hot-comb on her hair worn in an old fashion French twist.

She placed the book opened on the desk and suddenly, looked up as if sensing she was not alone. Surprise flashed across her face, with her eyes wide and mouth open. In that instant, a vaguely sensuous light passed between them.

"How did you get here? Nobody's supposed to be here," she said, her soft, elegant voice rushed as if breathless.

"Not even you," Jules replied, smiling. He pushed away from the door and sauntered deeper into the room. "It's after four. I figured you'd be out of here by now."

"I had to wait for our order of seafood," she said nervously. "The driver was running late."

"And you just happened to remember a recipe you wanted to try," he said, nodding toward the book opened on the desk.

She smiled sheepishly. "I want to try the peanut butter milk frosting for tomorrow's chocolate cake."

""Be sure to save an extra slice for me," Jules replied. He wondered about the man she had married and was divorcing. Had he not lived up to her expectations?

Thanks to Baderinwa, he knew her husband was not the father of her child. Did her teenage daughter factor in her decision to leave that man? He knew children were important in these kinds of situations as Sean was learning.

"I'm going by Sam's to get a couple of things," she said, referring to the local wholesale grocer.

"If you're done, I'll walk you out."

She bobbed her head. "Yes, I'm done."

Jules noticed that she didn't move; neither of them moved as seconds ticked off an invisible clock. Could he be what she wanted in a man? Did she find him as attractive as he found her? Or would she be turned off by his balding, his age, his profession?

"I just need to get my things."

"Okay. Take your time," he replied.

He never felt so insecure about himself since he became an adult; yet, never so sure about what he was feeling.

Chapter Fifteen

With each interview he had conducted today on the eve *of du petit Taylor* and her mother's funeral, Sean noticed his concentration waned.

It seemed that since he secured Helen's commitment to be his lover, justice dropped to second place.

Wednesday evening, he was still pondering the sense of persistent urgency he felt toward her. Confusion lingered in his gaze, adding definition to the frown lines on his forehead. He accepted that his interest in Helen had changed. The macho desire he once embraced with relish for the chase had become lost, replaced by a need for more.

He felt both mentally and physically twisted in knots by the growing assault of passionate need. The likely reason of his zealousness really had little to do with logic, he thought, as his stored images of her flashed across his mind.

Sean filled his cheeks with air, and blew it out as he shook his head. With determination set on his face, he recaptured his lost concentration and focused.

"I'll kill your daughter if you don't do what I say."

Sean scripted dialogue as he imagined it impacted the order in which the killings could have occurred. Only the words, not the tone of voice held menace or intimidation.

A threat, such as the one he considered, issued by a vicious assailant, he knew Helen would comply without hesitation even though obeying would assure her death. Likewise, it would hold true for Elaina, as well.

The frightening possibility chilled him to the marrow, and he shuddered.

But there was no reason to think either of them, Helen or Elaina, was in harm's way, he told himself. It was actually just a timely coincidence, he rationalized, recalling that he met Helen and Elaina shortly after discovering the murders.

Confident in the explanation of his transference, he redirected his attention to the purpose that brought him back to the Butler home. Stealing under the yellow police tape that still blocked the front door, he headed straight for Taylor's room. It was shortly after six now, roughly two hours later than his initial visit of the scene of the crimes four days ago.

Initially, he had considered that Joann was murdered first, because as an adult she naturally posed a bigger threat to her killer. He now conceded that it could have happened in the reverse just as easily. Dr. Clemens believed *du petit Taylor* was killed first, he recalled. However, either mother or daughter could have been subdued by a mere threat to the other if one didn't cooperate with the killer. Or killers.

Yet, that was not what most bothered him.

Sean stroked his chin several times as reluctance warred in his expression. As unpleasant as the thought was, he couldn't overlook the possibility that the mother, Joann Butler was somehow involved in the murder of her child, *du petit Taylor*.

Dishonoring the family name provided the motive in a number of female killings on the continent of Africa, he mused. The remains showed murder as vicious and horrible as this one. In a number of them, the police found the mother of the murdered woman as culpable as the man who usually committed the actual crime.

He shook his head, having no substantial reason to believe it was the case here.

Still, he knew that it was a misnomer that **all** mothers were loving, nurturing caregivers and cultural dispensers for their offspring, he mulled. Some went so far as to kill their children - - the reasons ran amuck from insanity to protection. During slavery, black mothers preferred to kill their children, rather than to raise them in the insidious institution of slavery.

But this wasn't slavery.

And the staging of *du petit Taylor's* murder seemed like some kind of punishment. Regardless, he sighed frustrated because he still lacked sufficient information for either theory. And then there was concern for who killed the mother even if she killed her child.

"I had a feeling you'd show up back here."

Sean spun on his heels startled as Sgt. Paul Diamond joined him in the girlish bedroom. He felt a high voltage energy surging from the street clothes, wearing cop. "Tell me that you've found the killer, and I'm spinning my wheels for nothing."

Sgt. Diamond muttered bitterly. "I wish. Well, could he have done it? Could Ray Butler have committed these murders?" He stood next to Sean, staring at the empty bed.

"And if he didn't, was the killer already in the house before Joann Butler arrived? How did he get in? Did Taylor Butler let him in? There were no signs of a forced entry. And then there's this little matter of motive."

Sean's mouth curled into a smile that reached his dark eyes, and it seemed to have released some of the tension from his body. "That's quite an exhaustive list of questions and thoughts to ponder. I'll have to consult my crystal ball and get back to you," he chuckled, joining Sgt. Diamond in a moment of levity.

"Now that we have that out the way, what are your thoughts?" Sgt. Diamond was all business once again.

With a crevice of a smile on his lips, Sean replied, "Ruby Poindexter wants to know why you haven't picked up Chester Mason for the murders."

Sgt. Diamond sighed as if exhausted. "That woman damn near drained me. I'm not an expert, but it's my opinion that Ms. Poindexter needs to get a life, because what she's doing to herself is suicidal."

"Expert or not, I concur with your assessment," Sean replied somberly, recalling his futile interview with the overweight woman who was committing slow suicide with food.

Except for vile conjecture against Chester Mason, she was filled with hatred for men and possessed no substantial information. Mason turned out to be a worm of a man who had never been involved in his child's life. *Du petit* Taylor was lucky in that regard.

"Now, back to business. A moment ago I would have sworn you had some assumptions of your own."

"Yeah, I do, but something brought you back here," Sgt. Diamond replied. "So, let's start with Ray Butler. Did he kill his wife and stepdaughter?"

The next of kin always topped the police's list of suspects when murder struck other family members.

Still, Sean was surprised that a man of Ray Butler's influence and stature in the community fell under the suspicious heading so quickly. That told him Sgt. Diamond played by the book.

"You interviewed him," Sean replied. "What do your instincts tell you?"

Sgt. Diamond's face sagged with disgust. "That's just it. My instincts haven't had a chance to work. He's still stalling. At first he was too upset," he added mockingly in an effeminate tone. "Meanwhile his campaign manager, Barry Barnes, called the Chief, who called my captain, who then instructed me to back off. Butler's supposed to come to the station tomorrow to answer our questions."

Sean muttered noncommittally.

Most parents would have been eager to talk: full of remorse, believing their absence prevented them from saving their family, they would have bent the police's ear off. Those that didn't automatically convicted themselves as far as the police were concerned.

Except for Mason, a selfish child trapped in a man's body, he thought disgustingly.

"Since I'm doing this circular dance here," Sgt. Diamond said, cutting into Sean's thoughts, earning his attention. "Can we rule out females as suspects?"

"I wouldn't. Even though I would love to."

Sean fell silent, questions without explanations scrambling his mind. The inconsistencies that suggested overkill in the way Joann Butler died in particular.

Advice given him by a former forensics professor popped into his head: *Analyze the evidence, and the why will take care of itself.* It rested in his conscious as he mulled Sgt. Diamond's question.

"We know for certain that a man . . . no, not a man, " he corrected, "but some sicko masquerading as a man did indeed sexually assault Taylor. Did Joann learn who and threatened him? Did she know? Or more importantly, did she care?"

"I'm sure if she knew she would have acted," Sgt. Diamond replied confidently.

"Are you sure about that?" Sean quipped. "Sometimes mothers remain silent because they fear reprisals from the police or some other authority. Some mothers simply refuse to believe their child's claims and remain in denial. And then some," he added with significant emphasis, "allow the perpetuation of the shameful act to continue because they were brought up that way."

"I'd love to argue," Sgt. Diamond said with a touch of sadness in his expression, "but I've seen the damage of incestuous families. I just didn't want to think this could be one of them. We still don't know if Ray is the father of Joann's baby."

"Maybe he'll give you a sample tomorrow," Sean quipped sarcastically. "The room hasn't changed …" he fell silent. Although the body had been removed, he could still see Taylor Butler lying nude on the bed in a more advanced state of rigor than her mother. Her hands were fastened on the sheet she'd gripped while enduring the savage ravishment of her young body.

"But I did find something different today that we missed the other day," Sgt. Diamond said, stalking from the room.

His mouth opened in question, a frown on his face, Sean followed. The investigator led the way past the bedroom, making a left up another hallway that he didn't notice the other day.

"Been holding out on me, Sgt. Diamond?"

Sgt. Diamond replied," I didn't know you the other day, Dr. King," as he pulled the string that was hanging from the door in the ceiling. He pulled open the door, and then reached up to grab what Sean knew would be a short ladder.

"And you do now?"

"The Internet is a wonderful thing," Sgt. Diamond replied, climbing up the short, three-step ladder.

"I thought only the air conditioner was up there," Sean said puzzled.

"Hurry up, will you?" Sgt. Diamond called down.

Sean whistled shortly after stepping into the attic space that had been converted into a bedroom. He wouldn't go so far as to stereotypically declare men junky creatures, but this decidedly male's room was a catastrophe, what his mother would call a 'pig's sty.' The only uncluttered object was the framed print of a woman's ruby-red, puckered lips, perched on the back rail of the teak daybed.

Clothes were strewn just about on every surface, from the daybed with a blue checkered comforter, to the computer desk and chifferobe whose opened doors revealed a TV connected to an Xbox Video Game atop a portable food tray. Clothes were even on the plywood floor.

"The room belongs to Stanley Butler," Sgt. Diamond said, discriminating touching items with his ballpoint pen. "They call him Stan. He's nineteen and a sometimes college student."

"Still trying to find himself," Sean muttered absently as he continued to inspect the room. Wires looped overhead connected between a black Aiwa stereo receiver, with speakers suspended from the slanted ceiling. A glass shelf in a corner held the kinds of trinkets won at a carnival. He thought it odd that the only kind of books Stan Butler seemed to own were game magazines. He didn't even see a backpack.

Sgt. Diamond found something of interest on the inside left door of the chifferobe. "The young man has a juvenile record," he said, flipping open his notebook. "But the DA's not willing to stick his neck out to get it unsealed without sufficient evidence."

Meandering around the room, Sean asked, "Is there a naked woman holding your attention? You've been staring at something a while."

"There are some dates circled on his girly calendar from last month," he replied, flipping the calendar with a handkerchief, "all the way to August."

Sean nodded absently, his attention elsewhere, noticing different styles of clothes, from what Stan Butler, still a teenage, might consider "cool" and those that looked as if his father would have insisted he wore. He nudged aside some clothing on the floor with his loafered foot. "He works at the Houston Zoo."

"How do you know?" Sgt. Diamond asked hastily, as he spun to stand alongside Sean near the daybed.

"Uniform shirt under those Tommy jeans."

"Two pairs of eyes are always better than one," Sgt. Diamond said, making a note in his booklet.

"Do you seriously think this kid could have committed the murders?"

"Look at the room," Sgt. Diamond instructed. "What do you see?"

"The maid doesn't come up here."

Chuckling, Sgt. Diamond replied, "Beside that."

"Okay," Sean said, drawing a deep breath. "Stan smokes a little pot. I guess that's why he keeps the air purifier under the desk over there. The way the clothes are thrown about, it looks as if he may have packed in a hurry."

"My thoughts exactly," Sgt. Diamond said. "I'm betting he was here the day of the murders. If he didn't commit them, then maybe he saw the bodies and split."

"Why don't you just ask him?" Sean replied, recalling the legal and moral quandary about incest. If a man sexually assaulted a woman or child it was considered rape, and he would be sentenced to jail time. But if that same man assaulted his daughter or sister, it was considered incest, and he would be given counseling.

"Under Texas law, he would still be charged with a crime," Sgt. Diamond interjected somewhat proudly. "As for the young Butler, I only spotted him today."

Sean shook his head, clearing his thoughts of the dilemmas posed by incest. "Where was he?"

"He was with his old man," Sgt. Diamond replied, leading the exit from the room.

On the way down, Sean thought the case so far seemed reminiscent of his foray into the field of forensic science, which was predicated by the death of his best friend, John McIntyre. He was in his fourth year of college, at Temple in Philadelphia, a semester shy of graduation with a BA in cultural anthropology and African American Studies. John, who by then had four children, remained in Lufkin, where they had met in high school. News of John's death reached him shortly before Thanksgiving.

The police called it suicide by hanging at a time when the suicide rate among black men was negligible, and hanging too preposterous to believe. He was devastated, even more so because he didn't know how to prove otherwise.

Ill-equipped to prove John's death a murder; hence, exonerate the McIntyre family from the stigma of suicide altered the career path he subsequently pursued to a doctorate.

While wholly committed to discerning what happened to a person based upon the condition of the body, he worried whether the killer would ever be discovered. Although he had learned to accept that he would always be too late to prevent the theft of an innocent life, Death's victory sometimes got to him.

Despite the sunset hour, the sun shone as if it had no intention of leaving soon. It was still hot when he and Sgt. Diamond walked outside. They could definitely use some rain.

Looking up and down the street in front the Butler's Third Ward home, he felt safe assuming that every neighbor on the block knew of the murders by now. They would be extra cautious for a while, maybe a couple more days. Once the fear died down, they would return to business as usual.

"You said you spotted Stan with his father today," Sean said. "Where was that?"

"He accompanied good-old dad, with his trusty campaign manager to his lawyer's office."

"Who's representing him?"

"Oh that one is really rich, let me tell you," Sgt. Diamond replied with a sarcastic snort. "He went back to the woman he was once engaged to marry."

"That's nervy," Sean commented, pulling car keys from his pocket. "Who is this generous woman?"

"Name's Parker. Helen Parker."

Sean's mouth fell open, and he dropped his keys.

***

Helen heard the door slam shut, and then the bolt slid into position to lock.

It was supposed to be a secondary, protective measure against the unlikelihood that someone broke past the security measures that had been installed in their home. That her daughter apparently considered her the enemy did not amuse her.

"Elaina, open this door," she commanded.

Even though they had been home for over an hour, she still felt suspended between relief that her daughter turned up safely, and anger that Elaina had stolen off campus with a couple of friends from school.

Helen couldn't remember being so scared in her life as when Miriam informed her that Elaina was not where she was supposed to be. She didn't think she had breathed from the time of the call until she walked into the university's security office to see her daughter, alive and well, being scolded by Miriam.

"Mama, no!" Elaina cried from the other side of the door.

After speaking with the Houston Police Officers who had arrived, as well as the Director of the summer program, she and Elaina were allowed to leave.

Still upset after they arrived home, she spent the first half hour just trying to calm down. She had been so angry that she seriously considered spanking Elaina.

Instead, she lingered in her room, leaving Elaina to stew in anxiety while she decided on a suitable punishment. Now that she had, she knew she couldn't back down, for the deed could not go unpunished.

"Girlfriend, if you don't open this door right this minute," she threatened between her gritted teeth.

She heard the lock click, signaling the door had been unlocked as instructed, but the door didn't open. She twisted the doorknob.

Elaina's room had a lone picture window that faced the front of the house. Several hues of purple and gray butterflies painted over pink walls, white furnishings, light gray drapes and dark purple comforter shared the room with a bookcase and every piece of electronic equipment imaginable. Except a cell phone. Helen felt she had to draw the line somewhere.

"Mama, I promise it will never happen again; please, mama. Please don't take anymore stuff," Elaina beseeched her as she stood protectively in front of the entertainment center, tears running down her face.

"I know it better not happen again," Helen retorted. "Get out the way."

"Mama, please don't take it. You've already taken my computer."

The room contained everything Elaina ever asked for, and then some, like the South African baskets that formed an "E" shape on one wall, an expensive gift from her godmother.

Her child only had to leave the room to eat, for she had her own bathroom, along with phone line - - a convenience for Helen, as well - - computer, stereo, and flat screen TV perched for a direct view from her four poster bed, cluttered with pillows atop the quilted purple comforter.

Banishing Elaina to her room would have been too much like a reward for her disobedience of a much-preached rule.

"You better move, girl," Helen said undaunted by her daughter's tears. She pulled the plugs from the electrical socket behind the entertainment unit. Facing the unit, she slid the stereo receiver off the shelf and turned to exit.

Walking out with the receiver in her arms, she admonished, "And don't lock this door. I'll be right back."

"There's nothing left to take," Elaina cried belligerently.

"The phone is next," she said over her shoulder from the hallway where the opened banner provided a partial view of the great room below and the fading light of day descending over the patio.

"Aw, mama, no! Please, no!"

Ignoring her child's fervent cry, Helen proceeded down the circular, carpeted stairs.

Unusually shaped rooms with angled door placements initially attracted her to the contemporary floor plan three years ago when she and Elaina moved out of the home that was owned by her parents who moved to Oakton, Virginia five years ago.

The second attraction were the wonderfully open spaces that allowed glimpses into the great room with its pebbled brick fireplace, the high ceiling above the gallery and the formal dining room right off the foyer, all floored with colonial oak hardwood, vanilla columns, and white doors.

The decoration of earth tone area rugs that highlighted the chocolate and mauve color scheme added a sense of calm and understated elegance.

As she entered the combination study/library with a fireplace, she mused that she earned a good living for herself and her daughter. But there were times when she thought she'd exchange all her tangible possession for absolute peace.

With a sardonic chuckle and a musing smile on her face, she laughed at herself for the preposterous thought as she put Elaina's stereo in the closet with the other possession she had confiscated.

Achieving such an esoteric concept was a pipe dream.

Like the professional music career her father once aspired for her, she thought smiling as she gazed over the assortment of string instruments she had collected over the years, from her first violin to her latest toy, a Stratocaster. She enjoyed music immensely, but she never wanted to be a professional musician.

Her eyes naturally gravitated to the bouquet of purple, pink, and white tulips in a round, red glass vase that for the third time this week awaited her return home this evening. The lovely bouquet instilled in her a feeling that was attainable.

She crossed the room to the bouquet that sat on the desk next to the music stand and guitar case.

Emitting a wistful sigh, she lightly fingered the flowers and examined the cursive crawl of his name on the small card.

No last name, no doctor, just *Sean.*

An unconscious smile slid into her expression as she opened the black leather case to remove her sky-blue bodied, electric guitar.

The flowers, like the sender, made her feel truly special, desirous, a sensation, she shuddered, she definitely wished to reciprocate in total.

She slipped the strap around her neck, plugged the guitar into the amp and began her routine scale exercise, all the while thinking that reciprocity was something to look forward to.

Chapter Sixteen

The evening was quiet except for the strands of a sad guitar drifting across Sean's thought, mimicking the melancholy that thrummed in his chest and the distressful expression on his face.

He found himself sitting in his parked car on the street in front of a contemporary, two-story home, in disobedience of his first thought upon leaving the Butler home. He knew Elaina had swim practice, so they probably weren't home.

He stared at the house on a corner lot that was three blocks from the south side of Mac Gregor Bayou where some of the most expensive homes in Third Ward were located.

No matter how many ways he looked at it, there was only one conclusion to draw. Sean swallowed the lump in his throat, reluctant to attribute the disgust bubbling inside him to jealousy.

But neither emotion would be calmed by the realization that Helen was still in love with Ray Butler.

He remembered the last time they were together when a sweet tenderness broke through her cool reserve, and he saw her confusion, an inkling of fear that drove him to push her further for a commitment.

He had guessed - - and now he suspected - - that her

fear of trusting him was because another man had broken her heart.

A broken engagement, he conceded, was sufficient enough to break one's heart. Still, he thought stubbornly, tapping a beat on the steering wheel with anxious fingers.

Glancing at the front door, he debated whether he wanted to broach the gate of the security fence, walk up the pebbled tiled sidewalk, climb the six steps to the recessed door tucked within a high, brick archway, and ring the doorbell.

He didn't want a woman who wanted another man, especially one she rejected before ten years ago. So why was he still sitting here in his car, growing hotter by the second with windows rolled down, parked in front of her home as the evening slid into night?

He seriously considered driving off, whispered a vow in French - - "Jamais plus!" - -never to see her again. A "but" held him still.

At least he could say that she didn't play the "other woman" typical in the break-up of marriages. But - - and there was that but again, he thought snidely - - there was no proof of that either at this time.

Proof or not, he knew the way homicide investigators thought. Even when the idea pained them as it did him. A case that was growing cold as this one often didn't lend itself to rational thought. It caused him to wonder whether Sgt. Diamond was leaning in the direction his thoughts were headed ... that Ray Butler killed his stepdaughter and wife in order to be with Helen and Elaina.

Sean swore bitterly, chiding himself for the horrible thought, even though he knew the homicide investigator would definitely consider her a suspect. For certain, he didn't believe Helen murdered anybody.

Why did he care? He only wanted an affair. Remember?

Still, he thought, he couldn't let her get away with the deception.

***

The doorbell rang on the very next note Helen played. But she didn't stop.

Her mind no longer heavy with thoughts, the ritual practice completed, she was just settling into the music, its notes, her tone, the Oliver Nelson composition, "Stolen Moments," in a rendition covered by Carmen McRae and Betty Carter.

She could hear the duo, soprano and alto songstresses as they sang, "They are such precious stolen moments, ..." as her sure, nimble fingers glided over the nylon strings with fine-tuned musicality.

The damnable interloper at the front door was persistent. Sighing irascibly, Helen stopped. She unplugged her Strat from the amp on her way to the front hall closet to turn off the alarm. Disgusted by the interruption, she hastily opened the door.

Her impatient irritation fled instantly seeing the identity of her unexpected guest, replaced by a feeling of extreme intensity. She wasn't expecting him. He had set a pattern of calling her late at night, whereupon afterwards when she fell asleep, he was on her mind, turning her dreams of him into fantasy.

A sense of joy sprang to her heart and sang its delight throughout her being, and burst into a smile on her face. "Sean," she said, with a hint of surprise in her tone.

Her eyes feasting on him, she realized that the composition she had been playing was a mere manifestation of her thoughts of him. His presence gratified her even more. "Come in."

***

Sean faltered in the silence that engulfed them as his eyes, roving the length of her, spoke of things hot and bothered. But it wasn't anger.

Helen looked so utterly exquisite; downright sexy

with the blue guitar slung at her side. She took his breath away and stole the reason for his presence. Even though he had seen her in a bathing suit, confirming to the wolf in him that she had a desirable body, seeing her now in a midriff top with puffy sleeves and a pair of well-worn cutoffs that caressed her lovely thighs increased his excitement, sending his pulse heaven bound.

Come on in," she invited again, her eyes warm with welcome.

Entering, he shoved the door behind him, and the bark of the closing reminded him of her betrayal. "You could have been honest and up front," he shoved at her, rallying with renewed anger. "I thought you were genuinely interested in us, but I learn you really have a deep love for the past."

She looked at him with a wide-eyed startled gaze as she stepped back from him. "I don't know what you're talking about."

Although she looked puzzled and a little nervous, he refused to be fooled again.

"You still have the nerve to lie?" he shouted with indignation, closing the distance she had put between them. "Is this some new kind of lawyer-client privilege action that I don't know about?

"Something that prohibits you from admitting you're

representing Ray Butler? As far as I know, he hasn't been charged with murdering his wife and child.

"Is that simply your way of worming back into his life?" he shouted.

"Mama, you want me to call the police?"

Both turned toward the stairs where Elaina stood steps above the floor landing. Her big brown eyes took them in their fear-glazed depths, her lips trembling.

***

"Elaina, not now," Helen said, attempting to eject a calm she wasn't feeling in her voice. Her mind was reeling with confusion.

Sean was furious, irrationally so, she thought, noticing a muscle flicker at his jaw. And while the ferocity of his passion was frightening, it was also exalting. She shivered subtly.

Sean's demeanor changed instantly. He passed a frustrated hand across his contrite and chagrinned expression.

Piecing together his accusatory remarks, Ray Butler's name on his lips, her stomach clenched tight.

His eyes softened as he spoke to Elaina in a lowered tone, "I'm angry, Sha, that's all," he said apologetically.

"I shouldn't have come. But you can be assured that

I'll never hurt your Mama. Never," he repeated in a fervid near whisper. He crossed his chest.

With questions about Sean's behavior volleying in her head, Helen saw her daughter rake him with a fierce stare. She gnawed her lips in debate, and then searched Helen's face for a decision. "Mama?"

"He's not going to hurt me," Helen replied. She didn't know how she knew that, but she did. "It's all right." She forced a smile to her face, but as soon as Elaina was mollified, she intended to let Sean have it. The audacity of him, coming here, scaring her child!

Elaina stared at her an extra beat, and then satisfied, skipped back up the steps. Helen knew she would stay hidden at the top of the landing.

When she faced Sean again, their eyes were locked in open warfare. "Sean," she said softly, with steel in her voice.

"I better go," he snapped, jerking open the door.

Her heart was beating crazily furious in her bosom. And he was talking about leaving! "Don't you think we need to talk about this?" she demanded forcefully.

"I shouldn't have come," he said, his back to her. "I won't bother you again."

Helen felt numb, hearing the note of finality in his voice. Even her emotions seemed paralyzed with shock.

With his final statement resonating in her mind, she suddenly realized she didn't like this non-feeling; she wanted joy back.

She rushed to the door and out onto the porch. Sean was at the gate, about to walk away to his car.

"Will I hear from you again?" She hated the note of plea in her voice, but didn't know what else to say. Watching a man who inspired her to dream of intimacy without panic walk away was too much to bear.

Sean stepped into a halt and his chin dropped to his chest. As angry as he was with her, and she with him, she felt that letting him go without trying would be worse for her. After what seemed like eternity, he looked at her, his head at an angle, his expression blank. "I don't know, Helen. I don't know."

His voice was absolutely emotionless and it chilled her. With her lips trembling as she watched her dreams walk away, Helen turned and went back inside. She wondered what happened, with the sting of tears in her eyes.

***

Claire felt a sense of freedom she couldn't explain, an excitement at seeing Honey she never felt before. Or at least, was conscious of.

Feeling Toni's eyes boring a hole between her shoulder blades, she severed the embrace. Even though it was a customary form of greeting, a welcome, guilt singed her conscious because it was such a pleasant touch. Confusion sprang to mar the moment of enjoyment.

Her sweet smile in place, Claire stepped aside to let Honey into her home. "Come in." After bolting the door, she turned to see Toni unfolding her long taut body from the couch.

"Hi." Toni's mouth barely moved when she spoke to Honey; her voice so low it was a strain to even hear her. She rolled her eyes at Claire, then sauntered from the room. All the tension didn't leave with her.

"What's wrong with her?" Honey asked. She was carrying a shopping bag that promoted the name of a local electronics store. She plopped it on the sofa.

"You mean this time?" Claire replied, her eyes glazing over with sadness.

First it was moving in general. Then it was the small A-frame house with one bathroom she had to share, followed by more complaints about the furnishings upholstered in orange velvet, and the boring, empty beige walls and carpet.

Claire shook her head dismayed that Toni considered their cozy place crummy. Her daughter failed to see the potential, refused to attempt making this home.

"This time, because she can't go to swim practice."

More than anything, however, she suspected Toni was stricken with homophobia - - a new word in her vocabulary. It was a nasty word that hurt, and she blamed Howard for instilling that hatred in her daughter. "She's leaving for swim camp in two days. Being out the water for that short amount of time won't kill her."

"Have you heard from your attorney yet?" Honey asked, staring intently at Claire, a hint of impatience in her tone, her hands on her hips.

Claire looked at her with a sheepish little smile on her mouth. She should have realized that Honey would know the main reason she kept Toni home.

"I tried to call earlier today, but I didn't get an answer." Actually, she called before 8 this morning and hung up without leaving a message. I'll call her tomorrow when I get to work."

"You don't have to wait that long," Honey said, reaching inside the bag. "Viola!" she exclaimed, holding up two cell phones. "One for you and one for Toni."

Thrill burst through Claire's demeanor. "Oh, Honey, you shouldn't have," she said excited, clutching the tiny silvery cell in her hand. "It's way too late now. It's almost nine. But this really is too much, Honey."

Honey flicked her wrist. "Nonsense. I know how you worry when Toni is out of your sight. This way you can stay in touch as often as you need to.

And," Honey added, least Claire offered another rejection, "it's cheaper than having a regular phone."

"Toni! Toni!" Claire called to a back room. "Come here a second."

"What's cooking?" Honey asked, making her way to the kitchen. "It smells great."

"Just a little something I threw together, she replied.

Listening to Honey meander in her kitchen, Claire felt an odd sensation in her bosom; it was gloomy like sadness and quick in its attack. She looked across the way to see her friend, lifting lids from the pots on the stove.

"Shrimp curry?" Honey asked.

Claire bobbed her head in reply. She didn't know how she could ever repay Honey for her kindness and generosity: in addition to allowing them to stay rent free until Claire got on her financial feet, Honey extended her use of a car. She vowed to do something special for her dear friend when she received her first check.

"Toni," she yelled again, forcing her gaze to the opening that led to the back of the house where Toni had vanished. She wondered if her daughter would come.

"What?" Toni asked, appearing in the opening.

Claire hated that dry as sandpaper tone of voice, but she didn't want to get into another argument. Her heart was already thumping, anxious about how Toni would receive Honey's gift. Too late to back out now, she swallowed.

"Look what Honey brought," she said, forcing an extra dose of cheer in her voice as she held up the phones, one in each hand. "This is yours." She held her breath. "If you want it."

Toni's mouth dropped open and a look of pure delight animated her expression. "Oh, wow!" she gushed, hurrying to take a phone from Claire.

"All of the information about the numbers and the plan and whatnot are in the bag," Honey said from the kitchen, where she was lifting tops from pots.

"Oh, thank you, thank you," Toni said excitedly. "Can I use it now?"

Honey nodded as she replied. "Yeah, it's good to go. I took the liberty of signing on before I came over."

"Thanks," Toni said before she dashed from the room.

"That ought to make her a little easier to live with," Honey said.

"How can I thank you, Honey?"

***

Ever since Sean left, Helen had been pacing the floor of her bedroom, berating herself. Why didn't she demand that he stay and explain himself? She should have been more forceful and less mindful of losing something she never had, she thought, as she walked from one side of the room to the other and back again.

If she didn't know better, she mused, Sean acted like a jealous lover.

The thought blew her mind open and brought her to a pensive standstill. Frozen, her mouth gaping open like a fish out of water, her heart began an erratic beat in her chest.

She cautioned her beleaguered mind to think rationally. Representing clients in divorces, she knew that a jealous lover could be a dangerous animal.

It was a trait any woman, or man with common sense didn't desire in a lover or mate.

But in the next instant, a dreamy cast came over her gaze, softening her expression as she nursed the thought. The idea of having someone care enough for you to behave jealously was not all wicked and sinful.

Did she dare let herself think that Sean was jealous of Ray?

As her thoughts continued a wistful path, she

wondered what Sean would think of her dramatically romantic bedroom: in cream and burgundy, it represented a fantasy that made her life bearable even as it revealed her subconscious wish, one that would fill the emptiness in her soul a child alone couldn't or didn't.

The bed, although queen-sized, would comfortably sleep two. Coral broadloom carpet complimented linen drapes covering the French doors that led to her balcony.

The doorbell rang.

Her heart changed beats, from erratic to pounding in her chest as she swung to face the bedroom door.

She held herself still, listening, fearing yet hoping that she had actually heard the announcement of a visitor.

Could it be Sean returning? She wondered, her mind racing.

This time she would put her indignation aside, patiently allow him to vent, and then calmly explain about Ray Butler.

If he was still angry after that, she thought, swallowing the lump that lodged inside her throat, there was nothing she could do about it, she concluded sadly. It would force her to admit that Sean King wasn't the man she originally thought he was.

"Probably a lousy lover, too," she whispered in a swearing tone to the air. Despite her sarcastic, under-her-breath mutter, she exhaled a melancholy sigh.

The very next sound ended all speculations and ponderings. Helen practically flew from her room and down the stairs, eager and excited for Sean's return. She fumbled turning off the alarm in the hall closet, and then jerked the door open, his name on her lips. Before she completed uttering the initial sibilant, excitement fled with her voice, and she frowned at the stranger standing there.

"Ms. Parker ... I'm Sgt. Paul Diamond, HPD Homicide," he said, his badge opened for her review. "I'd like to ask you a couple of questions in connection to the Butler murders."

Chapter Seventeen

With his body sluggish in retaliation from a two-day alcoholic binge, Sean watched the object of Helen's affection on the screen with a wounded look in his red-rimmed eyes. It had the effect of a knife twisting in his gut.

Ray Butler lost his lunch.

Sean felt the tight muscles in his face relax into a grin.

When Ray returned from the restroom to the interview room, he looked nominally restored. But the confidence that gleamed in his eyes and starched his demeanor had faded, casting an ashen parlor over him. His eyes strayed to the photographs that had soured his stomach and were now safely back in a manila folder on the table.

The fourth floor, conference room at Artifacts, Inc. was dark like a movie theater. Popcorn was not on the menu for this feature show. It could have been nails for the number of times Sean gnashed his teeth as he reviewed the videotape of Sgt. Diamond interviewing Ray Butler that occurred last evening.

He sat at the end of the conference table watching the television suspended from the wall across the room, with the control mechanisms at his fingertips.

Butler did not visit the scenes of the crime the day he returned home to learn his wife and stepdaughter were dead.

Hence, the politician retained his last image of them alive and well until Sgt. Diamond showed him the photos.

It had been Butler's charge that the police should be looking for a serial killer, which had stolen the last of Sgt. Diamond's patience, causing him to show Butler the photos. Some would call what the homicide investigator did to the aggrieved husband and father cruel and merciless. But the time for niceties had passed, and it was Butler's own fault if he felt punished, Sean thought, as he made a note on the pad in front of him on the table.

For the past half hour of Q and A, Butler had made an issue out of every question, toying with Diamond. He expelled twenty minutes worth of verbiage instructing the police how to do their job.

After denying that he killed his wife and stepdaughter he seemed to have lost interest in the interview.

With his attention waning as well, Sean wondered what Helen had seen in Butler.

He almost wished that Sgt. Diamond hadn't told him about the engagement Monday evening, two days ago. For certain, it tainted his objectivity, and exacerbated the acidity of disappointment in the pit of his stomach.

He had felt such high hopes for them, he thought tiredly, having covered this ground before. Even had no challenge of a conquest seemed likely, he was completely bowled over by Helen Parker the first time he laid eyes on her. He shook his head regretfully, and then redirected his attention to the tape.

"Do you know Helen Parker?"

Sean's head snapped: he felt as taken aback as Ray looked on screen. While his face brightened alertly to hear the politician's reply, Ray frowned curiously. His gaze shot to his attorney who was not captured on the video.

"You already know I do," Ray replied cautiously.

"What's your relationship to her?"

"There is no relationship," Ray replied forcefully, his gaze locked into the homicide investigator.

"Huh?" Sean muttered. His mouth suddenly dry, he swallowed, troubled. His mind racing, he wondered whether he'd jumped the gun, believing Helen was still in love with Ray? He had thought like a criminal investigator with feelings steeped in aggressive male hormones that somehow had gotten away from him, morphing into an honest desire of need.

"Then why did you go see her?"

"Yeah, why?" Sean echoed eagerly, his expression pained. Somehow, he knew the reason didn't support his accusation of Helen's betrayal of the commitment to him.

"It was a personal matter," Ray replied.

Sean inhaled deeply and hung his head in regret.

"What could be more personal than the death of your wife and child?" Sgt. Diamond quipped, with frustration in his tone. "Mr. Butler," he continued hastily, "were you, or are you now, having an affair with Helen Parker?"

With his error burning a hole in his chest Sean absently knuckle-wrapped the side of his head repeatedly, where Ray's denial beat against his mind, *No relationship ... No relationship.*

Suddenly, the overhead lights clicked on, but the illumination was in Sean's expression. Jules and Baderinwa sauntered into the room. Jules was eating from the saucer of biscuits he carried.

Sean paused the tape, and Ray Butler's frozen face filled the screen.

"Let some light in here," Baderinwa exclaimed, strolling to the bank of windows. "The dark only clouds your objectivity.

"You need the light to keep your mind open," she said as she opened the blinds, all three sets until the middle of the day streamed through, illuminating the bright room of sky blue walls, the sun casting a streaking ray across the oval walnut conference table, surrounded by suede beige armchairs. Three detailed maps covered the paneled walls on one side of the room, while a full grown skeletal man dangled quietly at the opposite end.

Jules sat at Sean's left, and shoved the plate of biscuits between them.

"Haven't seen nor heard from you these past couple of days. Everything okay? You're not letting this Butler thing get to you, are you? Remember you're supposed to be on vacation. In case you don't remember, vacation is time off to restore and renew your energies that you've been complaining about not getting for the past year."

"It was reported on the news last night when they showed a clip of the funeral that the little girl had been sexually assaulted, according to a so-called anonymous source close to the investigation," Baderinwa said in an even tone, staring at Butler's image.

He had already buried himself with Helen, Sean thought. He dropped his chin, his head shaking from side to side in despair. He knew Sgt. Diamond would not be pleased by the disclosure, which was to have remained secret in the event that the perpetrator, if he were ever caught, would somehow tip his hand.

Jules stared at him pointedly. "Something's wrong, what is it?"

Sean shook his head. "Nothing." He was too damn embarrassed to share his grand faux pas. Absently, he grabbed a biscuit from Jules' plate and bit into it. His stomach growled, reminding him that he'd forsaken it for alcohol. "Not bad." Something more appetizing than food was on his mind, he thought.

"Our new manager in the cafeteria is also a great cook," Jules declared, dipping a biscuit in the syrup on the plate and popping it into his mouth.

"Sounds like she's found a way to your heart," Sean said. He wondered what it would take for him to get back into Helen's good graces?

"Jules is more than a little taken with her," Baderinwa said.

"Who is this woman?" he asked conversationally. It had been years since Jules showed a serious interest in a woman. When he accepted the teaching assignment at A&M, the woman he was engaged to marry didn't want to leave D.C. for Texas, he recalled. That had been ten years ago.

"Name's Claire," Jules replied, chewing. "She has a teenage daughter."

"I see," Sean said. He smiled with bitter amusement, thinking he and Jules were attracted to women with children.

"And she's in the process of getting a divorce," Baderinwa added, casting a sidelong secretive smile at her brother.

"How are Helen and Elaina?" Jules asked, slipping into their Creole tongue.

Sean shot Jules a hard stare, a quip about fair play and turnabout on his tongue, "Fine," he shrugged, "I guess. I haven't seen her in a couple of days."

"Oh-oh. Do I detect a retreat?" Jules asked jokingly.

Sean replied in Creole, "I made a mistake." A major blunder, he upbraid himself. How in the devil could he fix it?

"As great a catch as you are, cousin, " Baderinwa said patiently in their native language, "sometimes I swear that you don't pay attention. Or maybe, it's just the living that you have a difficult time with seeing since you mostly deal with the truly dead."

He glowered at her, and she laughed at him with her mouth and her eyes.

His mouth full, Jules chimed in, "I can't believe that you would allow a preadolescent teenage girl run you away. Elaina is just not use to seeing *sa mere* with a man." He swallowed, and picked up another biscuit. "I'm surprised to see you giving up so quickly. And without a fight," he added with a scoff in his tone before he popped the biscuit in his mouth.

Sean sneered at him. "All of a sudden, he's an expert," he said to Baderinwa. She had been watching him, studying him, reading him.

"Flowers won't work this time," she said with solemn repose.

"Huh?" Jules asked, his gaze volleying between them.

Sean bit down on his bottom lip as he returned Baderinwa's steady stare, his expression still and thoughtful. "Baderinwa," he announced, "I need a gift basket."

He was determined that even if he had to fall down on his knees in a preying position, he was going to convince Helen Parker to give him another chance.

***

Helen toyed with her fingers. As if physically drained, she slouched in the chair facing Dr. Greer who sat across from her. With puffy eyes ringed with black circles, her whole body was engulfed in tides of weariness and despair.

She didn't have to wonder at the cause of her weariness. She knew her nightmares didn't bare the sole blame.

Except for her broken engagement to Ray, she never cried over a man since, or before, she mused despondently. Until now, she had forgotten what it felt like to be hurt by a man you cared about.

It was only the responsibility of motherhood that got her out of bed this morning. After dropping Elaina at school, she had returned home to indulge in a good cry while waiting the time of her appointment with Dr. Greer.

It was Friday morning, shortly after eleven. Almost two full days had passed since she'd heard from Sean, when she had come to expect his call for lunch.

"What do you think the dream was about, Helen?"

Helen was more unnerved by Dr. Greer's question than she would ever know. The painful recollection that there had been no flowers from Sean, and no phone calls, either was the first thing that popped into her head. What she did know was after spending nearly two days of fuddled longing and two nights' sleep of horror that she needed psychological help for certain.

"I don't know," she replied.

While she had been as pissed at Sean as he had been outraged with her, she couldn't have another night like the last two, she thought.

She spent hours tossing and turning before she finally fell into a restive sleep. Each night began where she felt as if her life stopped with Sgt. Diamond, questioning her about the calls Joann made to her office.

His questions, she soon realized, explained where Sean had gotten the notion she was still attracted to Ray. Germinating as suspicions did, it wasn't a big leap for him to assume she was possibly having an illicit affair with Ray.

She didn't think she was in love with Sean, but undoubtedly, he hurt her by believing she was capable of such awful deceit. She couldn't believe she had wished such torment on herself. It made her wonder if what she had felt for Ray was indeed true love.

"Do you want to know?" Dr. Greer asked.

Helen looked up at her with anxiety in her tearful gaze. Anger with Sean had not been in her sleep, she recalled.

Rather, she dreamed of him romantically. But when the romance turned sexual, the *Slave Master* replaced Sean as she then dreamed a nightmare of unprecedented horror. She shuddered, remembering it anew.

"I felt very afraid," she said in a small voice. "And," she gulped, "guilty. A horrible, horrible sense of guilt and shame."

"Why guilt and shame?"

"I know you like this."

Hearing that taunt, Helen shivered as if cold, remembering the *Slave Master*, with his liquor breath and leather belt. With her expression a distant gaze, a keening moan escaped her throat. The shivering intensified, and she wrapped her arms around her, pulled her legs in the chair.

"Helen, you're all right; you're safe."

Dr. Greer's calm voice reached her, and she breathed a quick intake of breath like someone who had plunged into icy water. Setting her feet on the floor, she rubbed the fabric of her dress covering her thighs.

"Take a deep breath," Dr. Greer counseled. "That's it. A long deep breath."

Helen did as she was instructed, and slowly, her pulse returned to normal. Now, she felt embarrassed on top of everything else.

"Who did you date in high school?"

Helen's head snapped up as if surprised by the question that seemed impetuous. She answered nevertheless. "I didn't."

"Did your adopted parents forbid you to date?"

Shaking her head from side-to-side, she replied, "No. I had such a busy schedule with school, and violin lessons, and swimming that I don't think it ever occurred to them that I wasn't dating."

"What about college?" Dr. Greer queried further. "Or did you bury your head in the books there, too?"

Helen smiled in response to the amused look on Dr. Greer's face. She pulled up her college years; they were mostly fun, she thought, and then a look of deep thought crossed her expression.

She squirmed as if uncomfortable in the chair, recalling an incident she'd completely forgotten about.

"Yes?" Dr Greer prodded.

A suitemate, a woman whose face she could recall but not her name, she remembered teased her with being a lesbian in her junior year at UH. In retaliation, she accepted a date with a football player.

"Dennis Hardeman," she whispered as if astonished.

"What happened?"

"Disaster." She frowned distastefully and visibly shuddered. "I was lucky," she said, her voice faltering. "He called me a tease and took me back to my dorm."

"That's enough for today, Helen. We'll pick up from here next week. If," Dr. Greer added with a pointed look, "you're sure you want to continue."

More than ever, Helen thought, she wanted Sean back. She wanted another chance to prove to herself that she was capable of deep affections for a man unencumbered by fear.

***

Helen drove the 40-miles trek from Dr. Greer's Woodlands office to her midtown office building, with a hunger gnawing at her heart.

She couldn't say what sights she passed, nor did she hear the music playing on the car radio, for she was listening to her internal communications and seeing her past with Ray.

He didn't pursue her with fervent persistence as Sean did, making her more aware of her femininity than ever. She never felt vulnerable or unsure of herself with Ray as she was with Sean.

Ray didn't inspire her with sensations of a holiday tingle, or aspirations for more desirous emotions.

In hindsight, she and Ray had a pleasant, but nonetheless practical, passionless relationship.

Her parents had been proud at the idea of having a community organizer with political aspirations join the family, she recalled. But she couldn't blame them for that, either.

It was two O'clock when she parked and got out of her car. The parking lot was full of vehicles, but everyone was inside the building, escaping the atrocious heat.

With shades blocking the sun from her eyes, Helen sauntered toward the building entrance, her mind locked on Sean.

She had been conscious of an emptiness that wasn't even loneliness for so long that the degree to which she responded to him came as little surprise. And even if it wasn't love, she told herself, reaching the cool, air-conditioned foyer, it was still better than the self-imposed sterile life she had lived for far too long.

Catching the elevator up to her floor, she mulled ways to convince him to talk to her, see her. She could be quite persuasive, she thought, pleased by her newfound sense of determination to get him back.

Getting off the elevator, an unconscious smile of enchantment on her face and rejuvenated energy in her steps, she headed for her office.

"You meddling bitch!" Helen heard just as she was grabbed from behind, too late to do anything but cry out alarmed. "I'll teach you about meddling in other people's business," her attacker yelled as she screamed.

Fear curled around her heart like a snake as a big-handed, claw-like grip prohibited her from running. Helen fought back as she cried, "Help!" It seemed useless. It was just like the dream that provided no option to escape. Still, she tried to fight him as he hurled obscenities and fisted power at her.

"Where's Claire, goddamnit?" he demanded voraciously. "You better tell me where she is!"

With terror beating in her bosom, Helen tried to run and went nowhere but down as she tripped over the straps of the briefcase and fell.

The *Slave Master* stole the light from day, as Helen felt catapulted into darkness, in the shadows of that small cramped room. She remembered from times before that its lone window was nailed shut. She was trapped, ensnared between the small bed and him. The door was miles away, even if she could reach it, which she couldn't.

"Where's my wife? You're the one who convinced her to leave me! Where is she, you meddling bitch? Tell me where she is, right now! If you don't tell me where she is, I swear I'm gonna ..."

Helen heard: *"You fast, little heifer! Don't run from me! I'm go be your teacher tonight! You fast, little heifer! I'm go be your teacher tonight!"*

Patricia, the hateful woman she called Mama was passed out in the other room. She always claimed she was exhausted, but she never did anything more strenuous than sip those funny smelling cigarettes, hold a bottle of sweet liquor to her mouth and guzzle down long swallows. She never heard Corinda's cries and pleas for help. Corinda didn't call for her now. She submitted to her awful fate.

Helen lay on the floor in a fetal position, whimpering, waiting for the brutal assault to continue.

Corinda waited for the sting of the leather strap as she cried. Although there was nowhere to go, no way to escape, she twisted and turned to elude the Slave Master, a giant towering over her, pulling at her, cursing her, demanding things of her she didn't want to do.

"Hey, what the hell do you think you're doing?"

***

Sean asked no more questions upon seeing Helen assaulted by a strange man. Roughly five nine or ten, the man was tenacious like a pit-bull, barrel-chested, and solely intent on carrying out his cruelty.

Sean raced up the corridor, with his zero-tolerance for hitting women, small children, and vulnerable animals. He was no fighter, but he knew how to throw a punch. His fist, empowered by every pound he possessed, landed in the man's face, connecting nose and mouth. The man's head jerked back, and in that micro-instant when it returned, another fist in the face knocked his head back, and then something small and white sailed through the air and blood gushed from his face.

"My nose," the man cried, clutching his face. "You broke my nose." He stumbled backwards, nearly tripping over Helen, trying to get away. He grabbed the wall to support him as he retreated.

Sean heard a female voice cry out behind him, and on some conscious level, he assumed it was Miriam as he pursued his prey. He was not going to be too late, he thought, over and over.

He grabbed the cowardly man by the shoulders, spun him around, and jabbed … and jabbed … and jabbed until the man fell like the giant Goliath, yammering something indecipherably. Tears and snot mixed with his blood as he begged Sean to stop, holding up a hand in surrender.

Sean was not in the prisoner-taking mood. He didn't know what the man was trying to say, nor did he care.

He kicked the downed man in the side, and then stomped … left foot, right foot into the man's chest. *That one was for du petit Taylor*, he subconsciously thought. Left foot, right foot. *That one was for Joann*. Left foot, right foot. *That was for Helen*.

He heard footsteps running up the corridor, but he had his feet working. Left foot, right foot. *And this one's for* …. Arms were all over him, dragging him. He fought them back, the rage of an animal deprived of its catch coursing through his mind.

"All right, come on, now." The male human voice reached the sane part of Sean's brain. "Calm down. It's over. We got him."

Sean's harsh excited breathing slowly descended as he took gulps of air into his lungs, exhaled, and drew another deep breath. Reality shot through him in a flash, and he cried out, "Helen!" breaking away from the guards who held him.

He scanned the corridor quickly. Helen was no longer in the hallway, so he raced to her office.

His pulse slowed slightly as relief came over him when he found her sitting on a chair in her reception area, sobbing uncontrollably. Although her hair was mussed, the jacket of her blue dress torn and ripped, her face wet with tears, she was alive.

Miriam held a towel to her nose that was bleeding as she tried to console her.

He rushed to her side, and she took one look at him, and started screaming hysterically.

Chapter Eighteen

"His name is Howard Jackson. He owns *Almeda Café*, which is a couple of blocks over. We used to lunch there all the time, but not recently."

Sgt. Benson was scribbling furiously in his notebook as Helen's secretary Miriam proved to be a willing and talkative witness. Sean listened quietly, amazed. In the hour or so he had been waiting for Helen to arrive, Miriam barely said two words to him. She had been neither impressed by his charm - - and he laid it on like Cane Syrup - - nor his business card. She was the personification of professional decorum.

"Attorney Parker is representing his wife in a divorce," Miriam continued, her voice bearing all the traits of a competent, assured woman. "She was concerned that he'd do something like this, but she figured it would be directed towards his wife, or his stepdaughter, not towards her. …"

The three of them were standing right outside the door of Helen's office in the corridor.

By the time Houston Police Officers - - six of them - - arrived, the bedlam had been sorted out by the building's security guards and the high point of activity quieted.

The only pandemonium that remained existed in

Helen's head, Sean mulled pensively. And while his own ambivalence over the violence he took perverse delight in dispensing disturbed him, he was deeply concerned about Helen's reaction.

Like everyone else who had seen her - - rocking back-and-forth, her gaze vacant and mind elsewhere - - he desperately tried to discern what brought on this fugue state she seemed locked in and how to break it.

Recalling her terrifying scream that was still in his head, he thought that sound alone was enough to vindicate his animalistic tirade against another human.

"People make jokes about attorneys all the time, but no one has ever attacked one. At least, no one's attacked one for being an attorney. Who would get them out of trouble?"

It was the first time Miriam unveiled her dry sense of humor, Sean thought. Her face never cracked a laugh.

"What's the wife's name?" Sgt. Benson asked. "You should probably notify her."

"Her name's Claire," Miriam replied, fiddling with the pearl necklace at her neck. "Claire Jackson. But we don't know how to contact her," she added, alarm in her expression.

"Claire Jackson?" Sean echoed. He paused

thoughtfully a second, the time it took to snap a finger, thinking mouth-watering biscuits. "Is she a cook?" he directed to Miriam, recalling Badarinwa mentioning a cook, a paragon of food preparation.

The most salient thing he remembered about the name was that it belonged to a woman who had found the way to Jules's heart. And as only providence would have it, he thought, if it were the same woman, she prepared foods that were found in the Butler's freezer.

Both he and Sgt. Diamond had been looking for her.

"Yes," Miriam said, her face pinched in amazement. "Do you know her?"

Sean felt a moment's elation that was not squashed by the suspicion in Miriam's eyes as she stared at him, questioning whether he learned of Claire Jackson, a client, one whose information was privileged, from Helen. "She works at my company's restaurant, The Cook's Chamber."

"I'd appreciate a number, Dr. King," Sgt. Benson said, his pen at the ready over his notebook.

Sean didn't know the number at the restaurant, so he pulled out his business card and scribbled Bararinwa's name on it, and passed it to Sgt. Benson.

"If that's all officer," Miriam said, "I want to get back to Helen."

"Yes, ma'am," the uniformed police officer replied as he dragged his gaze up from the card to acknowledge her with a polite smile. "Thanks a lot. You're been very helpful."

As Miriam ducked into the office, Sgt. Benson turned to Sean. "It's a good thing you were here."

Sean shuddered inwardly as he recalled seeing Jackson cursing Helen viciously and taking swipes at her as he stood over her threateningly. He had been sitting in Helen's waiting room, trying hard to make an impact on Miriam when they heard the commotion. "I imagine you see a lot of this," he said, his voice soft with bitterness.

"More than we want to," Sgt. Benson replied regretfully, flipping to a blank page in his notebook.

"What's going to happen to Jackson?" Sean asked. If the Calvary had not come, he suspected that the police would have been taking him to jail tonight. As was his luck, only Howard Jackson had been taken away, albeit with a couple of broken bones.

"He'll be booked, and then we'll take him to the infirmary," Sgt. Benson replied matter-of-factly. "He'll stand before a judge tomorrow on assault charges, and depending on whether or not he has money, he'll likely be released."

"I imagine you can't lose him in the system somehow," Sean suggested with hope.

Sgt. Benson stared at him, his gray eyes boring into Sean's face, as if debating whether or not to trust himself to speak. "I need to get a statement from Ms. Parker," he said, reaching for the door handle.

Sean acquiesced with a sigh, thinking that he had to try. Jackson was no doubt a menace, but he had civil rights, too. Before Sgt. Benson reached the handle, the two emergency attendants filled the doorway.

"Can I talk to her now?" Sgt. Benson asked the senior of the two men.

"I doubt it. She won't let us touch her. I don't think anything is seriously wrong. Not physical anyway. We told her secretary that she should contact her doctor to make sure."

"Thanks," Sean said.

"Sure thing."

The attendants walked off, heading for the elevator, and Sean entered the reception with Sgt. Benson.

Clutching the folds of a blanket that had been wrapped around her shoulders, Helen remained in the chair where he'd last seen her, still rocking. Sean cursed to himself and drew a deep breath.

Sgt. Benson's expression sagged with disappointment. "Maybe she can come to the station tomorrow," Sgt. Benson said with a trace of rue in his voice.

"Yeah," Sean replied, his own spirits dipping deeper into dejection upon seeing Helen in the same condition. "I'll make sure that she does."

Sgt. Benson pulled a card from his shirt pocket and scribbled a number on it. "Tomorrow," he said, giving Sean the card.

Sean nodded as Sgt. Benson walked out. He stared at Helen with his own thoughts confused and wistful. Although relieved and gratified that he'd been present to prevent Jackson from doing irreparable physical damage, he was utterly helpless to fix the injury in her mind.

He wondered where Helen's thoughts were, what she was thinking, what did she see that scared her so badly. He wanted to go to her, but feared her reaction.

Miriam returned from a room in the back of the office. She stared empathetically at Helen, her eyes filled with sadness, and then walked to Sean, a sheet of paper in her hands.

"Mr. Cavanaugh is in a meeting right now, but I was able to reach his wife, Pauline. She asked me to ask you if you would take Helen home, but I told her that I can do that."

"I'll handle it," Sean replied. "What about Elaina? It's after three. She'll be worried."

"I already notified the school; they're going to keep Elaina in the director's office," Miriam replied. "I was going to run and pick her up right quick, and then take them both home."

"I got that, too, Miriam," he said. "You just need to contact the school and let them know that I'm coming instead of you."

Miriam bit down on her lip, nervous indecision clouding her gaze, as she looked sidelong at Helen. "But what if Helen ... I mean Ms. Parker doesn't take to you?"

Sean inhaled deeply. "There's one way to find out," he replied. Cautiously, he walked toward Helen, whose gaze at that very instant, met his. He held his breath.

"Sean?"

He rushed the rest of the way to her, and took her hands in his. "Yes, Helen?" he asked, his heart beating outrageously in his chest. Her eyes were red, but they no longer had that dazed and confused look.

"It is you, right?" she asked, her smile awkward and incomplete. "You're not going to change into the *Slave Master*, are you?"

Sean felt the sting of tears in his eyes. He swallowed them away, and with the brightest smile he could muster, he replied, "No, I'm not going to change, Helen. It's me, Sean, the fool who made those outlandish accusations a couple of days ago. I hope you can forgive the bumbling, jealous idiot that I am," he added, a lopsided grin on his face.

He watched her chest heave with the exhaustive breath she took, and then she smiled in earnest, and his heart slammed into his ribs.

"Thank God for that," she said heartily. "I need to get to the hospital."

"But ..."

Helen cut him off, the lawyer in her awakened. "I wasn't thinking straight then, but I am now. Miriam," she directed to her secretary, "go home. I'm fine." Miriam looked dubious. "Trust me. I know what I need to do."

Sean thought that Miriam was going to balk at the instruction for a second, and then the two women exchanged was some type of code that he didn't question.

"Call me."

Helen acquiesced to the command with a nod of her head, and Miriam was out the door.

"Now what?" he asked.

"Just drop me off," Helen replied, rising, holding the blanket around her shoulder, "and go pick up Elaina. By the time you return to the hospital, I'll be done."

"Can't this wait until tomorrow?" he asked.

"I want that restraining order in place before Howard Jackson appears in front a judge in the morning."

Chapter Nineteen

From the fourth wall of French doors encased in wood, Helen stared absently at the tenacious beam of the sun in the early evening, azure sky.

It was half past six now, and in a couple of hours - - about as long as she had been self-sequestered in the room - - the sun would descend into the quiet, sleepy waters.

She still wasn't ready to face her daughter who she spotted fishing with Baderinwa at the end of the long peer jutting over the water that extended from the adjacent yard next door. A partial view of its patio as well was visible from Sean's second story bedroom.

Hell, she couldn't face herself, she thought. The flashback was a bitch. There was no other way to describe it.

Yet, she went back to that ugly, black place, a time of utter despair and humiliation in her history, replaying everything she remembered over and over in her mind.

Helen momentarily buried her face in her hands and sighed.

Still, she remembered no more than a slice of the past that came to her during Howard Jackson's attack.

Once Sean intervened, her memory stopped, refusing to fill in the blanks that would answer **all** the questions even now.

However, the emotions she felt then didn't stop. Only now, they were worse.

Sitting on the brown-and-off-white zebra pattern divan positioned in the L-shape between the glass doors and a solid papyrus wall at her back, she picked up her purse that was next to her briefcase. A bold, flower print caftan - - on loan from Baderinwa to change into - - lay across the armrest. The first thing she did upon arriving was shower.

Although her body had been cleaned, her mind wasn't, she thought fleetingly as she looked though her purse for her cell, with the impetuous intention of calling her Mama - - her adopted mother, not Patricia Diagre.

She had a pretty good feeling that Candace Parker knew of her past and could fill in the pieces missing in her memory.

The cell in her hand, she punched in the Maryland number without thought, and then just as quickly, closed the phone shut before the call went through.

The second she thought about it, she realized that calling her mother made her feel less than competent. She had to ask herself whether she wanted to pile another mar against the degrading and shameful feelings already battering her.

No, she decided, putting away the cell, she had to face the fact that she had been sexually abused as a child alone. After all, she was an adult, a grown woman, imbued with the education and intellect to handle this on her own.

Helen pushed herself up and walked to the center door, leading to the patio. She tightened the belt of the long, navy silk robe - - she couldn't stand to stay in the clothes she had worn today - - and then reached for the doorknob, with a thought to open it.

Even from the distance, Elaina looked as if she were enjoying herself. She was probably talking Baderinwa's head off, Helen thought, a wee smile on her lips.

She knew her child's history and was grateful that no abuse of any kind tormented Elaina. Her biological mother realized within two years of Elaina's birth that she was ill prepared to raise a child and had put her up for adoption. When Elaina turned 18, Helen was to give her the letter the mother who birthed her wrote to her, explaining her decision.

Helen turned from the door, crossing her arms as she began to walk aimlessly around the room, acting out her conscious thought to find a peace of mind.

She couldn't stay holed up in Sean's master bedroom forever.

Sean lived in the coastal town of Seabrook, roughly twenty miles from Houston. His home sat on the far left, one of the three homes on the four-acre lot he owned with his cousins, Baderinwa and Jules, she recalled him telling Elaina when they arrived.

Royal blue, white and gold seemed mainstay colors throughout his oceanfront, two-story home. She recalled the exterior was composed of stucco and stone, while beams, crown molding, and glass, with a combination of playful antique and contemporary furniture abound the interior. His bedroom was uncluttered; a king sized bed on a platform and an artful, gold chifferobe that depicted children fishing in a pond were visible. She knew double, walk-in closets and a marble encased hot tub were beyond the swinging doors on the other side of the room.

There was only one picture, a large color photograph of his family, framed over the bed. It looked recently taken as age showed in their smiling, happy faces.

Sean and the oldest, his brother Jamie, inherited their mother's fair coloring. His sisters, Ida and Isabel were lovely shades of brown, a mix of their parents' dark and light complexion.

Even though she envied that his history was no secret

to him, she admired his strong sense of family. His home seemed crafted with family in mind.

She doubted a designer created his wonderful setting, for Sean was a man definite about what he wanted. Still, she could no longer say that included her now.

She could but only hope.

"Helen ... are you decent? It's Sean. May I come in?"

Helen froze where she stood near the foot of the bed, eyes wide as she stared at the bedroom door. Nervous flutterings pricking her chest, she pressed her hands over her heart as if to still its beat. She wondered if the dirt on her flesh would be visible to him through the robe, even knowing it was a foolish thought. But she couldn't help it.

"Just a minute," she said, hurrying to the divan to get the caftan. Disrobing to reveal her sky blue teddy, she stepped into the caftan and adjusted it over her body. "Okay. I'm decent now."

Sean pushed open the door with his hip, his hands occupied. He smiled at her upon entering, his dark eyes bright with pleasure, as if just seeing her gave him some kind of joy.

Her heart flip-flopped in her bosom, and with the reaction, a sensation that brought a warm tingle to her depths.

In one hand he carried two long-stemmed glasses filled with a clear liquid, and in the other, a long stemmed rose with thorns. "For you, ma belle," he said, offering the flower.

Helen felt the sting of tears in her eyes as she accepted the flower, careful of the thorn. "Aw, Sean, this is so sweet," she said, swallowing the tears in her throat. Her gaze on the flower, she silently counted the petals, reciting, *He wants me; he wants me not. ...*

"A little wine before dinner."

"Thank you."

Accepting the glass, she noticed he had changed into a white, ribbed Polo that distinctly outline the exquisite expanse of his chest, with beige shorts teasing her with his fine bow legs, and black sandals.

She quenched her sudden thirst, drinking a sip of wine. Seeing him well-groomed, wearing his usual natural air of authority, she wondered if he could indeed carry the weight of the world on his broad shoulders, or at the very least, the burden of her sordid past.

She noticed that after giving her wine, he stepped almost a social distance away. It occurred to her that even had he stood further, she would be able to feel the surging power of his presence. She had felt it the first night they met. But that spoke of him, the magnitude of his personality, not his feelings about her, she rationalized.

"Are you feeling any better now?"

"This is lovely," she replied, the rose at her nose as she sniffed its sweet fragrance. She took another sip of wine. "This is nice, too."

"Let's sit on the balcony," he said, leading the way. Helen laid the rose on the coffee table as he opened the door, and after she joined him, he closed it behind them.

The temperature difference was immediately felt from the cool indoors to nature's heat where the sun won over the mild breeze blowing off the water. The balcony flooring was soft and warm under her bare feet as she walked passed the aqua colored patio furniture, the umbrella open over the two chairs at opposite ends of the round, glass top table.

Helen leaned lightly against the white waist-high, guardrail, looking down where her daughter was still at it under Baderinwa's instruction. But it wasn't her child on her mind. Rather, she was wondering how she could feel such want and desire for a man knowing what she did about herself, knowing it must show, and knowing he couldn't possibly want her back.

The perceptions shrouded her in questions, forcing her to concede that human nature was as big an enigma as she ever thought.

"My daddy used to take mom and me fishing. I'd forgotten how much fun it used to be."

"Bee's favorite pastime," he replied, sitting in one of the two chairs at the table. "Even if nothing's biting, as I suspect is the case now, she loves being by the water. I don't know why, we're both earth signs," he added with a chuckle.

"I hope she's not bothered by the imposition. I'm sure Elaina is grilling her ad nauseam. But I certainly appreciate the time she's spending with her," she said, turning to face Sean.

"Beside, I don't want Elaina seeing me like this now. Thanks for not running away."

Sean's head snapped. He set his glass on the table and rose to go to her. "Are you're sure you're all right?"

"I'm as good as can be expected," she replied, sipping her wine, shuddering at his nearness. He smelled good, an herbal scent on his flesh, and his breath of mint.

"Would you mind telling me what you're talking about … Elaina seeing you like what?" he asked, a puzzled frown on his face.

Helen lowered her eyes to the bottom of the wineglass. She felt ambivalent about him forcing her to say it out loud when he surely knew. But that was Sean, persistent to a fault, she thought, recalling their first dance together.

"Helen?"

Slowly, from under her long lashes, she looked up at him. His head was slightly cocked at an angle, a look of intense, clear light shown in his eyes. She didn't know what the look meant.

She knew what she wanted it to mean. Fractionally, she held the deep breath she drew in, as if to strengthen her resolve, and then released it slowly.

"I'm sure you can tell," she said plainly. "I don't know if Elaina could. God," she added with heartfelt emphasis, "I hope not."

Sean looked pained by his confusion. "Helen, I don't know what you're talking about."

"Come on Sean," she cajoled, "you don't have to be polite about it. It's an ugly thing," she shuddered visibly. " I'm just glad you stayed around to get my child from school. Bringing us to your lovely home is a bonus. I really, truly appreciate that. I'll call Marcellus and Pauline to pick us up so we won't be in your hair any longer."

"Helen, make sense, please. I'm not following you.

Baderinwa said I was dumb to the living, and obviously that's true, because I haven't a clue what you're talking about, what you think I see. I mean," he added abashed, "other than the woman I want in my life."

His accent was more pronounced with his deep feeling, and she shivered imperceptivity. Gosh, she wanted to believe him, wanted to believe his guile, the look on his face that suggested deeper than mere masculine interest, wanted to believe he still wanted her, but feared her wish for a fairy tale romance too fragile for the reality of the situation.

"I know you see the incest on me," she insisted, her voice a plaintive cry.

***

Sean felt as if he had been kicked in the gut by a mule.

His heart raced to catch up with his pulse, speeding like a stampede in his chest. And for several long seconds, he couldn't speak, as if he had a mouthful of grout, his breathing laborious as he tried to digest what Helen just admitted.

He was at a loss for words. He didn't know how to rectify his perceptions from the truth, the two different images of her clashing in his memory. She had been injured party with an obvious emotional scar one minute, and in the next, damn near a superwoman, possessing a single-minded determination to go to the hospital, explaining that photos of her bruises were needed evidence in securing a restraining order against Howard Jackson. After he picked her up from the hospital, she returned to her stoic self, breaking character only to assure her daughter that an anomaly occurred and she needn't worry. And now, she cavalierly announced that she suffered from the most insidious victimization a male father could perpetuate against a female daughter.

He gripped the top of the rail, unfeeling of its hotter than fire touch to his hand. Helen was staring out, seeing nothing but her tortured soul, he thought. He agonized quietly, watching her observantly.

She pinched the corners of her eyes. "I can feel it even though I took a long, hot shower. I hope it comes off Baderinwa's clothes in the wash."

She looked guilty, like a child who had committed a major transgression, but he could tell she wasn't lying.

This was no joke; not even a bad one, he thought, looking at her intently. The delicate dimension of her face was enshrouded in humiliation, a wounded look in her eyes and mouth drawn tight, giving her the haggard expression of self-loathing. He didn't like the truth he saw.

The wineglass cracked in Sean's hand, the top breaking from the stem. He captured it before it fell below, undaunted by the wine that spilled.

"Did you hurt yourself?" Helen asked anxiously.

"Don't' worry about it," he said dismissively. He made a little pile of the broken pieces and set them on the table. He ignored the small cut, the pinch of blood pooling above his right hand's thumb. Wiping his hands on his shorts, he asked, "Helen, are you seeing a doctor? A psychologist, I mean?"

She bobbed her head woodenly. "Yes."

He knew quite a bit about incest, mostly through its victims that couldn't speak of the horrors they endured. Even still, those were usually just bones when he met them, buried mummies to hide their perpetrator's hideous secret.

Except for one … *du petit Taylor*, he thought, contempt slipping through his expression. His mind burned with the memory of her … the ravishment of her young body explicitly posed in rigor.

"I saw her today," Helen replied matter-of-factly.

He stared at Helen, her face imposed on that of *du petit Taylor*, and anger grew like a life form inside him, begging a guilty party upon whom to release the violence he felt. He ran a hand down his face, particularly his top lip where beads of perspiration formed. "Should I try and get her on the phone for you?"

"My next session with her isn't until this time next week."

Condemnation stole through his blank-television expression as he watched Helen struggle to maintain her composure. He wanted to go to her, to wrap her in his arms, but he feared making a wrong move.

"I'm sure she won't mind if you call her," he replied. He had to be calm, he told himself, although he didn't like the blame she assumed. "It seems like an emergency situation. What's her number?" He wanted to speak to the doctor, as well, if Helen would give her permission. He needed to know what to do, and what not to do to further exasperate her mental state, to help her get through this extremely rough period.

"I don't need to call her tonight, Sean." Her reply stopped him at the door. " I've figured it out. I know the answers now. Let me thank you …"

"Will you stop that, damnit?" he said emphatically, waving his hands like a conductor. He was angry for sure, but not at her. "I don't know what you're thanking me for! You don't have to thank me." And maybe he was angry with her, he realized. He reached for her instinctively, and then caught himself and pulled up abruptly.

"See? You do see it," she said sadly, and again, turned away from him to face the water.

Sean didn't hesitate to touch her this time.

"Let me tell you what I see," he said, turning her to face him. He took the glass from her hand and set it on the table, and then in a slow choreograph, he placed a hand on her shoulder, one at a time.

When she didn't balk, his hands slipped to span her waist, drawing her to him, his forehead resting on hers.

He had to suppress the urges raging inside him, least he frighten her with his want. But it was hell, being this close to her and unable to act on his desire to possess her. He drew a ragged breath, somewhat contented that she allowed him to get even this close to her.

"I see a woman I want. A woman I feared I couldn't have because I believed that she was still in love with Ray Butler, and ..."

Before he can finish the sentence, Helen's head snapped up, bumping his. They both chuckled in a moment of levity. "Sorry," she apologized amused.

"No problem. My mama used to tell me all the time I had a hard head."

"Where on earth did you get that notion from? Is that what Sgt. Diamond told you?"

Sean ducked his head, a chagrinned smile on his face as he stuck his hands in his pockets. "Not really. When he told me that Butler went to see you, presumably to seek your legal counsel, I jumped the gun."

"He did come to my office with an outrageous explanation that I didn't buy for one second. I had to kick him out," she said mildly annoyed.

"You did?" Sean asked surprised, his hands flying out of his pockets.

"Yes. Why would you think I was in love with him?"

Hesitantly, he replied, "I heard you two were engaged once."

"Ten years ago," she said. "I'm lucky he called it off. I know how fortunate I am," she said vehemently.

"What happened?"

As if all of her energy suddenly flew, she replied with sad introspection, "I didn't know what I know now."

"That's good enough for me," Sean said. He was grinning like a cat granted a bowl of cream, absolutely delighted by this bit of news. That she didn't want Ray Butler was eureka to him. "I don't need to know any more. I got all the information I need."

"You need to know. That is …," she stalled, looking at him from under her long lashes, "… if you still want that affair with me."

"Helen, I want to kiss you. Will that bother you?'

For a moment, she stared at him bemused, and he held his breath, wondering what she was thinking, whether he'd pushed too hard and too fast, like a schoolboy eager to get in his girlfriend's panties. He swallowed the lump in his throat, waiting.

"Why don't you kiss me and find out?" she asked, a coy smile on her face.

Sean hesitated with the excitement beaming inside him. Before he could move, they both turned, hearing ... "Hey, Mama! Look what I caught," Elaina cried jubilantly.

Elaina was running into the bedroom, and then out onto the balcony, with a fish dangling from the end of a fishing pole.

"Baderinwa said it's a sand trout, and I can eat it!"

Chapter Twenty

Twilight. The stars seemed stuck deep in the silvery, blue-black sky. While no wind stirred the humid night, an effervescent air wrapped Helen and Sean in the sweet aura of tender passions.

Helen felt the moment she had been waiting for all evening was near. Replete from a dinner of boiled crawfish, corn on the cob, and potatoes, fed her by Sean, a reciprocal delight she returned, they had gone walking.

The excuse fooled no one as they had given themselves away during dinner. Sean had kept her at his side all evening. He refused to let her stew privately in the past, forcing her participation in dinner repartee.

Hand in hand, they meandered in and out of shadows from tall lampposts intermittingly dispersing light along the deserted paved street.

And while expressions were barely discernable in the dark, they spoke softly, in tones of voices that bespoke the warm glow of their feelings.

Ever since Elaina interrupted them to show off her catch, she had hungered for the feel of Sean's lips on hers, coupled with a very strong need to find out how she would react.

With satisfaction looming in the safe distance and safety in numbers allowed by not only Jules and Baderinwa, but Marcellus and Pauline, only desire simmered in her on a low boil.

"You've been holding out on me," Sean said.

They were a couple of yards from Sean's, an area she called "the compound," as the three homes were within the confines of a security gate, accessible by a security code, much like the one at her home.

"What do you mean?"

"You didn't tell me you played the guitar. Oh, pardon me," he said, gesturing with his free hand, " I mean all strings instruments."

Helen laughed lightly, but pride swelled through her, recalling the haughty satisfaction in Elaina's voice when she insisted that her mama could really play upon discovering Baderinwa's acoustic guitar. Forced to prove it, more for her daughter's sake than her own ego, she did, serenading the group with her musical talent while they congregated on Baderinwa's patio. Sean and Elaina, it seemed, were of one accord when it came to ensuring she stayed active in the group.

"You play beautifully. I never would have imagined it of you."

Helen blushed. "That's nice to know." A woman needs her secrets, she recalled her Mama advising her at a time when the secrets were already locked inside her head.

"What's nice to know?"

He gave her hand a tight squeeze, no longer than a hiccup, as if sensing her thoughts sliding downhill, away from him.

"That I can surprise you."

"What other secrets about yourself are you harboring from me?"

The street was narrow, one car per side could travel, but none were on the street. The homes, spaciously parted from one another, were built high as protection against heavy rains that ultimately caused flooding. And while their vehicles were street level, many had elevated driveways. The neighbors were inside their cool, air conditioned homes on this warm night, the light from the television screens visible.

"In due time," she said playfully, but felt it was a lie. All of her secrets - - the dirty laundry most didn't air - - were out.

Or, at least, the one that mattered most.

Now … again, …alone with Sean, her hand

possessively held in his, her heart thumped-thumped like the rotors of a helicopter, stirring up the dust of memories she desperately wanted to forget. She swallowed and silently pleaded with God to make it right.

"What do you want in a man, ma belle?"

Actually, Helen was startled by the question, but chuckled.

"What's that for? Did I say something funny?"

"Not at all. It's just that I answered that question during dinner," she replied. The laughter faded, replaced by the invasion of a serious vein as she recalled thinking that she could love this man. But it was an affair he wanted, not love.

He squeezed her hand gently. "And the answer is?" he prompted.

"Respectful. Considerate."

"That's it?" he feigned amazement. "You just want a respectful, considerate man?"

"What else is there?" she asked, recalling that her list was much longer. He was handsome, good-looking, and his nearness excited her. Her heart thudded.

"Intelligent, financially secure, and a sexy lover."

"Is that how you see yourself ... as a sexy lover?"

In seemingly one movement, Sean stopped, pivoted her around facing him, and his arms slid around her waist. "It's how I hope you see me, ma belle," he said, his face inches from hers. "I've been waiting all evening. The anticipation is about to drive me mad. I want to find out now."

"Find out what?' she asked breathlessly.

"This," he said, lowering his mouth to hers.

His lips touched hers with a featherlike lightness. His mouth was surprisingly soft and sensitive as his lips settled on hers with a soft sigh.

It was a test. A tantalizing one that she passed with a muffled cry for more as she wrapped her arms around his neck and pressed against the length of him. His mouth moved over hers in a sensuous exploration, teasing her lips apart with his tongue. Languidly, his tongue entwined with hers, and caressed the inner walls of her mouth. She clung to him, her hands at the back of his neck pulling his head closer, wanting the kiss to go on forever.

Reluctantly, he pulled his mouth from hers, and their foreheads rested together, as his ragged breathing mingled with hers. She felt him trembling, or maybe it was the tremor coursing through her body that she felt. Regardless, part of her question was answered.

"Wow," he whispered. "You're dangerous, ma belle."

"No more so than you," she replied in that same breathless whisper.

Slowly, he recaptured her hand, and they resumed walking.

"What do you want in a woman?"

"You," he replied effortlessly.

Facilely, sorrow slipped into her thoughts with her claimed memory, and belittlement into her voice. "I'm not so sure I'm a bargain."

He brought her hand to his lips and kissed it. "We will work through that, ma bell, don't worry."

A breath skipped in her bosom nervously. "Are you sure it doesn't scare you?"

"It scares me to death," he retorted in Creole, his tone sarcastic. "You wouldn't believe how much it scares me, but I'm sure it's not what you would think.

" There have only been a few times in my life where I was afraid of my own reaction to the horrors men perpetrate against women, children especially." He stopped walking to stare at her headlong. "Like your monster, the evil man you call the Slave Master."

Helen wasn't sure if he shivered, or she did, and it passed through both their bodies. Her mouth felt suddenly dry as she stared into his face where twin bulbs of pain blazed in his black eyes.

"I can imagine your pain, your fear, your utter vulnerability and helplessness. I want to kill the man that stole your childhood," he said fiercely.

Suddenly, he dropped her hand, shoved his hands in pockets and resumed walking, leaving her to skip to catch up with him.

"I feel that I'm always too late," he admitted solemnly, his head down.

She reached for his hand, and held it in both of hers as they continued walking. "What do you mean?"

He flashed her a rueful smile "I was almost too late to save you; certainly, too late to save *du petit Taylor.*"

"Du petit Taylor?"

"Taylor Butler. When I saw her body like that ..." he broke off. "I would have gladly saved the state the money for an execution. At least, until I had a chance to see what it feels like. I still haven't resolved the matter in my mind."

"You're talking about Howard Jackson."

"Oui."

"But that's the nature of your job. Putting together the broken pieces of victims back together, making them whole for death. I figured you were used to it by now."

"I am. Mostly. But there are times. . ." He let the words trail off, and then sighed. "We all have our warts, regardless their origin."

"Oh, and what are your warts?" she replied lightly, thinking he was just trying to make her feel good.

"I'm a possessive, jealous man, ma belle. When I heard about you and Ray, which I now know was just a figment of my imagination," he smiled broadly, " I was enraged."

"I could tell," she replied chuckling. "I'm glad we got that straight."

Sean stopped again, and pulled her into his embrace. "You should know that sharing your love with Elaina is not a difficult thing. Beyond that, and the child we'll likely have together, I want your affections reserved for me."

Helen had no words, no response to his declaration, and he gave her no time to find them, as he reclaimed her lips, and her mouth burned with the fire of his passion.

***

Under a glorious blue sky, white fluffy clouds, a ball of yellow sun, and the covetous look in his wanting black eyes, Helen gave herself to Sean. And received tenfold feelings of steaming hope in rampageous reactions she no longer feared.

Since Sean came into her life it seemed as if she had no frigid past. In a stolen moment from work and motherhood responsibilities, she discovered exactly what desire meant, and there were no limits to it in his arms.

"Je vous veux tout pour moi," she now knew meant "I want you all to myself."

While his deep sexy voice spewed a lover's muttering in Creole, his lips burned against her throat. He had promised her joy and was delivering.

She had but to relax and enjoy, which she did with her eyes closed as she inhaled the scent of his body, relishing the indescribable essence of him.

She was swept away by wave after wave of excitement, feeling his tender-tempered strong hands caressing her body. His palms closed around her breast and whatever common sense she possessed skittered into the shadows, and then he teased the taunt nipples with his mouth and stars shot through her in broad daylight.

He returned to her face and his warm lips smothered her mouth as his hands stroked the bush of hair between her thighs. She cried out with want, begging him to take her, to possess her there, to make her complete. He complied sliding an exact finger into the core of her.

"I know you like this."

Her eyes flew open hearing the rough voice, the vulgar implication of his words, on a face that belonged to the Slave Master, and Helen cried out in intense fear.

In the darkened bedroom, Helen clutched the sheet covering her, bemoaning its meager protection as she writhed violently against very strong hands and the pending horrible fate awaiting her.

No one stirred to help her.

Why didn't her mother hear her cries?

"Don't you run from me!"

Somehow she knew the answer. The Slave Master had come for her, with his liquor breath and leather belt.

He began beating her, slashing her body indiscriminately, all the while barking commands and calling her names. "You fast little heifer. I'm go be yo' teacher tonight."

She didn't know what to do! Escaping was not an option for there was no way out. She was trapped in this small space with the big Slave Master, a giant of a man, powerful in build and mean in spirit.

"I'm not go talk in school no mo,'" she begged as she squirmed this way and that. The snot running from her nose mixed with the tears steaming down her face.

"Take 'em off now, goddamnit! You fast, little, hardheaded bitch! That's why the teacher sent that note! Hurry up and git 'em off!"

But the Slave Master was not deterred by her pitiful cries that her mother could not hear. He just kept swinging his belt that lashed her body like bee stings as she struggled to remove her pajamas. Even though she was obeying, the Slave Master never stopped lashing her with all his strength.

"You ain't go sass no more. Git them goddamn clothes off!"

The tiny luminance from the nightlight revealed Helen twisting and writhing on the bed. She cried in her sleep, tears steamed down her face, as the promises and pleas that spewed from her lips finally turned into whimpers.

With a scream in her throat, Helen bolted upright in bed.

She breathed harshly in the seconds it took her to realize that she was safe . . . in her own bed and not the horror of her nightmare.

Averting her gaze, she looked at the clock on her bedside table that set the time at 1:32AM in green light.

Sean had brought her and Elaina home three hours ago, and in another four hours, he would return to pick them up.

Even though she missed two days of swim practice this week, Elaina was determined to compete in a local meet tomorrow.

Thinking about her daughter's complete change of attitude toward Sean, she laid down to stare at the ceiling. She wasn't ready to try to sleep again right now, she thought, unconsciously shaking her head.

Yet, she closed her eyes fractionally, wishing the nightmare away. Opening them, she pulled her fond memories of Sean to the fore of her mind until they were pure and unsullied, and smiled. "*Je vous veux tout pour moi,*" she heard his sexy Creole voice croon.

"I want you to myself," she whispered, shivering, as the dull ache of desire warmed her loins.

With a look of peace and satisfaction on her face, she closed her eyes, with Sean on her mind.

A distant ringing invaded her pleasant musing, and she frowned as her eyes popped open. Rising on her haunches, she scanned the room for the source of the interruption. It was coming from her purse on the dresser.

Would Sean call this late when he would be returning in a few hours? She wondered. The cell peeled off again, and she tossed the covers asides and padded across the room to the dresser. She withdrew the cell and checked the Caller ID.

"Ray, do you know what time it is?" she answered irately.

"I meant to call you earlier, but I couldn't get away," Ray replied as if she should have expected his call, regardless the hour. "We had another strategy meeting, and with the funeral arrangements, it's just been a nightmare."

He spoke as if exhausted by his schedule, emphasizing the drought of his time when his wife and child would have no such worry again, she thought bitterly.

She dropped to the side of the bed and looped an arm across her chest. "So what do you want?"

"Helen, we need to talk." He cleared his throat, his voice a little louder. "Seriously. Just you and me. Let's meet," he said as if her agreement was a foregone conclusion. "Some place discreet."

Helen was incensed by his audacity. "Ray, I'm not meeting you anywhere."

"Come on, Helen," he implored with sympathetic weariness. "This is serious. I know about Howard Jackson. You're representing his wife in a divorce."

Helen sat uncomfortably still, unsettled by the remark hanging between them like a lead weight. Uneasily, she asked, "How do you know that?"

"He'll be out on bail just in time for breakfast."

There was no more than matter-of-factness in his tone,

she thought, her heart beating faster than ever. She searched her mind anxiously for meaning behind the words, wondering if the mention of Howard Jackson was a threat somehow.

"I'll clear out my schedule anytime you want to."

Presumptuous bastard, she thought. "I'll think about it," she said tightly.

"Helen, I need your answer now," he insisted firmly.

Her bottom lip folded in her mouth, she questioned whether she should agree to meet him, as maybe she should have answered his wife's call.

"Ray, are you in danger?" she asked, softening her position a bit.

"I could be, Helen. I could be. Look, I gotta go. Call me at this number tomorrow ... around three."

"Ray . . ." she started, and then clamped her mouth shut. He was no longer on the phone.

Helen closed her phone, her expression cloudy with indecision. What kind of danger could he be in? Was he serious or was it a ploy to get her to agree to a meeting?

And then there was something else ... what was his relationship to Howard Jackson?

Chapter Twenty-One

The sun was enjoying its second cup of coffee by six o'clock, Saturday morning. With a cheerful whistle in his heart, Sean rang the Parker doorbell.

Helen opened the door, and her presence answered the masculine call in him that responded with a skittering pulse to her femininity. He stared covetously.

A flicker of a smile rose at the edges of her mouth, and then died out. She backed up as she opened the door wider for his entry. "Good morning."

"Morning," he said with his sense of good feeling as he sauntered inside the foyer. He tried to kiss her, but she averted her head, and instead of a quick kiss to her lips, his mouth caught her cheek. It wasn't until then that her dull greeting reached his consciousness.

Instantaneously, he reached out and caught a finger on her hand before she completely eluded his grasp, his brow arched with confusion. "Helen …?"

Elaina bounded enthusiastically down the stairs, with her swim bag, announcing, "I'm ready. Let's go. Morning Sean," she said chipper and eager on her way out the door.

Speaking, "Morning," Sean adjusted his expression to neutral and suppressed his annoyance. Questions circled his head as he helped carry overnight cases, cooler, and lawn chairs to the car.

A steady flow of chatter from Elaina to the northwest Houston's Dad's Club where the meet was held made the ride bearable.

It was easy to see that Helen was trapped in some distant place he couldn't breach. He knew something must have happened between the time he dropped them off at home last night and this morning, but not the what. However, it wasn't difficult to guess that incest was at the basis of it.

He didn't have to cull far in his memory for information about incest. The occurrence of it in the Creole culture was not a myth. Nor was it the genesis of his ancestry, for there was a concept known as the incest taboo, which occurred in every human culture in the world at some time in history, beginning with the ancient Egyptians.

Arriving, Elaina led the way, maneuvering around like a pro, checking in with her coaches and signing in. He was awed by the multitude of people - - parents, and in some cases, whole families who accompanied the roughly four hundred competing swimmers.

They settled in a corner where Dolphin swimmers and parents congregated in lawn chairs, surrounded by coolers filled with water and energy food.

Helen was dressed for the meet, a white tee shirt with a blue dolphin in the center tucked into blue calf length slacks that revealed her perfectly slim body, and she behaved like the typical sweet team mom - - cheering for every Dolphin that stood on the blocks, hugging disappointed ones as well as winners with a kind and encouraging word and dutifully noting times in the souvenir booklet.

He found no fault with her looks, or even the forced happy attitude she exhibited, but he was terribly disappointed that she would not share her pain with him.

Nevertheless, their public persona indicated that all was right between them and the world; consequently, the other parents embraced him as if he were one of them.

And he had to admit that hearing the bravura of proud fathers bragging about their sons **and daughters'** times filled him with an indescribable sense of admiration and pride.

Incest had not always been viewed as a sexual sickness of fathers abusing their daughters, or mothers their sons, he mused, as the meet began with freestyle heats.

In its early existence, money and protecting the gene line of the family were powerful forces for accepting the practice.

Slave masters who desired to increase the size of their slave stock forced enslaved Africans of the same blood into the practice.

And Creoles, "free people of color," indulged in the practice because to mate with a slave resulted in an offspring born into slavery. Today, its continuation was largely out of ignorance of family or worse.

Although the meet was an all day affair, it ended too soon. He was as excited as Elaina who earned a "B" time in her butterfly stroke and shaved three-tenths of a second off her breast stroke time.

Having promised Elaina her own fishing gear, they went to Academy, a local sports store. Elaina kept the sales clerk busy, sampling reels from the locked glass cabinet, while he and Helen lingered next to a stack of rods.

He pulled one from its holding and gently shook it. "You want to tell me what happened?"

"Nothing," Helen replied lightly, a quick smile. "I just have a headache," she added, massaging her forehead as if proof of the malady.

With his expression working around a look of disgust, Sean struggled to retain his casual persona. "I don't believe that," he said in a low firm tone as he returned the rod to withdraw another.

Helen fiddled with the thin gold chain around her neck. "Well, I don't know what you want me to say."

"Baloney," he whispered gruffly. His knowledge about the incest taboo was not helpful to victims left debilitated by the occurrence of incest in their lives. He shook the rod, testing it. "What happened last night? Tell me the truth this time," he urged, staring pointedly at Helen.

Her bright eyes darted to Elaina at the counter, and then back to him. She swallowed as if with difficulty before she spoke, her voice barely lifted above a whisper. "I had the dream. I didn't get any sleep."

"What dream?"

"Not really a dream," she said, "a nightmare. The Slave Master came. And .. and," she stammered.

"And what?"

"I'm sorry," she said, bowing her head as she shook it from to side. She inhaled deeply, and then looked up at him, with a smile wobbling on her lips. "I've behaved horribly today. Will you forgive me?"

The smile that then came to her face illuminated her beauty and turned bright lights on inside him. Although relieved that she had snapped back to normal, a tiny hole of concern made his sense of satisfaction incomplete.

Elaina ran to them, holding up a black reel that fit in her hand, asking, "Sean, can I have this one?"

***

Helen struggled to recapture yesterday's mood when she believed herself falling in love with the man who wanted her in spite of her incestuous history.

When torment invaded her sleep and permeated her entire being all day, she thought, not even Sean could penetrate her wall of sorrow. She had behaved cowardly, she realized now. She was ashamed, and determined to make it up to him.

She and Sean, hand-in-hand, strolled into Baderinwa's great room later that evening. It was like stepping into an art gallery.

As in her kitchen, an artfully executed blend of soft wood and hard stone prevailed.

African American Classical Music in its most esoteric forms played from hidden speakers throughout, coaxing the live plants and flowers to grow and bloom prosperously.

Helen marveled at the wonderful blend of bold prints, and wood and metal sculptures representing several cultures exhibited in a fusion of light and shadows. The theme centered on strong women.

Baderinwa, Jules, Marcellus and Pauline were seated around the card table in the center of the room on the porcelain-tiled floor in a dark brown mesh pattern in front of the tiled fireplace.

Jules and Marcellus faced each other at the card table, opposite of Baderinwa and Pauline. A red, leather sectional sofa surrounded them; a glass-topped coffee table had been moved to the far side of the room next to a six-foot tall African door.

Pauline was shuffling a deck of cards.

"The lovebirds have returned," Marcellus teased.

Sean was looking at her as if she were the most precious thing in his life, the only one that mattered in his world. She wanted to be that person he saw with his compelling gaze.

Helen plucked the back of Marcellus' head.

"Ouch!" he exclaimed, rubbing his head as the rest of them laughed. "That hurts, girl."

"Then behave yourself," Pauline chided playfully, dealing cards around the table. "How was the swim meet? And where is our little swimmer?"

"Elaina swam the butterfly stroke in thirty-three point sixty one seconds, and the breaks stroke at thirty-nine seven," Sean replied with proud amazement.

Marcellus whistled. "The little dolphin was flying."

"Now, she's fishing," Helen added with a chuckle.

Elaina who insisted on trying out her new gear headed straight for the pier behind Baderinwa's yard. "Sean equipped her with the latest, and I might add, the most expensive fishing gear in the store."

"Well, you need a new hobby," Pauline teased laughingly.

"No," Helen quipped, "Sean has a new hobby."

"Well, he's been dying to play papa," Baderinwa added, winking at him.

Jules and Marcellus teased him with comical expressions, and laughter rang around the table. Helen smiled softly, remembering how Sean had showered her daughter with attention she could never provide. And there wasn't a shadow of a doubt about his sincerity. The doubts of her ability to return his affection in a meaningful way were all hers.

"Misery loves company, my friend," Marcellus said. "I'll be happy to lend any parental expertise you need."

Helen noticed Sean duck his head and a stain of embarrassment colored his neck.

"What yawl playing?" Sean asked.

"Bid whist," Jules replied. "Yawl wanna play?"

Sean looked at Helen sidelong with an arched brow. "Can you play, Helen?"

"Mm, a little bit," she replied, and they all laughed.

"We know what that means," Baderinwa said, amusement in her voice.

"She's my partner," Sean declared possessively as he pulled Helen by her waist closer to him.

"I dare say none of us would have it any other way," Jules quipped dryly. He quickly protected his head, crying out jokingly, "Please don't hit my bald head," earning laughter all around. "I'm tender-headed, and don't want any lumps when I go to Africa in a couple of weeks."

"I didn't know you were going to take that trip," Sean said.

"We need the money, cousin," Jules replied, inspecting the cards dealt him.

Sean explained to Helen, "Jules is one of the guides on an educational tour of the Pyramids in Egypt every other year."

"How fascinating," she replied impressed. "Maybe Elaina and I can go the next time. It's a trip I've been putting off for years."

"Not without me," Sean whispered next to her ear, his breath fanning her neck.

A tiny mewl escaped her lips, and Helen shivered, a reaction that didn't escape the others who laughed and joked about her and Sean, acting "like two teenagers in heat."

Helen could but join the mirth as the heat of embarrassment warmed her face.

She wondered why was it only in the presence of others that she felt free, relaxed enough to feel and bask in the sweet sense of joy Sean transmitted to her?

***

It was highly plausible that she was fooling herself and Sean was simply too polite and his sanguine nature too stubborn to face the truth, Helen thought regretfully late that night.

She was sitting on Baderinwa's eerily quiet patio, a shadow in the dark as the only light came from the kitchen inside.

With her borrowed caftan pulled up to her thighs, she created ripples in the water on the shallow end of the pool, her feet twirling nervously. The action matched the bevy of anxious emotions stirring inside her.

Sean had showed her innumerably how much he wanted her, she argued. She knew from the bottom of her heart the feeling was mutual. And even though she didn't doubt that lust contributed greatly to their emotions, for as he once told her … "Desire is the first sign of attraction," she couldn't say with that same sense of certainty that it would be enough. It was much like the old song Tina Turner popularized: *What's Love Got to Do With It?*

But the feelings instilled in her felt so good, so utterly delicious, she shivered ... Until the Slave Master came and took them away, punishing her with feelings of guilt and shame. She feared ever overcoming him, the inexplicable horrid emotions he created in her.

He returned again tonight, she recalled somberly. Unable to sleep, she had crawled out of the bed she shared with Elaina, unwilling to risk another episode as before at her cousins' home.

Helen sighed and shook her head as if to erase the unsettling thought settling there. She guessed it was sometime after four. If not for the image she retained of the patio as a green lushly, romantic cove with purple and white furniture intimately placed among the lilacs and scrubs surrounding the rectangular shaped pool with the pyramid design in the bottom, it would be a scary setting.

And the evening had been going so nicely, she silently moaned with regret that it had ended so abruptly with the nightmare. Ironically, she and Sean had been an awesome partnership, she recalled, a smile slipping into her forlorn expression as a kernel of joy popped inside her.

The moment's joy dissipated with the ever-present prudent thought that she would have to give Sean up.

Her feet began to stir the water again, and then stopped when a musical interlude interrupted her thoughts, indicating her cell was ringing. She brought it out, debating whether or not to call her parents, regardless the hour. They had left several messages on her cell and also sent a message by Marcellus, she recalled, picking up the small, silver phone that lay on the towel next to her. Only they knew what happened to that little girl, Corinda, she thought.

"Ray," she answered, displeasure in her tone. He had been a ghost in her head as well, she mused disgusted.

"You were supposed to call me," he replied with annoyance. "Why didn't you?"

"I'm not at your beck-and-call," she replied bravely. Still, dreaded anticipation whirled inside her. "What is Howard Jackson to you?" she demanded, recalling he mentioned him last night. "How do you know him?"

"You should have met me," he replied. "It's too late now. I'm on my way out of town."

Her expression hard and unyielding, she replied, "If you know something I need to know, tell me. Otherwise, I want you to lose my number."

"Aw, Helen," he replied exasperated.

"What's your relationship to Howard Jackson?" she repeated firmly.

"Damnit, Helen," he swore bitterly. She could hear him take a deep breath, as if preparing himself for something horrible to come. "He is my wife's ... my late wife's brother," he said with sympathetic weariness.

Helen respired astonished; the information seemed too incredible to believe. Her mouth was still open as Ray continued talking. She tried to recall what he had said about his wife before, remembered thinking he was troubled about something, but not wanting to get involved.

"The family is pretty angry right now. I tried to talk to you before, but you refused to hear me out."

Helen clutched the cell with both hands. . "I'm listening now." Despite her denial of involvement with his wife, she realized that she somehow was, and was anxious to learn more.

"All I know is that some woman named Patricia Daigre called Joann, claiming that she was her mother. ..."

Helen felt as if she had been kicked in the gut. Her eyes widened trepidant, and her breath trembled in her bosom as the name bobbed across her mind like the proverbial bad penny.

Where had she heard that name before?

"Well of course that's crazy because Shirley Singleton

is her mother," Ray was saying. "But the woman was insistent. I don't know what she has to do with my wife's family, but they're pretty mad. My guess is that she's an old girlfriend because Shirley was livid that she called. That's all I know. I just hope this doesn't affect my campaign. Look, they're calling my flight. I must go. I'm taking my son back to his mother.

"But we still need to talk," he added, sounding rushed. "I don't want this woman to crop up and bite my campaign in the butt." With demanding in his hurried speech, he said, "You're going to tell me what this is all about … what she wants."

"Ray . . ." she started.

Again, he hung up on her, imparting with parcels of information. She still didn't know what it all had to do with her. She bit off a curse as she closed the cell and she pulled her feet from the water. With the cell under her chin, and feet on the towel, she thought about what she had just learned, tried to piece it together.

Nothing made sense.

She blew out her cheeks and shook her head from side-to-side. She wondered how differently things would have been had she responded to Joann Butler's phone calls.

"Who were you talking to?'

Startled, Helen jumped. Sean was so quiet she didn't hear him steal upon her. And it was apparent that there was another entrance from his home to his cousin's that she wasn't aware of. "You scared me half to death," she said, her hand over her heart.

"Who were you talking to this late?' Sean repeated, his speech warped by whiskey.

Helen looked up at him sidelong as his aggravated tone of voice reached her consciousness and even in the poor light, she noticed the stormy expression on his face. "No one."

Alcohol defaced his usual nimble, gracefulness as he weaved slightly to the light box adjacent to the back door.

Flipping the switch, lights bathed the area. Returning, he dropped onto one of the lawn chairs, splashes of his drink spilled over his hand.

His expression was tight, mouth pressed together, with a frown line stretched across his forehead as he stared at her headlong with a squinty eyes. She even felt a thread of anger emanating from him.

"Say it's none of my business," he said brashly, "but don't lie."

He already knew more about her than she wanted him to know. But that was her fault, she thought, displeased with herself.

"Alright," she acquiesced, slightly miffed, "it's none of your business."

He snorted disgustedly, obviously dissatisfied with her response.

"What are you doing up?" he asked.

"I should ask that of you. I thought you had a long day tomorrow." She recalled that he had mentioned as much before he left for home, several hours ago, even though he didn't say what he had to do. Despite her curiosity, she refused to pry.

"The Slave Master." He answered his unstated question to her, rather than hers to him.

Helen bobbed her head as she rose. She sauntered to the table where he sat and dropped into the chair across from him.

"I was thinking," she said hesitantly, absently tracing the design in the table.

She stopped, wondering how to put this to him, wondering whether she should wait for another time when his head was clearer. But it wasn't her fault that he was inebriated.

And then again, maybe it was.

"I was thinking that we should take a rain check," she said calmly, hiding the pain just the idea brought her.

"A rain check? What do you want a rain check for?"

"Not me," she replied emphatically, "us. Postpone us."

He stared intently, studying her, with his head cocked at a familiar angle and confusion in his expression.

"I know I've had a few, " he said, lifting the glass in reference, "but I don't understand what you're proposing we postpone."

Helen shivered under the intensity of that look. It told her that he knew full well what she was referring to and refused to accept it. That he could devalue her idea angered her, yet more than equally thrilled her that he sternly disagreed.

It raised a question about herself, making her painfully aware of a weakness in her character - - a lack of trust that a man would actually want her as his woman, knowing what he did about her childhood.

Sean rose and began pacing, carefully attending to his balance, as if trying to walk off the fog of the alcohol in his head. "Since we seem to be thinking, I've been thinking, too."

He stopped moving to look at her headlong, his expression serious. "My idea is one hundred percent better than yours."

"Sean, no idea can erase the past," she said softly with rue, even though she appreciated his persistence.

"I'm not about to suggest that we even attempt to do

that," he replied, with a wave of his head in dismissal. "What I am thinking is something that will help you get over it in a meaningful way. I'm sure the statue of limitation has probably expired, so I want you to consider suing."

A bovine frown flashed across Helen's face. "Suing?" she said dumbly.

"Yeah, sue the bastard," he said with conviction.

"And who am I supposed to sue?" she asked, thinking the alcohol consumed because of her had seriously affected his mind.

"The Slave Master," he quipped. "Your father, the man you call *Daddy*, the one person who should have protected you before and from all others who would harm you, the first man in your life who should have showed you how to love by example, not introduce you to a woman's life, stealing your childhood," he argued passionately.

Helen didn't move a muscle. Forget that the statute of limitations on a civil suit would have also passed now, her mind whirled as she thought about the man she called *Daddy*, James Parker.

For a long time, a year at least, or maybe two - - she didn't remember anymore – she feared him. He was a big man, larger than even the Slave Master in both physical stature and honest emotions. She never stayed in his presence without Mama, Candace Parker.

She must have said something about liking music - - she wasn't sure about that either - - but on her tenth birthday, James Parker, her Daddy presented her with a violin.

It was spanking brand new, and she didn't learn just how expensive it was until much later. But it changed their relationship forever, cementing a bond between them that couldn't be broken.

"You think you know everything," she said annoyed, getting to her feet. "Go to bed, Sean. Sleep it off. I'll see you in the morning," she added, walking off.

Sean hurried to halt her exit, spinning her around facing him, holding her lightly at the shoulders.

"You have to stop protecting him, Helen," he insisted zealously. "He stole your childhood, one of the most precious times in a person's life. I know it would likely pain your mother, but you've got to show him that you're stronger now, no longer that little girl he violated."

Infuriated by his refusal to listen, she shoved his hands off her, and he lost his balance. With his arms waving like propellers, he tried to prevent the inevitable, but it was too late, and he fell into the pool in a splash.

Helen walked off, leaving Sean sputtering in the water, calling her name.

"Helen! Helen, come back here, damnit! We're not finished talking! Helen!"

She flipped the light switch on her way inside, throwing the patio into darkness.

Chapter Twenty-Two

"Do you really want us to be together, Chere?"

Helen shivered imperceptibly as she stared at Sean with wet eyes. She swallowed, and then moved her head up and down in a series of nods.

Early Sunday morning before the crack of day, Sean found her in the kitchen, picking up bits and pieces of broken glass. Baderinwa only had teas in her home, and tea wasn't what she needed. So she had stolen across the way and located his liquor cabinet and an unopened bottle of Remy Martin. She had been crying so hard, she sloshed the liquid on the floor while trying to pour it in a glass, and then the glass slipped from her hands.

Now, she sat on the barstool, her foot in his hands and desire in her throat while he tended the cut.

It had been morosely quiet in the cool room off the kitchen when she arrived. So quiet that the tinkle of glass breaking seemed as loud as a cannon.

She didn't know whether Sean heard the noise or if he had simply sensed her presence. It was quiet still, but the air had begun to sing a sweet song, a sensual ballad.

Maybe it was just the beat of her heart she felt that was accelerando, gradually thumping faster in her bosom.

"If that is so," he said in an imminently reasonable voice, "then we are going to have to do something about it." He cut her a sidelong look, a sly smile on his firm lips.

She tried not to squirm. It wasn't the peroxide he cleaned the cut with that brought about her discomfort. Sean had come down in pajamas, a pair of colorful pants with a drawstring. No top. Barefooted.

"What?" she finally managed to ask.

It was difficult holding still ... so near to him ...the scent of manliness wafting her senses ... shoulders powerful enough to bear the weight of her troubles ... fine sculptured torso of his wide-chest curving down to his slim waist ... the smooth, black chest hairs, like the hair on his head, lying down as if he had brushed them. Tempting.

"I presume the Slave Master drove you from bed again," he said, her foot still in his gentle grasp.

"Uh-huh," she replied weakly. She suppressed a moan, folding her lips in her mouth.

"He comes between us at other times, too."

He released her foot to close the cap on the bottle, and she breathed, but his remark floored her. "How so?" she stammered in reply.

"Do you think I have not noticed the flashes of anxiety you experience when we're alone, away from the safety of others?" he replied sotto voiced that accentuated his Creole tone, looking up at her sidelong, her foot in his hand and a band-aid in the other.

She had thought herself adept at hiding her insecurities. "I'm sorry," she said remorsefully as her hand instinctively reached out and stroked the side of his face, as if it had a mind of its own.

And its mind sought to soothe hurt feelings she may have caused, a mind with a ravenous need to touch him. Sean trapped her hand next to his cheek, and the light stubble tingled titilatingly, and she sighed as longing knotted in her loins. He planted a lingering kiss in her palm, and she tasted his hunger on her tongue. It tasted like the delicious shudder that coursed through her.

Unable to bear his sexual healing that created a sweet ache of wanting, she exclaimed, "Sean," breathlessly before she bit down on her lip. Wanting was bad. The Slave Master showed her that time and time again, she thought, as fretfulness flashed across her gaze.

"It's all right," Sean said coaxingly, his lips smiling beneath his mustache. He returned to his duty tending her foot, but the covetous look in his eyes showed that he had by no means relinquished his desire of her.

"No apologies needed," he said, slightly breathless, as he placed the band-aid on her cut.

Without severing contact, her foot still in his hand, he pulled the adjacent stool closer and sat. "Tell me about him," he requested with the bedside manner of a sexy, caring doctor. "How does he make you feel?"

"Dirty." She replied as if the word were engraved on her tongue. "He says horrible things."

"Is your mother in this nightmare? Where is she?"

Helen drew in a breath so deep her entire body moved. "I remembered," she said, her eyes with astonishment. "Her name is Patricia. Patricia Daigre." Sean frowned, and she hastily explained, "Ray said that she called his wife, claiming to be her mother. That's probably why Joann called me," she said in a rush of eureka. Then her expression darkened pensively. "But how would she know to call me?"

Sean bit off an obvious curse in his Creole tongue as he shook his head confused. "I thought your mother's name was Candace Parker. Who is this Patricia Daigre?"

"Sean," she said again with astonishment, "I thought you knew. I was adopted. Candace and James Parker adopted me when I was six years old."

"So," Sean replied, his head twisting from side-to-side, "James Parker, the man you call Daddy is not the Slave Master?"

"No." Helen slowly shook her head. "I don't know who the Slave Master is. I remember what he says, what he does," she shivered. "But I don't remember him. I barely remember this Patricia woman, who so obviously didn't care about me at all," she added embittered. " But I definitely don't remember him."

"Then here's what we're going to do. ..."

***

It was not just another Monday morning. Still, the sun rose early and blazed a laser heat across the city as Sean navigated his Jag through the rush hour traffic.

Helen was coordinating vacation time with Miriam from the passenger seat to his right, while Elaina, riding in the back, had borrowed his cell to contact her friends, allegedly about a class project. So under the din of Zydeco music playing softly in the background, the Parker females were yammering on the phone.

Shades protecting his eyes, he hummed right along with the music from the car's CD player, the Zydeco Wailers, a spirited tune that matched his cheerful mood.

Sean relaxed. A smile played at the corners of his mouth. He felt a sense of rightness about the familial atmosphere surrounding him that was uncanny.

He could just see them in the future, having a day like

today, moving together with purpose. While he hadn't given permanence, commitment, marriage, and a family of his own **serious** thought before, it didn't frighten him in the least. Earlier he told her that she was going to have his child.

With his eyes judiciously on the road, Sean managed to steal a stealthy glance at Helen, her legs crossed at the knee, a black heel dangling.

After securing her confession that she did want to be with him, they hammered out a plan yesterday. One that he was confident would be fruitful for the both of them. Helen would pick up her car from the office, and then drive it back to her home, while he took Elaina to school.

He realized that Helen bestowed upon him an honor that he never expected anytime soon, if ever. It couldn't be matched by any accomplishment he had ever achieved in his life. It was a major step that pleased him immensely.

He would then meet Helen, and together, they would drive to Dr. Greer's office for an appointment in two hours.

Elaina giggled from the back seat. No sooner than Helen ended her conversation with Miriam, her cell rang again.

Approval beamed in his hidden eyes for the snazzy ensemble in three pieces she chose to wear today. The mandarin collared jacket folded over the back of her seat matched the short skirt in perse, a blackish-purple, with a violet V-neck, sleeveless shell. She applied a judicious use of make-up, with her nails freshly polished a clear coat. Except for the slim, black-banded watch on her delicate wrist, she wore no jewelry. He stole another peek at her thighs revealed by the short skirt, and nearly grunted.

"No, that's boring," Elaina exclaimed. "Let's do something unique."

"Claire, don't worry about it," Helen said to her client whose distraught voice he could partially hear. "I'm going to file a restraining order this morning. ...Claire, he's already mad," she replied calmly to the woman's strident objection.

"Claire," Helen pleaded, "please don't let him get away with this."

Claire? Sean echoed silently, his eyes squinted behind the shades. He sat up alertly, casting a curious sidelong look at Helen as she animatedly conversed with a woman named Claire who seemed reluctant to accept Helen's proposal.

He tapped Helen on the shoulder. "Where does Claire work?" he asked.

Helen shook her head and frowned annoyed at him.

"I need to know," he insisted.

Helen held up her hand to prohibit any further attempts on his part to intrude upon her work.

He was too preoccupied to be offended, thinking of biscuits and Jules as if they were companions.

Could it be the same woman Sgt. Diamond was looking for? She was just wanted as a witness as she cooked for the Butlers. He shook his head amazed, realizing she had been under his nose all this time.

"Think about what I said carefully," Helen said to her client. "Meanwhile, I'll get the papers to you for your signature. I don't want you to risk coming to the office."

"I don't like that idea either," Elaina told the friend she was talking to.

"Now, are you sure you're safe and he doesn't know where you live or work?" Helen asked her client.

A block from Helen's office building, the traffic slowed. Inching the car closer to their destination, Sean wondered if there had been an accident as he tried to see something that would clue the sudden hole-up.

"I'll have thought of something by the time I get there," Elaina said. "See you in a few."

"What the . . . ?" Sean caught himself before the profane word on his lips slipped out, as he stared with open-mouthed amazement at the incident occurring on the parking lot of Helen's office building.

Drivers trying to get onto the parking lot were being diverted by a police officer standing in the street in front of the building. On the parking lot, firemen were spraying white form onto the black smoke and blazing fire emitting from a vehicle.

Helen noticed it, too. "Claire, I have to get back to you," she said, promptly ending the call as she stared out the front window at the fire trucks and police cars crowding the parking lot of her office building.

"Wow!" Elaina said, scooting up to fill the space opened between the two front seats.

Sean rolled down his car window to speak to the police officer guarding the Almeda St. parking lot entrance.

"Sorry, you can't park here now, sir," the police officer said.

"What happened?"

"Someone's car caught on fire, and that's all I know. There may be some parking spaces across the street, but you can't get in the back of the lot either."

"Do you know what kind of car it is?" Helen leaned over to ask.

By the tone of dismay in her voice, Sean guessed she already suspected the answer. While he hoped it wasn't so, he didn't believe in coincidence.

"It was a burgundy Toyota Camry. Do you know the owner?"

Sean and Helen exchanged a poignant glance.

"Yeah, she knows the owner," Sean said with disquiet, as his gaze took in the disaster. "It's her car."

"Who would do something like that?" Elaina bemoaned.

Sean met Helen's gaze head-on. Howard Jackson came to his mind, and he assumed by the deep frown on her face that she believed the same. He reached out and squeezed her hand. "Don't worry," he mouthed to her.

Elaina draped her arms over the seat to wrap around Helen's chest. "I'm sorry."

Helen patted her daughter's hands. "It's just a car, an inanimate object that can be replaced."

"You've been talking about getting a new car anyway, Mama," Elaina offered although her expression didn't match the bright tone of her voice.

Helen clasped Elaina's hands to her affectionately. "Yep," she said sadly with resignation, her eyes strangely veiled, "that decision has been taken out of my hands."

"Move along, please," the officer said.

"My office is in that building," Helen said to the officer. "Will I still be able to go into the building?"

"Yes, ma'am," he replied.

Sean drove to the next block, his left blinker flashing. "Why don't we take Elaina to school, and then come back? I'll go up there with you and we can talk to the officer together."

"No," Helen replied absently.

Sean noticed she wetted her lip just as he turned on the side street. Her brows were knitted together in a pensive frown.

" Sean, I want you to take Elaina to school," she said, her voice calm with resolution. "You can just let me off here, and I'll walk across the street.

"No, Mama," Elaina cried. "Let me stay with you. Please. I can miss one day."

"No, you go on to school," Helen replied. "I'll be all right," she added reassuringly.

Sean felt his mouth dry as he gripped the steering wheel and braked the car to a stop. Helen opened the door and got out. She leaned over the seat and kissed Elaina on the forehead, and then stroked her cheek.

"We'll see you at three," she said, slipping on her jacket. She gathered her handbag and briefcase.

"Aren't you forgetting something?" Sean asked, his brows lifted.

Helen smiled shyly, and a wee chuckle slipped from her lovely lips. Wordlessly, she leaned over and kissed him on the mouth. "That ought to hold you for a little while," she teased softly, her eyes sparkling.

"I'll be right back," he promised. If only they were all he had to think about, he thought, the car still on his mind. "What are you going to do?"

"Going back to law school."

She jumped out of the car instantly without clarifying her remark. Sean wondered what it meant as he watched Helen skirting the traffic as she crossed the street. Hesitantly, he shifted into first and eased out.

"I heard Mama early this morning, Dr. King. She was crying again. What's wrong?"

The tone commanded his attention. It was not the voice of a frightened little girl, but one who knew something was amiss and wouldn't be put off.

"And don't tell me that she will let me know in her own time," Elaina added, looking at him with a mature, determined expression.

Sean didn't want to cross Elaina at this stage of his relationship with her mother, which was tenuous at best. Still, he knew with certainty that Helen would not appreciate him divulging her secrets. "Wrong question," he replied judiciously.

He watched her worry with the rejoinder, gnawing at her bottom lip a moment, and then she returned his headlong stare. "Are you responsible for making her cry?"

"No."

"Are you serious about her?"

"Yes. Very."

"We better hurry, or I'll be late for school," she said, scooting back against her seat.

***

She had put it off too long, Helen told herself as she pushed opened the door to her office. As soon as she addressed matters concerning her torched vehicle, she intended to call her parents.

Miriam, who was sitting behind the desk, looked up, an "Oh, my" look on her face.

"I was hoping you wouldn't have come in," she said, her expression collapsing into a frown. "I've already notified the insurance company. And, you have a visitor."

No sooner than Miriam made the announcement, the question in Helen's raised brow was answered. Sgt. Diamond who sat in the far corner of the receptionist area, stood.

Helen sighed and shook her head, thinking trouble marked her with laser precision. Even awake, she felt the powerlessness of Corinda.

"I only have a few questions, Ms. Parker," Sgt. Diamond said as he shortened the distance between them. "Sgt. Benson is on his way up."

Helen frowned. "And what would Sgt. Benson want?"

"He got the call about your car," Sgt. Diamond replied.

"Send him in when he arrives, Miriam," she instructed, leading the way to her private office. On the way, she reminded herself that she wasn't Corinda any longer. And while Patricia Daigre never believed she was worth fighting for, two brave and caring people, James and Candace Parker, saw something valuable in her.

If not for herself, she thought, dropping her purse on the desk, for them, she had to believe she was strong enough to overcome every obstacle that came her way, regardless how painful it was. After all, she had another champion in her corner, she thought, as a smile stole into her expression. A quick flick of her wrist to note the time, she knew Sean would return shortly.

"Have a seat, Sgt. Diamond," she gestured. "What can

I do for you this time?"

Sgt. Diamond flipped a page in his notebook. "Do you know a woman named Patricia Daigre?" he asked, reading. "I think I'm pronouncing that last name correctly," he added, looking at her expectantly.

Helen swallowed, her mouth suddenly gone dry, and blinked several times.

"You do know the name," Sgt. Diamond said, as if impatient with her silence.

Helen bobbed her head, and he, surprisingly, sighed as if relieved.

"Nobody knows this, so I'm taking a big chance sharing this information with you. We found the name stuck in Mrs. Butler's phone book. The woman's not in our system as either a visitor to our fine jail, or as a missing person. What do you know about her?"

Her hand absently fiddling with the collar of her top, Helen replied, "I heard the name from Ray Butler."

"What?"

"Your reaction tells me that he told you he never heard of her," she replied, dropping into one of the chairs in front of her desk. "He called me twice this weekend. The last call, he mentioned Patricia Daigre."

She cleared her throat and stared headlong at the homicide investigator who remained standing.

"As for this woman, Patricia Daigre," she paused, her tongue between her teeth thoughtfully, "I know her and I don't. I assure you that's not double-talk."

Remembering Ray's call sparked another query she hadn't considered before. Although he pretended ignorance, she wondered if he had become aware of her past.

Sgt. Diamond took a seat on the sofa, his pen poised over his notebook, ready to record her response.

Helen swallowed the lump in her throat and wetted her lips. "The short version is simple. I believe she was my mother. My biological mother."

The intercom on the phone desk buzzed, and Helen got up to answer. "Yes, Miriam?"

"Officer Benson is headed your way."

Chapter Twenty-Three

Claire's pulse began to descend, her insides that clamored in a tumultuous upheaval moments ago settled. Except for her brief absence from the kitchen, which wasn't too unusual as she was the boss, no one could tell, for she showed no cause for alarm. Besides, no one had the time to notice.

"We need more potato salad up front," somebody called out loudly.

"Be right there," another replied.

The kitchen in the Cook's Chamber was noisy. All wore hairnets, gloves, and starched white uniforms. They moved with the quick efficiency of emergency care attendants in a hospital, barking out orders as they moved to and fro the kitchen and serving counter around the corner. Their hands full as they exchanged hot empty pans for pans loaded with hot foods.

The staff was busy with the lunch crowd, even the busboy - - no one would break for bathroom or cigarettes until quitting time, 2:00 pm. It was the same way at breakfast.

Stragglers would amble in just as they were about to close, wanting to know if there was anything left. Some of the scientists who worked upstairs didn't mind leftover lunch for their dinner.

"Claire, where did you put that other pan of cornbread?"

"Look in the bottom warmer," Claire replied absently. She stood at the wooden block counter, lathering a three-tiered chocolate cake with a brownish-yellow frosting. Her concession to sanity was the large apron worn over her simple, navy cotton dress and the plastic gloves on her hands.

She was careful assuring the round sides were covered. She took her time because this cake was for Dr. Jolivet. The other one was already gone.

As soon as she got off the phone with her attorney, she called her daughter. Toni, away at camp at Texas A&M was on her way to morning workout. Toni had been talkative and excited, two things Claire feared she'd ever see again from her child. But Toni loved the campus, her dormitory room. With two years left of high school, she was talking about college. Wonders never ceased, Claire thought, pleased.

While the information calmed her considerably, she was still worried. She never would have guessed that Howard would attack Ms. Parker.

Did she really expect Howard to think of her escape from him as "good riddance"?

"More clean plates out front, please."

Except as the cook that made his business grow and his personal slave at his home, he didn't want her, she mused. He hardly let time go by without reminding her that he didn't need her, either.

"Dr. Clay is here," someone called out. " Get that veggie burger ready."

For so long - - she had lost count - - she felt worthless, used. There was certainly no love in their marriage, and over the past couple of years, even the kindness he showed her before they married slowly eroded until it was non-existent. He taught her a woman's place in his life, and that's where she was to stay - - in his business as cook only, and in his bed, where she played a role no woman in her right mind would play.

Still, she realized that it was not wise of her to think that Howard would let her go so easily without fuss. What on earth was she thinking?

Her hand faltered a second, recalling the injunction Ms. Parker wanted to file. She swallowed, thinking it was only going to make Howard madder now.

Damn! She cursed silently. Why couldn't Howard have been different?

Dr. Jolivet seemed like such a nice man, she thought, an unconscious smile slipping onto her face.

She sighed with the mellow sensation that coursed through her. He wasn't the most handsome man she ever saw, but every time he looked at her with his big brown doe eyes, her heart melted.

Why couldn't she attract a man like him?

The cynic in her head reminded her that she thought Howard was a good man initially.

Yeah, she conceded, but there's something different about Dr. Jolivet. In Howard, she had just ignored the signs, believing that her daughter needed a father. And of course, not to blame it all on Howard, she thought she needed a man.

Claire shook her head. She refused to believe Dr. Jolivet was anything like Howard.

Just about everyone in the building had something nice to say about him, even though they claimed he was hardly in town, she recalled. She had even heard that he was leaving in two weeks to conduct some kind of digging tour in Africa.

"You put anymore frosting on that cake, and it's going to fall over," Ms. Gonzales who made the best tamales in the world teased as she passed Claire.

"Yeah," Claire said softly, Dr. Jolivet still in her thoughts, "I guess this is enough."

She covered the cake, and placed the label she had typed earlier on top, and then set the cake in the place where she kept her lunch. She knew no one would bother it.

"Ms. Gonzales, I need to make a call," she announced.

"You go on," the sweet, matronly Hispanic woman, replied, waving her hand in dismissal. "We got this."

"Thanks," Claire replied, pulling her cell phone from her apron pocket as she walked out of the kitchen. Heading to her office across the hall, she dialed Honey's number from rote. Just as Honey answered, she closed her office door behind her.

"Honey, did you know about Howard? That he attacked my attorney because she wouldn't tell him where I was?" she asked.

"I can't talk now?" Honey whispered in reply.

Claire frowned, creating deep indentations across her forehead. "Honey, is everything all right?" she asked, concern for her dear friend replacing her own.

"Look, he's coming," Honey whispered anxiously in reply.

"Honey, who's coming? Where are you?" Claire asked as apprehensively as Honey sounded. It scared her because Honey was afraid of nothing.

"Howard," Honey replied quickly. "I gotta go."

Howard, Claire mouthed puzzled. What was Honey doing with Howard?

Chapter Twenty-Four

"I now know who the Slave Master is not," Sean said with bitter amusement. He recalled that it had taken a chlorine bath and tensed moments wondering the state of his relationship with Helen before he found out however.

Although he would have chosen a different doctor for Helen, he discerned quickly why she selected Dr. Greer. The distance from the city assured her the anonymity she believed she needed - - so like her - - and Dr. Greer was an impressive practitioner.

"When she called," Dr. Greer replied, her mouth up-tilted at the corners in a tiny smile, "she told me you thought it was her father, James Parker."

"I didn't know she was adopted," he said defensively. "She never told me. I simply thought she was protecting him, as kids are prone to do. But of course," he said, throwing up his hands as if in defeat, "you know about that better than I do. I thought suing was an answer. Hell, I didn't know. Still don't."

"You hated seeing her hurt," Dr Greer stated, citing his concern.

"Yes," Sean replied forcefully, feeling as if he'd found a like mind in Dr. Greer.

"You wanted her to do something about it."

"Most definitely," he replied vehemently. "Sue the son-of-a-bitch, and let the chips fall where they may."

"You wanted her to prove that she didn't want the "son-of-a-bitch" that molested her."

Sean squirmed in his seat in front of Dr. Greer's desk, and swallowed the sudden lump in his throat. "I don't know." He gleamed her perceptive remarks in total, which accurately clarified the thoughts and feelings he had. "Maybe," he admitted uncomfortably, realizing he had inadvertently blamed the victim and challenged Helen to prove her innocence. He felt ashamed. "But now that you mention it, I swear it will never happen again," he said, looking at her headlong, his expression serious and sincere.

"Be careful, but be natural, Dr. King," Dr. Greer advised. "I don't know Helen that well, but she seems a strong, determined woman. Trying to fool her or patronize her will do neither of you any good. So above all else, be honest, tell her how you really feel. If you are not safe enough to air your thoughts and feelings bluntly, then I predict your relationship will come to a dead halt.

"There are several stages she'll likely progress through."

"I think I've already seen one," he acknowledged, recalling his confusion when Helen insisted that he could see the incest on her.

Dr. Greer nodded in confirmation, even though he hadn't detailed the occurrence. "It's called the Emergency Stage," she said. "The victim sees incest everywhere and believes that everyone around her can see it on her, too. …"

Sean listened intently as Dr. Greer outlined the other stages and what could likely happen in each. He felt like a student again, and this time, he paid attention.

"You also need to remember that a relationship is about give-and-take," Dr. Greer said. She looked at her watch, and then directly at him. "You can't be the sole one giving or taking. It's a joint venture. Now, let's get Helen back in here."

He couldn't fault Dr. Greer's suggestions. Not wanting Helen to brood over her parents, past or present, her car, or anything else but them, for the two hours they had before Elaina was to be picked up from school, he suggested a picnic.

Pink and white flower blossoms of crape myrtle scented the half-acre of live oaks, so thick the sun couldn't penetrate the depth of them, even midday.

Anticipating the guarded trees' growth, some ingenious landscape artist installed wooden picnic tables and benches in private alcoves.

It was where Sean and Helen practiced the fine art of necking, a prelude to foreplay.

Secluded from even nosy eyes of joggers who frequented the nearby trail that surrounded the manmade lake in Tom Bass Park, they were free to explore the depths of Helen's range for intimacy and Sean's tolerance during the discovery.

Helen wore those well-worn cutoff jeans he liked so much, and a halter-top in reddish-orange that complimented her complexion.

Sean knew he was supposed to take it slow … but having endured her delectable fanny and attentive bosom for the past hour of their picnic lunch, he didn't know how much slower he could go.

They straddled a bench facing each other. With her hands on his shoulders, his head was buried in her neck. Her scent more intoxicating than the sweet bloom of myrtles, aphrodisiacal to his senses.

Touching allowed him to sense any discomfort she might have. Any tension he felt from her was a sign of fear, and a red light for him. He felt no such tension and buried his face deeper in the crevice between her taut breasts.

Helen sipped a breath, but there was no tension … except for the budge between his legs.

"Sean."

She cried his name harmlessly … evidence of wanting in her tone. Gratified, and in dire need of his own, he didn't stop. Stealthily, he tugged the fabric covering her left breast a way and then captured the nipple between his teeth and lavished it with his tongue.

Helen froze, and her muscles tightened as if strained, transmitting her distress.

Sean swallowed his moan of disappointment, and with Herculean strength suppressed his ardor as he lifted his head to meet her line of sight. Her eyes were bright with anxiety that slightly dulled by her self-disgust.

"I'm sorry," she cried with anguish in her tone. "I'm sorry."

"Shh," he shushed her, stroking her face and hair. "We have plenty of time, mon chere." He kissed her gently on the mouth.

***

The next day, a more subtle kind of exploration, she and Sean sat in the darkened IMAX Theater at the Museum of Natural Science.

Elaina and some friends from school occupied a top row of seats, leaving them, the adults on the third row from the front.

It was the seating pattern for the modest crowd

composed. It was a seating pattern designed so neither was able to see the actions of the other.

They had the row nearly to themselves. The next closest patrons were a senior couple on the opposite end. In the dark, Sean held her hand in his, drawing circles in her palm.

Helen sat stiffly, her lips folded in her mouth. Her eyes opened and closed, with desire blinking in her pupils. They had come to see the documentary on the anomalistic brown, polar bear, but she couldn't remember a thing she'd seen so far. The feel of Sean's fingers making sensual twirls on her flesh had her suspended in a tableau of arousal.

She grunted deep in her throat, holding back the cry of want writhing through her body. His intrepid hand moved, but never lost contract with some part of her as it slid from her palm to her waistline. Strong fingers, persistent and tender, tugged her shirt from her pants, and then slowly crawled up her stomach, along her hot flesh to her firm breast, the nipple already at attention.

He worried the nipple with his fingers.

The moan of desire that had been building concurrently with each touch of his hand on her flesh slipped from between her lips, and she quickly covered her mouth with both hands. She grunted as the moisture built between her legs.

Meanwhile, the animal on screen chewed its bony prey, and Helen sighed ... with relief.

Chapter Twenty-Five

Every moment with Sean was an occasion to touch and be touched ... to learn and explore the full range of wanting sensations ... wholesome lust ... strong desires that created a vivid, salutary picture of their intimate togetherness in her mind.

The cure seemed to have worked, for she thought of little else, Helen chuckled to herself as she pushed open Elaina's bedroom door.

Surrounded by pages of information and a history book, Elaina sat in the middle of her bed, the phone at her ear. "Mom, I'm busy now," she exclaimed, covering the phone. "Why don't you go call Sean? His meeting ought to be over by now. Or go practice your music?"

The situation was much too funny for Helen to feel insulted, or get pissed at her daughter. "Excuse me," she said, backing from the room as she closed the door.

And she had thought this a typical, pre-Sean Wednesday night, she amused herself as she sauntered downstairs. Standing at the edge of her office, a finger in her mouth and debate in her expression, she felt out of sorts, didn't know what to do with herself.

It was almost ten, but too early for bed. Reading was out as well. Sean promised to call her when his meeting was over, and he had never squelched on a promise.

She looked at her wristwatch and calculated that approximately nine hours had passed since she last saw him. It had been a full day for the both of them.

He was ensnarled in a slew of committee meetings developing a number of joint projects between his company and several universities. He promised her that after today, she would have his undivided attention for the rest of the week, she recalled, a warmth invading her senses. The idea pleased her more than she ever thought possible.

She cleaned up the house while Elaina was at school, met Sean when he braked for lunch at Artifacts, Inc., where Baderinwa gave her a tour of the facility.

She got Claire's signature, dropped the paperwork off with Miriam, and then returned to pick Elaina up from school. A trip to the salon for hair, nails and feet preceded swim workout for Elaina, while she practiced with the band.

In a matter of days, Sean had become such a fixture that it was hard to remember what it was like before he came into her life.

Since launching their courtship ritual, she thought smilingly, she promised him that she would indeed make time for herself.

"Steal a moment just for you, mon chere," she shivered, recalling his advice. A shopping spree was planned for tomorrow, and dancing tomorrow night, and a sense of delight coursed through her.

This man was good for her.

With the thought lingering, Helen sauntered into her office.

Impulsively, she turned on her computer. As it powered up, she picked up her old acoustic guitar and sat with it in her lap.

While the Mac configured her screen, she strummed a chord. The guitar was out of tune, and she began adjusting the tuners at the head of the guitar, stopping only to double-click her online connection to her email.

She adjusted, plucked a string, and tuned it as her eyes scrolled down the long list of messages, mostly junk mail. At the bottom of the list, she recognized Doug's address: Doug Pearson at DBLegalSearch.Com.

She had forgotten that on Monday, right after the police left her office and before Sean returned, she had emailed Doug.

He was a computer whiz with a law degree. It was one of the reasons she had hired him to computerize the legal paper documents her office handled, although he'd yet to pass the bar after two tries.

Even though it was not a legal search she wanted him to conduct, she was confident in his skills that he would ferret out whatever information was available on Patricia Daigre.

She saw that he responded earlier today, and she felt excitement and a sense of trepidation, as well. She set the guitar on the floor next to the chair, and clicked open the mail.

His report contained a three-sentence paragraph detailing the life and death of Patricia Daigre juxtaposed against blue links to the history and culture of Beaumont, Patricia's hometown.

Beaumont was roughly ninety miles east of Houston. Coupled with nearby Port Author and Orange, Texas, it formed the Golden Triangle, a major industrial area on the Gulf Coast.

She drove past the town many times on her way to and from Lake Charles, Louisiana where she occasionally gambled at one of the casinos located there. Still, Beaumont was hardly a blimp in her mind, its history insignificant before now.

Patricia Daigre, at the age of 52, died in Beaumont on June 19th.

Helen slumped against the back of the chair as ambivalence sliced through her. Public opening of the *Henrietta Marie* was on Juneteenth, she recalled.

She had blamed her nightmare on the slave ship, but now considered that her psyche must have known that her blood relationship had been severed by Patricia's death.

Her expression tightened with anger. The opportunity to confront Patricia and demand why she hated her so had been stolen from her, as well.

Absently, she reached across the desk to the phone, and dialed a number committed to memory.

"Hello, Helen, is that you?"

"Mama, why didn't you tell me?" To her ears, she sounded every bit like a whining child, she thought, cringing. Unable to sit any longer, she got to her feet, and began pacing back and forth the length of the room.

"Helen, what are you talking about?" Candace Parker's strong pearly voice commanded. "Your father and I have been trying to reach you since Sunday. Didn't Marcellus tell you?"

"We learned from Miriam that a client's husband attacked you last week and torched your car," her daddy's booming voice interjected. "Who's this Sean King she told us about? Said he was in your lobby and heard the attack. Are you home? Why haven't you been answering?"

Helen merely massaged her forehead as they turned the questioning in on her when she was the one in need of answers.

Her mother stepped in. "What a minute, James. You're going too fast. Let her answer my first question. Are you alright?"

"Yes, Mama, I'm fine," she replied with forced patience.

Candace sighed with relief. "Marcellus told us you were all right, but we're glad to hear your voice."

"I remembered, Mama," Helen said tiredly. "Not quite everything, but the ..." Her parent's silence sounded like guilt. They knew something they didn't want her to know. Emitting a puff of air, she continued, "I remember Corinda. The name she gave me." Woefully, she dropped back into her chair and curled her leg under her body.

Following an extra beat of silence, Candace announced firmly, "We're coming home."

"Mama, I don't need you to come home," Helen insisted, sliding her leg from under her to sit with her feet planted solidly on the floor. "I just need you to fill in the blanks."

"I'll call you with our flight and you can pick us up from the airport," her mother replied.

"I don't need you flying down here to hold my hand," Helen snapped impatiently. She drew a deep calming breath. "Please. It's not necessary. If you'll just tell me about her, I'll do the rest.

"Why did she hate me so?"

***

The song opened on a riff. Pickless, Helen's fingers flew up and down the neck of the Strat, coaxing high, low and double notes from the strings in an intricate and melancholy opening of *Why Not*. It was as complicated a piece for guitar as it was for the piano, the instrument for which Michel Camilo wrote it.

But it didn't matter to Helen. She had an inexplicable and desperate need to master the complex piece. It seemed synonymous to her feelings. Mistakes she made, but she played over them, completing the entire song before starting again.

It was midnight, and she was determined not to cry.

Even though her parents did cry as they recounted how she came to be their daughter, she recalled with her eyes closed to feel the soul of the music. She tried her darnedest to absolve them of their guilt, swore with every fiber of her heart that she held them blameless, that she loved them still, and even more.

There would be no tears for Patricia Daigre from her. She was determined to bear the black memories that scorched her soul even now, 27 years later.

She had all of the pieces save one - - the identity of the *Slave Master*. He remained hidden in another compartment of her mind. Nevertheless, she remained undaunted by what she still didn't know.

She played for them, James and Candace Parker, the parents who assumed responsibility for her damaged soul, with notes crackling the air, crisp and clean with her lightening quick plucks of the strings. She played for herself, and her tomorrows with Sean, uncaring the length of time that turned out to be.

Through her thoughts of him, she could hear herself mastering the composition. She felt it coming together - - her fingers, the strings, the notes symbols of her and Sean and conquering her demons - - became one for the perfection of the piece, for the purity of the feelings they shared.

Her entire practice was conducted in conscious oblivion of the tears that rolled down her face.

So into the solacing music she played she barely heard the intrusion. If not for its off-key sound she wouldn't have recognized that someone was ringing her doorbell.

***

The sporty Jag ate up the distance from Kemah to Houston. Roughly 30 miles from his house to Helen's separated them. Neither the speed limits nor the cops who may have spotted him speeding deterred Sean.

A ticket was the least of his concerns.

Reaching Helen … finding her and Elaina safe … was uppermost in his mind.

His heartbeat accelerated right along with the maximum capacity he drove his car. He wished it could go faster than 170 mph.

The meeting lasted longer than he would have liked, but it couldn't have been put off any longer, he swore, zooming off the exit ramp at 45 and Calhoun. The results ensured Artifacts, Inc. would continue to thrive, and profit with its survival.

But while in his whirlpool, a tall drink on the side, a strange sense of foreboding struck him as he was reading the dangers an incest survivor faced when going through the stages toward recovery. Inexplicably, *du petit Taylor* Butler invaded his thoughts, and memory of the crime scene edged his teeth.

It occurred to him that Helen was somehow tied up in the case, and a cold chill rolled up his spine. Determined not to be late this time, he hurriedly dressed, and was now racing for her home, with a prayer on his lips.

Utter relief joined the incredible esurient need he felt to see her, to be with her. He considered that he mistook foreboding for something else as he gobbled her with his eyes and a rush of elemental feelings coursed through him.

A wide grin on his face, he struggled to get his aggression under control, but he couldn't take his eyes off her or arrest the decidedly wanting sensations he felt. She wore his favorite outfit - - halter top with tight-fitting cut-offs that only added to her feminine allure. Yet, he detected something different about her. In spite of the small smile on her lips, the tracks of tears on her face, a murky glaze of sadness shadowed her expression.

But, she was alive, and that was the most important thing. Next to …

"What are you doing here?" she asked, although she neither looked nor sounded displeased by his presence.

"Because you needed me, mon chere," he replied as he crossed the threshold and closed the door behind him. "As much as I need you," he added, pulling her into his embrace.

In his arms, he felt Helen tremble. He knew instantly fear was not the cause as she began to cry softly in his chest.

"Non, non, non, my belle," he crooned, squeezing her tighter next to him. "Tell me what's the matter. Let's talk about it."

"Nothing," she replied, sniffing, embarrassed as she wiped her nose with the back of her hand. "I'm just feeling crazy today." She tried to laugh, instead emitted a sob before she sniffed again and inhaled deeply. "Pay me no mind, I'm just being silly."

Guessing the reason of her angst, he whispered over her head as he cradled her in his arms, "It wasn't your fault. Please, please, please, I beg you, don't blame yourself.

"Dr. Greer warned me to expect you to have uncontrollable flashbacks. She said you might even cry all day long and be unable to go to work."

"Isn't remembering supposed to be healing?" she said sarcastically as she sniffed again and wiped the tears from her face.

"I believe, my belle, you already know that remembering is just a part of healing. I imagine we'll be seeing a lot of Dr. Greer for a while.

"For now, we have to get through the emergency stage." He kissed the top of her head. "You're not going crazy. It's going to be a tough ride, and alcohol doesn't help except to depress you even more."

He also knew this period was one in which suicide could occur as the self-blame grew too great a burden to bear.

"What are the rest of the stages?"

"She identified remembering the abuse, confronting your family, and forgiveness, although they are not applicable to all women.

"In a book I picked up after leaving her office, the writers mentioned trusting yourself, anger, grieving and mourning, resolution, and a few other things I can't recall off-hand. Maybe you'd like to read the book?" he subtly suggested.

"What's it called?"

"The Courage to Heal."

"Okay."

"Okay, what?"

"Yes, I want to read it." She looked up into his face. "I want to heal, Sean, I really do."

"I'm no expert, but having the courage alone seems like half the battle."

She swooned into him, giving her lips to his, and offered herself to him with the sensual cry of his name, "Sean."

She fit perfectly in the circle of his arms as he crushed her to him, claiming her lips. Reliving the velvet warmth of her mouth, he felt heady with the sensation of her exposed flesh under his hands.

Parting was painful, and he did so with reluctance, severing the kiss as he drew away from her. His body was on fire, sizzling with desire, and it was the hardest thing he had ever done.

He inhaled a bucket of air and let it out. "That's a good start," he said, smacking his lips, a smile on his face. "When I take you to my bed, I want there to be no confusion about who you're with."

"Sean," she groaned in protest, trying to pull him back to her.

He held her off, folding her hands together. "Another time," he replied. "Now, I'm starving. How about you?"

Helen chuckled. She took his hand, leading him deeper into her home. "You'll see for yourself that the kitchen is the least used room in my house."

"I'll find the kitchen," he replied. "Why don't you put on some music?"

"Why? Do you think music will improve my mood?"

"I do my best cooking with music," he replied, as they went off in separate directions.

In passing, he admired her tasteful decorations, with artistic treasures from around the world, musical instruments in fine crystal, and sleek contemporary furniture in a pastel color scheme of lavender and off-white.

In the kitchen, he saw a quart-size bottle of Remy Martin opened on the counter. He hid it away and opened the refrigerator.

Luther Vandross began singing instantly, "Well, I think I'm going out of my head," picking up from the pause in the opening bridge.

"Eh bien, je pense que je vais sortir de ma tête," Sean echoed.

Chapter Twenty-Six

Nearing midnight, a sense of softness pervaded Helen's home as if nurtured by the smooth jazz, featuring the Crusaders Live, and dim lights. Like the ebb-and-flow of a tide, a serene rapture singed the atmosphere.

With her arms across her chest, Helen felt her eyes close. She wasn't sure she actually muttered the hymn-like moan of pleasure in her throat, but she certainly felt that wonderful sensation as Sean massaged her feet.

Replete from the delicious late-night meal he had prepared, they had retired to the great room, with brandy. Two crystal snifters rested on the coffee table adjacent to the couch where each of them occupied a corner. While Sean faced her, her feet in his lap, she was lying back, with her head resting on an end pillow

"If you're not careful, I'm going to fall asleep on you," she said lazily, a smile in her voice.

Sean ran his index finger up the middle of her foot, and a shiver of delight spiraled all the way up to her bosom, and this time, there was no question about her vocal reaction. "I don't think so," he teased.

Giggling, Helen tugged her foot from him, and Sean pulled back, keeping it captured in his hands and resumed attending it, one toe at a time.

"I think you made a good choice in selecting Dr. Greer."

Helen momentarily stiffened. The way Sean mentioned her shrink was too casual for it not to have been intentional, she thought. Dr. Greer was part of her ugly reality, and she wanted to keep that world at bay for as long as possible. In reply, she exhaled a long bored sigh, hoping he would get the message.

"Where you successful with the insurance company?"

Sean was changing tactics, she smiled to herself. Again, she ignored his remark, replying only to his tender ministrations to her other foot - - an elongated moan of pleasure. The Crusaders continued on the CD player with "So Far Away," Helen was lulled back into a purely peaceful state.

"Elaina called me."

Helen sat up with a jerk, this time successful in eluding his attempt to hold on to her foot as she looked over her head where she'd last seen her daughter in her bedroom. The evening raced through her mind, and she remembered her need to escape her parental responsibilities even as she chastised the mother who abandoned the motherly role to her.

"She called you to come over?" Guilt beat at her heart. How very much like Patricia Daigre, so absorbed in her own needs that she couldn't protect her own daughter.

"No need for alarm," he replied calmly, reaching over to pick up his glass of brandy. He drank a sip, and then set the glass back. "It was earlier today. Her history group decided on the project they want to present in class."

Intrigued, her head cocked at an angle, she asked, "What does it have to do with you?"

"She wants me to help plan an outing on the *Henrietta Marie*," he replied. "Her group decided to do Juneteeth as their history project."

"You know she's in summer school at Rice," she said, her brow arched curiously. It wasn't very long ago that Elaina wanted her to have nothing to do with Sean. "Not even you can move the *Henrietta Marie* from Galveston to Houston. That's a tall order for a project. I hope you told her so."

Sean seemed amused by her reaction. "No, that's not what I told her," he chuckled. Recapturing her foot, he continued, "The arrangements are practically complete already, thanks to my cousins. We're going to bus her class to Galveston, and once abroad the *Henrietta Marie*, her group will make its presentation, and then I'm going to conduct a tour. If," he emphasized, "she can convince her teacher on the class trip. We're planning it for next Friday."

Pulling her feet to her as she sat up, Helen looked at him intently, with her chin on her knees. She was rather uncomfortable with the commitment he offered her daughter; she didn't know if it was a good idea that Elaina thought she could depend on Sean.

"What is it?" he asked, seeing a debate ensuing on her face.

"Are you sure, Sean? That's some imposition."

"None at all, I assure you," he replied. "I don't leave again until August."

"Leave?" she asked, her legs sliding into a prone position. Her heart thumped. It was the first she heard of him leaving. "Where are you going?"

"Canada ... for a refresher course with a world famous forensic anthropologist," he replied. "I'm not too old to learn something new. Maybe you and Elaina would like to accompany me?" he added hopefully.

Helen reached over to get her snifter off the table. "Elaina is going to Belize with her godmother next month when school is out," she said, taking a sip of brandy, "and then she's going to spend the rest of the summer with my parents."

"Is the relief I hear in your voice due to Elaina's summer plans, or something else?"

Helen froze, and looked at him headlong, trying to read him. While there was suspicion in his expression, she detected something else in his voice.

She soon recognized it as hurt, and a wisp of melancholy thrashed against her bosom as she set her snifter down.

"I thought you trusted me with your daughter," he said softly as he leaned over to pick up his snifter.

Sean took a swallow of his drink, and as he raised the glass to his lips a second time, Helen moved. Taking the glass from him, she set it on the table, and then captured his face between her hands.

"I do trust you with my daughter," she said with sincere reverence, fixedly keeping hold of his face so that he could not turn from hers. "I swear to God I'm not suspicious of you, or your intentions. I admit that I still have questions about my life, but my daughter's safety in your hands is not one of them."

"Then what is it?" he asked, holding her hands in place on his face.

"You and I are supposed to be having an affair, remember?" The smile on her face wobbled a little, yearning tugged at her heart. "An affair is not permanent. I don't want my daughter expecting you to be a fixture in our lives, and hurt when you're gone.

"I can accept it for myself," she admitted, realizing how crazy that might sound to some. "I almost envy my friends who do it, but crying over a man who is worth the tears is something I look forward to."

"I hope I never give you a chance to regret you said that."

Seeing the want in the depths of his jeweled eyes, sparkling like diamonds in the dim light, she said, "There'll be no regrets," her lips brushing his gently.

He inhaled deeply and closed his eyes as if to hide his want from her. She kissed his closed lids, one at a time. She pressed her lips against the tip of his nose where he inhaled gustily through his nostrils.

Finally, her lips touched his in a breezy kiss, and a munificent moan respired from him.

She kissed him as she did in her dream when they were in that beautiful place. Only this time, she anticipated, and shivered so, that she would wake - - crying, yes; however, not in fear, but in passion.

Her mouth smothered his warm lips. Sounds of wonder escaped both their throats when his hand swept to the back of her neck and pulled her closer. She sampled his mouth, and greedy for more, thrust her tongue inside.

He was as hungry for this as she, demonstrated by his hands kneading her flesh, propelling her fingers to perform magic, unbuttoning his shirt and pushing it off his shoulders.

"Helen," he muttered breathlessly, with equal parts wanting and warning.

"Let's go upstairs," she whispered, lavishing his lips with her tongue.

"But ..."

"We'll be more comfortable there," she said, her mouth over his, her breath almost one with his as rapture thrashed against her bosom.

The master balladeer, Luther Vandross started up again, crooning throughout the house as Helen led Sean up the stairs to her bedroom, enticing and exciting him with the sensual sway of her hips, laughter punctuated with a kiss to his lips.

She was like a wanton vixen, mesmerizing him, and he followed as if headed to the Promised Land.

Helen was determined to bury Corinda, once and for all.

Arriving, admiration joined the excitement of anticipation in his gaze as he perused her bedroom. Pleased, she was about to turn off the lights when he captured her hand.

"Laissez la lumière."

Helen understood by his action what he said as his hand halted hers on the light switch. She was abruptly startled by the look on his face.

"Je veux vous voir."

There was no going back, and in that instant, she was stricken with fear and her knees quivered under his hot gaze, his dulcet voice, the French on his tongue.

Tenderly, Sean brushed her cheek with the back of his hand. "You don't have to do this, my belle. I can be just as content holding you in my arms, watching you fall asleep."

Helen smiled her appreciation as she held his hand on her face. "Are you saying you don't want me?"

"You know that's not what I'm saying," he chuckled softly in reply. "Je n'ai autant jamais voulu une femme que je vous veux." He kissed her hands. "What I said is that I never wanted a woman as much as I want you.

"But I don't want you conquering demons just because you think it's what I want. No bed is big enough for three of us. I want you to want me. Just the two of us in bed. Juste les deux de nous," he repeated.

"Sean," she exclaimed, swooning into him and wrapping her arms around his neck.

"Yes. Sean," he replied, his gaze riveted on her face. "Sean wants you. Make no mistake about it, but not until you're really ready."

Helen stared at Sean; she felt him; felt his nommo, a spiritual credibility that made words alone insufficient. She was ready, and they moved to her bedroom under a halo of passion-filled kisses and tender caresses. Clothes discarded, the age-old dance of woman and man resumed in bed.

She grunted in pain with his initial slow penetration, and an instant's fright widened her eyes. Sean stopped, and then eased his hips from hers.

"Helen … it's Sean," he said softly, as he stroked her hair from her face. "Do you want me to stop?"

"No, she replied urgently. The pain was slight, and it was much too late, for she was lubricated with desire. Thrusting her hips up, she pulled him down onto her … into her, with "Aw" singing in her throat.

She had no memory of moving, just feeling, a sense of rightness about the incredible sensual sensations driving her. Even in the light, the room ceased to exist as it was. Not a room, but a heavenly abode where the air was thick with passion born of an age-old ritual. Sean spoke French to Helen in bed, not a bed but a sweet haven where the freedom to enjoy and relish lust and passion prevailed.

There would be no regret, no recriminations as nothing was in the dark here, nothing hidden. Sean never let her forget whom she was with, and she felt overjoyed saying his name, which she had reason to cry passionately over and over again. "Sean."

"Oui. Sean. Sean vous aime. Je suis Sean, et je t'aime."

Sean's deep sexy voice spewed a lover's muttering in his Creole French, and his lips burned against her flesh, brandishing every inch of her with his special possession.

"Yes, Sean," he cooed repeatedly. "Sean loves you. I am Sean, and I love you."

Helen was swept away by wave after wave of excitement, feeling his tender-tempered strong hands caressing her body. His palms closed around her breast and whatever common sense she possessed skittered into the shadows, and then he teased the taunt nipples with his mouth, and stars shot through her in broad daylight.

He returned to her face and his warm lips smothered her mouth as his hands stroked the bush of hair between her thighs. She cried out with her raging desire, begging him to take her, to possess her there, to make her complete.

And he complied.

"Sean," she cried out.

"Yes. Sean."

Chapter Twenty-Seven

Helen trusted him with her daughter, but would she ever trust him with her heart?

The question weighed heavy on Sean's mind. It had been there from the time he woke at the doorbell's insistence around six this morning. Helen, exhausted from their all-night sexual workout - - she was insatiable, he smiled - - didn't stir a muscle.

It was fifteen after eight, he noticed in the car's clock. He was driving up Almeda, passing Helen's office building, Howard Jackson's café, heading north. He was looking for a coffee café called *G's & Z's* in a two-story, corner home.

He had just dropped Elaina off at school. She lifted an eye at his presence in her home this morning, he mused with a chuckle. After dressing for school, she kissed her Mama, who still didn't wake, on the cheek and then hurried him so that she wouldn't be late.

She chatted non-stop about her history project. In fact, he even met her history teacher, and was scheduled to meet with her later to discuss the plans Elaina's group had presented to her for their history project.

He never once wondered what it would be like to have a daughter, but already Elaina had him thinking he would prefer daughters to sons. Of course that was predicated on

Helen, he thought feeling that he had returned to square one.

What if she never felt comfortable enough to give him more than her body? Could he live with that?

Locating the establishment, Sean parked on the side street. He noticed the nondescript police cruiser, an ugly white vehicle with a big engine. Parking, he got out his car and walked around the corner to the front of the business.

The blazing sun followed him into the cool air-conditioned establishment. Music from a local jazz station greeted him. Although sunlight bathed the front of the shop, unstoppable by the front and side glass windows, artificial light shone over the serving area in the back. Several people were in line for coffee, the mainstay of the establishment.

Sgt. Diamond was seated at one of the small square tables near a set of stairs, reading a black weekly. As he folded the paper, turning to another section, he saw Sean.

"Get coffee and join me," Sgt. Diamond suggested. "Try the almond mocha."

Within a few minutes, Sean was seated at the table across from Sgt. Diamond. The police officer closed the newspaper and dropped it atop the adjoining table.

Following what seemed like a long scrutiny to Sean, he asked, "How's Ms. Parker this morning?"

Sean's cup froze at his mouth, and then he drank a sip. "She's fine." He knew he should have been upfront with Diamond about his relationship with Helen when he had the chance the other day, but he bet it was his clothes that gave him away. "How did you know?"

"I guess I'm not surprised," Sgt. Diamond replied laughing as he crossed his legs at the knee.

"What gave me away?" Sean asked, sipping coffee. Right after this meeting, he was going home to shower and change, he thought.

"You mean aside from the fact of the wrinkled clothes you have on," Sgt. Diamond teased in reply. Sean laughed as the detective drank a sip of his coffee. "There were a few subtle little things, pulled together from different occasion. A slight tensing at the mention of her name. An unconscious smile, the distant look, like a glaze came over your eyes."

Sean chuckled. "And all the time I was worried you'd think I compromised the case."

"I told you, Dr. King, I did my homework on you."

"What are you two gossiping about like two old married men?" Sgt. Benson asked as he approached from the front of the building.

Sgt. Diamond's head dipped a little as he flashed Sean a teasing grin. "And Benson told me. Get you a coffee and come join us," he instructed to the newly arrived officer.

"Sgt. Benson," Sean said, extending his hand. "Good to see you again." Shaking Benson's hand, he asked, "Have you found Jackson?"

"Not yet, but we will." Sgt. Benson replied. "Be right back," he said as he walked off to get in line.

"Thanks to Benson," Sgt. Diamond said, "we're looking at the Butler murders from a different angle. One you implied from the beginning."

"Oh?"

"Dr. Clemens provided a scenario how one person committed the murders. Remember, we thought there were two different chokeholds on Joann. But imagine the first if she were caught from behind and the killer applied pressure from the back. Joann passes out; the killer thinks she's dead. But Joann moves, and the killer gets on top of her, this time using two hands to choke her to death."

Sgt. Benson returned with his coffee, and sat at an adjacent table.

"Benson was an anthropology major in college with a minor in psychology," Sgt. Diamond said.

Sean didn't believe the information was just for conversation's sake. He nodded as if with requisite approval at Sgt. Benson, but he couldn't help teasing him a little. "Couldn't find a job in your field?"

"Part of it," Benson chortled amused.

"So what's this new angle?" Sean asked.

"Incest."

Sean didn't enjoy his vindication for instantly thoughts of Helen, not as his lover or with a lover's feeling, but as a victim of the amoral incident. He looked back and forth between the two police officers. "You've apparently uncovered new information?"

"You remember the MFSB scenario in kinship studies," Sgt. Benson said. "We're looking at Joann Butler's family."

"You were always suspicious about that little girl's condition," Sgt. Diamond reminded Sean. "I wish you would have been more insistent."

"What convinced you?" Sean asked. Until a year ago, first cousin marriage, a form of incest, was still legal in Texas. Despite progress women experienced in the courts, incest was still difficult to prosecute, explaining also why homicide investigators were reluctant to have anything to do with that particular occurrence.

"When we learned Howard Jackson and Joann Butler were brother and sister," Sgt. Diamond replied. "That, and the evidence that proved Chester Mason was not Taylor Butler's child as was claimed."

"Ah, the autopsy," Sean chimed in, aware that paternity would have been plainly visible at that time.

Sgt. Benson added, "So now we're looking at an incestuous relationship that's often overlooked because we've been primed to expect the father-daughter incest model. It also answers why Howard Jackson has been so determined to get at his wife. He's afraid that she'll tell and ruin not only his life, but his sister's good name, and you know who his sister was."

"Ray Butler's wife," Sean said thoughtfully. Since he knew Joann Butler contacted Helen, they had all assumed it was because she wanted a divorce. But maybe she wanted a different kind of legal representation. "Have you discovered the father of her child?"

"I'm betting it's her brother, Howard," Sgt. Benson said. "It's shocking but possible," he added with disgust in his tone.

"What about Ray? Do you think he's involved?"

"He's not out of the woods yet," Sgt. Diamond replied. "Ms. Parker told me that he's been after her for a meeting. It's apparent he wants to know what his wife told her, so that suggests that he knows something. Anything more than a guess on my part is mere speculation."

Sean concurred, nodding absently. Whether about the incest, he couldn't say, but for sure, Ray Butler knew something that Helen must need to know.

"And it's also motivation to explaining why Jackson went after Ms. Parker, as well," Sgt. Benson added, pulling Sean out of his muse.

"Crazy," Sean said, shaking his head. "Stupid."

"Yeah," Sgt. Diamond chimed. "That's murder for you."

***

Her hand reached over.

What she expected wasn't there, and Helen, lying in bed on her stomach, lifted her head. That side of the bed that was usually empty showed wrinkled sheets, indicating the presence of another body, and while it was unoccupied now, resting on the pillow next to hers was a single tulip atop a sheet of typing paper.

Oh, what a night, she thought, smiling, wondering where was Sean. If he were here now, she moaned aloud with an erotic pleasure.

Maybe it was a good thing he wasn't, she told herself, still smiling, still filled with delight, still wanting him nevertheless. She shook her head as if to shake out the cobwebs of sleep. She hoped he made coffee.

Pleasantly sore and wonderfully rested, she didn't want to get up. Groaning, she rolled over, capturing the tulip and paper, only to lie on her back. She sniffed the scant fragrance of the flower gazing across the room.

Daylight stole between the tiny opening in the curtains, and that was her first clue. Her expression twisted in a frown and she looked over at the clock on the bedside table. It sealed the truth, and she groaned: she had slept most of the morning away. And then the time really hit her - - 11:10AM - - and she hopped up.

Three hours late, she thought, realizing it was useless for Elaina to go to school at all today. She looked across the room at her bedroom door. It was opened.

She dropped her head and closed her eyes. *The horse was out of the barn now*, as Mama used to say, she told herself: Elaina already knew that Sean spent the night.

Shaking her head as the thought of how to explain Sean's presence to her daughter, she read the note written in his familiar scrawl: *"Taking Elaina to school Back by noon to take you to lunch. Your love, Sean."* Helen laughed out loud and held the note, an object of endearment, next to her bosom. With less than an hour to dress, she set the note and flower on the bedside table.

Her nakedness said it all, she mused, giggling like a schoolgirl. She blushed beautifully, recalling the things she had done last night and early this morning, the things she had let Sean do to her. While she wouldn't share those private and very intimate things with her girlfriends, she was one of them now.

She laughed out loud and thought to say sincerely, "Thank you, Jesus," clasping her hands together in prayer.

Only the two of them shared the bed, she thought, naked and unashamed as she traipsed to her luxurious bathroom with a Jacuzzi and tiles the color of plum and white.

Thank god she had never been ashamed of her body, she thought, turning on the showerhead. As the water temperature leveled, she got towels and her mango bottle of shower gel from a cabinet.

Standing beneath the streaming jets of water, she relived last night, the wonder and sensitivity of her lover. He caressed her with hands more tender than she applied now scrubbing her body. He was amazing, and she wasn't just referring to his sexual prowess.

Everything he said was what she needed to hear. She laughed out loud, mindful that she didn't understand everything for he spoke French, but the loving sentiment was present nonetheless in every word he uttered to her.

She gave a quick thanks to her doctor for planting the seed in her mind of sharing her childhood ordeal with the man largely responsible for her seeking help in the first place as she turned off the shower head and got out. She dried quickly, oiled her body, and then wrapped herself in the thick, fluffy towel.

She felt as if her body sang with the memory of last night. After-all, it too, she realized, experienced a change. She felt complete, like a whole woman.

That was the most important thing. She was confident the rest - - motherhood, career, and now a man in her life - - would fall into place.

She padded to her closet where her dresser was located. She slipped into panties and bra, standing before her racks of clothes. Selecting an outfit that matched her mood - - a purple pantsuit - - and one she thought Sean would appreciate, as well, with a pair of black, sling-back sandals.

She dressed quickly, eager to see how Sean and Elaina were getting along. Just as she walked back into her bedroom, the telephone and doorbell rang simultaneously.

She picked up the phone on her way out the door. As she answered it - - "Hello" - - the doorbell rang again. "Oh, hi Mama, hold on a minute."

She looked out the peek hole, and a grin spread across her face. Opening the door, she said on the cell, "Mama, let me call you back. Sean is here," as she floated into his opened arms.

Chapter Twenty-Eight

Honey had nothing to worry about, Claire thought, smiling pleasantly to herself. This evening brought another first for her, and she was giddy with excitement.

She and Honey were right off her small kitchen at the table from where breakfast, lunch, and dinner were served, adjacent to the living room. Rhythm-and-blues, the staple of Majic 102 FM's musical format played on the portable radio on the kitchen counter.

Claire wanted to but didn't dare tap her foot to the beat as her favorite Luther Vandross, "Going Out of My Head" played. As if schooled still, she sat in a chair pulled from the table as Honey stood before her, combing her hair as if she were a girl.

She couldn't remember her mother ever being so particular about her hair, she thought. But as this was her first perm, she couldn't even get melancholy about the memory.

Honey had been extra careful from the application of the chemical product to her hair to the styling. In fact, Honey had been so quiet, more serious than she could recall that she figured Honey might be a littler nervous about her reaction.

And speaking of reactions, she pleasantly mused.

"What's so funny?" Honey asked dryly.

Claire wasn't aware that the giggling feeling inside her had come out in a laugh.

"Just thinking out loud," she replied. Actually, she had begun to think about that nice Dr. Jolivet, wondering what he would say about her new hairstyle when she saw him again tomorrow, Friday.

It wasn't all she wondered about him, or wished for, for herself. She knew Toni would be shocked.

Honey stood back, inspecting her work.

"Can I see now?" Claire asked as she sat up alertly with anxious jubilation.

"Hold on another minute," Honey replied. She dug through her big handbag, and pulled out a small make-up kit. She laid items on the table for easy reach, and started by applying a powder to Claire's face.

Dr. Jolivet made her feel like a schoolgirl, she thought as an elemental, yet alien feelings rushed through her, a time in her life that had once been full of promise. Her eyes darkened as she recalled that it was all stolen in one afternoon when her mother's boyfriend had cornered her, and her life spiraled downward. She halted progression of the memory, reminding herself instead of the end result, the best thing in her life, her daughter Toni.

Honey stood back and inspected her. "You look so

beautiful," she whispered in awe, and then surprisingly, burst out in tears.

Claire stared momentarily frozen in alarm, her heart beating a wild gallop in her bosom. "Honey, what's the matter?" She sprang up and went to her friend, putting her arms around her. "It can't be that bad," she cajoled laughingly.

"I'm sorry," Honey sniffed. "It's just that I couldn't help thinking you look more beautiful than my sister. We buried her, along with her little girl."

Claire blinked, and then shook her head as if doubting her hearing. "Buried your sister?"

Her hands instinctively flew to her hips, and with eyes narrowed in disbelief, she stepped back from Honey. "I didn't know you had a sister."

Honey dropped into a chair at the table, tears streaming down her face silently, the comb held limply in her hand.

"We were just step-sisters, Joann and I. We weren't close at all. She didn't like me," she shrugged. "Still, she was my sister," she added, staring at Claire as if looking for understanding.

"Joann? Joann Butler, the wife of Ray Butler who's running for mayor? That was your sister?"

Claire was incredulous. She forgot all about her new hairstyle, and a murmur of uneasiness raced through her. Joann's little girl was a Tadpole. When she got better, she would become a Dolphin, the same swim team that Toni is on," she said as if astonished anew. "I let Toni go to the wake with some of the other swimmers."

With stark amazement in her expression, she unconsciously started to turn away from Honey, with no destination in mind, and then swiftly reversed her position. "You never told me," she accused confrontationally. "You never said a word. I even cooked for her and her husband when I worked at the café for Howard."

Claire dropped back into the chair she had risen from. It occurred to her - - not for the first time - - that she didn't know as much about Honey as she once believed. She remembered when she called Honey to tell her that Howard assaulted her attorney, Helen Parker, and Honey couldn't talk, saying something about Howard was coming. The frown on her face now was one of puzzlement and suspicion.

Honey couldn't even look at her, an infinitely sorrowful spirit locked in her grief. "I'm sorry, Claire."

"You're sorry? I thought you were my friend," Claire shoved at her angrily. "What were you doing with Howard?" She sprang from her seat again.

Honey lifted her tear-stained gaze, looking at her with a mix of emotions that scared Claire to death. She waited with patient desperation for Honey's reply, praying with everything in her that Honey would prove to be the friend she always believed she was, that this was all some terrible mistake and she was simply misreading the guilt on Honey's face.

Instead, her heart dropped, weighted by betrayal.

"I had to get him out of jail," Honey answered in a small, remorseful voice.

With her pulse climbing upwards as a hard fist of fear grew in her stomach, Claire asked, "Why did you have to get him out of jail?" Boy, she wished she didn't need to know the answer to that, she thought.

"Howard … He's my brother."

Claire felt as if she had been kicked in the gut as fear tightened in her chest, nearly choking off her breath. Howard and Henrietta. Brother and sister. Henrietta could change her name to Honey, but she was undeniably and forever tied to Howard. Urgently and anxiously, she asked, "Honey, did you tell Howard where I am?"

Honey snapped out of her glum lethargy, reaching out to Claire, and Claire took another step away from her. "No, Claire, I'd never do that, I swear. He asked me, but I didn't tell him.

"I never wanted you to marry him. But you were tired of cleaning white folks' houses, so I introduced you to him. I thought you'd just work for him," Honey said bitterly, her expression saying more. "That was it."

"Goddamnit, you never said he was your brother!" Claire stormed as she jumped up and began pacing back and forth in her small kitchen. She didn't like the thoughts she was thinking about her friend, right now; she didn't like her friend right now, either.

"You needed a job and you didn't know how to do anything else!" Honey retorted with sulky truculence, a teardrop hanging from her eyelash.

"And I didn't encourage you to marry him. Remember," she said, rising to go to Claire, "I told you I didn't think it was a good idea."

Claire halted her approach with a fierce look. As they stared each other in a declaration of war, her mind raced through her four-year history with Honey, three of them as Honey's brother's wife.

And she never knew the truth of their relationship, she thought, leaning over the stove.

She remembered Howard forbade Honey coming into their home. She simply thought it was because he disapproved of her lesbianism. Now, she had to wonder, casting a sidelong look at Honey's forlorn demeanor. There had to be more between them for that kind of estrangement.

"Claire, let's go away," Honey said anxiously. "I got a bad feeling. My stepfather and ..."

She abruptly stopped that thought, clamping her mouth shut. But silence didn't linger as she suddenly blurted, "Let's go away; let's get out of Houston."

She reached for Claire's hand, and Claire pulled away.

"Go away? Go where, Honey?" Claire pushed away from the stove, wrapped her arms around herself as she sauntered into the living room. "I came here, to Houston, running away from nowhere in Chicago," she said, the painful memory of why she escaped Chicago in her expression. "Where do you suggest I run to now?" she asked bitterly.

Honey followed and reached out to her. "We can start over someplace else. I have money. Wherever you want to go," she promised, her expression of anxious enticement.

With anger and disbelief in her expression, Claire put more distance between them in the small living room. "I don't want to run anymore, Honey. I'm not running anymore," she said firmly.

"What else is there that you're not telling me?"

Chapter Twenty-Nine

"No, Daddy, I don't want you and Mama to come," Helen stated firmly, rolling her eyes to the ceiling.

Sean loved to cook and it showed in his kitchen, Helen thought as she paced practically every inch of it while talking on her cell to her father. She bet he had every kitchen utensil there ever was.

"Yes, Daddy, I did. ... I did that, too. ... I can handle it," she cried, throwing up her hand.

Larger than her own, quite different in design from Baderinwa's, and in keeping with the color schemes that ran throughout his home, the kitchen was ceil blue. The azure color was caught in the silestone counter top - - which she banged with her fist in frustration as she listened - - against stainless steel and onyx appliances, giving the room an ultra-high-tech look.

But Helen was ever more aware of his virile appeal as he stood at the counter near the sink, dressed in a white body shirt and long, red swimming trunks, with Nike thongs on his feet.

She stared momentarily fascinated by his efficiency as he rolled a lemon between his big hands, softening it, with a half dozen more at his disposal.

She was entirely caught up in her own lusty emotions when he wiggled his ears at her, forcing her to cover her mouth to stifle the laugh bubbling inside her.

"No, Daddy," she replied as a chuckle escape. She spun away from Sean to meander into the adjoining nook that was sequestered behind glass, as was the family room opposite it. "But I haven't thought about the kind of car I want," she said, watching the sun slowly sink into the distant bay waters that was part of Sean's backyard scenery.

Moments later she returned to the kitchen. Sean was pouring cups of sugar in the tall glass pitcher with a red rooster designed. "Respect your parents; they know better," he whispered.

Helen stuck out her tongue at him. "I promise to let you know. No, Daddy, I swear I'm not mad at you or Mama," she said sincerely, her voice soft and tender. "I'll call as soon as I decide. I love you. Bye."

Ending the call, she declared peeved, "I hate it that my parents feel they have to call me every day now," dramatically waving the cell in her hand.

"Maybe you should surprise them with a visit," Sean suggested.

Helen thought out the idea a fraction, and then kissed Sean on the cheek. "I think I might just do that." She even considered flying to visit her parents a week before Sean was scheduled to go to Canada. But she didn't tell Sean her plan. Instead, she kissed him again.

Shuddering visibly, he said, "I like it, I like it, don't stop."

"After I get Marcellus," she added, her voice lowered with a threat. "He undoubtedly told his parents who ...

"Who called your parents," Sean picked up her line of thought with an amused chuckled, stirring the pitcher of freshly made lemonade.

"That's about right. I purposely," she enunciated, "didn't tell them about my car because I didn't want them to worry. That's what this call was all about. Daddy wanted to fly down just to get me a new car."

"Oh wow!" Sean exclaimed, eyes wide and a hand over his mouth in amazement. Pretending repugnance, "How insensitive of him."

Helen huffed, her mouth open in exasperation as she stared at him. Within seconds, she said, "Oh damn, I forgot to ask my Mama something."

Seriously, Sean asked, "What?"

"How to explain my lover to my adolescent daughter, particularly when he spends the night."

Sean froze fractionally, staring at her with an oh-oh look, and then Helen burst out laughing.

"Oh, I'm going to get you for that," he threatened and started after her.

With delightful giddiness, Helen raced out of the kitchen, pass his family room, and through the connecting, narrow glass walkway into Baderinwa's den.

"Oh, don't run, Miss Bad Attorney," Sean cried in chase. "Just wait until I get my hands on you. We'll see how you respond then."

By that time, Helen was out the kitchen door and onto the patio where Elaina, and her three friends, Jackie Kwan, Latoya Franklin and Christie Myers were playing volleyball in the pool.

Helen dove in seconds before Sean, and began swimming across the pool.

Sean was no match for her aquatic dexterity or speed, stopping midway the pool, nearly knocking the net out of place. Helen was sitting at the opposite end of the pool, laughing gregariously at him.

"Can't you two go play somewhere else?' Elaina cried. "You're interrupting our game."

An hour later that evening, Sean was ranting about Elaina's history teacher under another balmy sunset.

Playtime over for them and relegated elsewhere, Helen and Sean served their duty as chaperones from the second story balcony of his home. Splashing water and the girls' delightful squeals wafted up from the pool next-door, juxtaposed to his tirade.

"That woman is an idiot!" he declared vehemently.

Helen was amused by his parental outrage, but her mind quite frankly was elsewhere. Expressing dismay about the quality of education was new to him; she felt like a pro on the subject.

Snapping his fingers, he asked, "What's her name again?"

Taking a sip of her drink, she supplied, "Holton. Mrs. Elise Holton."

As if her new favorite position, she sat in the chair across from him, with her feet in his lap, which he absently stroked. She was wondering whether an affair would actually suit her.

The day had a familiar feel to it, she thought. It seemed as if sharing the day's events was just part of their normal routine, when in fact, it was around eight, and their first private moment together since before day this morning. She wanted the right to demand his attention always, and just an affair precluded that.

"Yeah, Holton. Synonymous with hold them back from acquiring a full and decent education," he rasped, his accent pronounced with his peeve. He drank a sip of lemonade, and sighed as if he had needed a thirst-quencher.

She knew Sean got embroiled with Elaina's teacher, no doubt charming her, that it didn't make sense for him to return until school was out in order to meet their lunch date. She wasn't displeased, however, for it allowed her the time needed to hear and digest her mother's explanation.

When they met up later, there was no time to discuss what she had learned.

Elaina and her friends wanted to spend the weekend together, so parents had to be contacted and the friends picked up. They came to Sean's home, which was closer to Galveston and the *Henrietta Marie*. The girls convinced their parents that it was necessary that they view the slave ship before their presentation.

Lucky for her, she had a rehearsal with the band tomorrow.

"How can you call yourself an American historian and possess the audacity to claim the reason you don't do much lecturing on slavery is because it's too painful?" he asked incensed with his disbelief.

A response was not required. Helen smiled to herself. She was still marveling by how comfortable she felt in his presence, extremely so, she thought of the sexy, two-piece bathing suit in lavender she wore. In one of those short bouts of disconnected thoughts, she realized that she never dressed like this in public before.

"I've never seen Elaina excited about anything historical before as she is about this project. I doubt very seriously that Mrs. Holton would have agreed to the class trip had I been the one to speak to her.

"I'm not sure you appreciate what you were able to accomplish," Helen continued, holding him with esteem in her expression. He had professed his love for her, but that's what lovers were supposed to do, she thought, poignantly aware that she had yet to reciprocate. As if a stone had dissolved inside her, she reminded herself that he didn't have to take on the challenge of her child's education. "Oh, look at you blush," she teased, experiencing a sensuously persuasive feeling as she leaned over and planted a sweet kiss on his mouth.

He sighed munificently as he pulled her onto his lap. "I guess you go through this all the time," he said, rubbing his cheek against hers.

"It's always something," she said with undaunted resignation as she settled back, enjoying the feel of his arms around her. "Elaina attends private school during the regular school year, and it's a little better. But parents whose children are in public schools have it much worst, trust me."

"But even with all your education and whatnot," he said casually, "you didn't learn to fight for your child by yourself. Your parents taught you how to maneuver the system, which people to talk to, and the right buttons to push. Learning and utilizing the system to your best advantage is half the battle. Many of us aren't blessed with the role models who possess that wherewithal."

"True, but you're not talking about education now," she said, the question in her gaze as she turned to look at him directly. Every minute in the company of this man deepened and intensified her want of him, her love for him growing, as well.

"No, I'm not," he replied with a gentle shake of his head. "I'm talking about your parents. I hope you're not angry with them, because what they did in essence was rescue you from a horrendous situation."

"No, I'm not angry with them at all," she denied, with a shake of her head. She inhaled deeply, with melancholy infecting her expression. She had told Sean some of the conversation she had with her Mama, Candace Parker, about her biological mother, Patricia Daigre.

"Basically, my mother committed extortion, a legal crime, regardless the reason."

In as matter-of-fact tone as she could muster, Helen recounted her mother's explanation. As the principal of the elementary school that she attended in kindergarten and first grade, Candace Parker noticed a significant change in her from the end of the spring term and start of the fall, her mother had explained.

The first grade teacher initially mentioned it to Candace who promised she could check into it.

Principal Parker's suspicion of abuse was confirmed when she saw the welt-like bruises on Helen and Helen's reluctance to talk or allow anyone to touch her. She confronted Patricia.

"And you would hold it against her because she forced your biological mother to give you up?" he asked, his voice rising with confused amazement.

"She's the one feeling guilty," Helen replied. "Nothing I said seemed to have absolved her. I'm sure she knew all along that she could have been arrested for what she did."

Still, she felt an inconsolable disconcertion. It was true that she held her mother blameless, although the justice system surely would have and her self-serving interest notwithstanding.

"I bet Patricia didn't suffer the same qualms your Mama did when she accepted that ten thousand dollars," he said with a snide mutter. "I'm sorry," he added hastily with sensitivity, hugging her tenderly to him.

"It's a bet I wouldn't take." Helen sided with the practical and rational part of what she was. She wasn't wholly sure about the whom, yet. "It's obvious now the money went straight to her drug supplier."

"But she was still your natural mother," Sean said, still holding her, "and you know there's something that was in her that is in you. That means all of her wasn't bad, my belle. Candace Parker sensed that, and wanted you because of it."

"I never doubted that my parents loved me," she said, remembering what her mother told her just today. "*We were resigned that we couldn't have children, and there you were, cute as a button and smart as a whip. You were always more than just a favorite student to me. There was something about you that touched me so deeply that I wanted you for myself, for your father and me.*"

"I just didn't realize how much until now." She would never forget it.

"Hey," he said.

His steady gaze bore into her in silent expectation. She had felt that same expectation. "What?" she replied gamely.

"Come here," he crooked his finger at her.

Helen eased onto his lap, revealing the joy inside her with a smile that brightened her face and put the sun in her bosom as desire wrought the want in her loins.

"I know someone else who loves you."

"Sean," she said, her lips against his.

"Oui, Sean," he said, claiming her mouth in fiery possession.

***

"Okay, you two; break that up. Fine baby-sitters you are."

Sean recognized Baderinwa's voice before he reluctantly tore his mouth from Helen's. With her gaze locked into his, she smiled beautifully at him, showing teeth and tongue. He grunted. "Baderinwa," he said, "your timing sucks."

"Not my timing," she replied, pulling the extra chair from the table. "There's a negative energy in the air, and it's causing destruction wherever it can." She sat.

Helen tried to move, but Sean refused to let her go. "Okay, talk to me," he commanded once Helen was situated between his thighs, his arms around her waist.

It was usually difficult to discern abnormal emotions in Baderinwa as she always exuded a calm and serene demeanor, Sean thought, attending his cousin.

It was in her hesitation, the painstakingly deliberate movements that told him something was not right. "What's happened?" he asked, schooling his own apprehension from showing.

"It's Claire."

"What about Claire?" he asked, his tone on the precipice of dread. Helen tensed in his arms, and he gently rubbed her sides, trying to instill a sense of calm.

Then he remembered that when Jules was home for summer vacation from school, he and Baderinwa were inseparable. He looked his bedroom inside, and then back at her. "Where's Jules?"

"That's what I came to tell you," she replied. "He's getting Claire set up in her new location."

"What new location?" Helen blurted, unable to keep silent any longer. "What's going on with Claire?"

"Helen is Claire's attorney," Sean explained. "It was Claire's husband that attacked Helen."

"Aw," Baderinwa replied, as if putting the pieces of a puzzle together. "Now I understand what she was talking about. She was at the office way before opening this morning. I could tell she'd been crying. She definitely was upset, but she didn't want to talk about it."

"Please don't make us play twenty questions," Helen said with forced patience. She pushed Sean's hands aside, got up and stood by the railing. "What happened?"

Baderinwa sat utterly still a second, and then took a deep breath as if preparing herself to comply. "A couple of police detectives came to The Cook's Chamber this afternoon to speak to Claire."

Sean interjected, "Diamond and Benson."

Baderinwa nodded as she continued. "Claire spoke with them alone, and then when they left, she told us, Jules and me, about her husband. The police were looking for him. One of them, the big one, implied that since her new address was on a report in conjunction with the Butler murders, it would be advantageous for her to find a place where he couldn't find her."

"Damn," Sean cursed. "That's my fault. I told them where she worked in the first place."

"She told us what her husband had done to you," Baderinwa said directly to Helen. "She didn't want another incident like that, so she was going to quit, but Jules talked her out of it."

Sean noticed Helen absently rubbing her hands, her bright eyes haunted and pensive. He'd like to wring Jackson's neck.

"Where's her daughter? Toni?" Helen asked anxiously.

"Oh, she's away at some swim camp or another," Baderinwa replied. "Claire felt confident that she's safe. She checked. Jules got her an apartment at the Wind Surf Apartments. He's still with her. He'll advise the security guards there to call the police if her husband shows up.

"We've already taken similar steps at the company," she added, speaking specifically to Sean. She shrugged. "Hopefully, she will be alright, but you never know."

Helen turned away from them, facing the water, her head lowered. Schooling his own angst at the havoc Jackson wrought, Sean stood behind her, his hands lightly on her shoulders. "Helen?"

"I'm all right."

He heard the anger in her voice, and knew what she knew. The safety measures that had been taken to keep Claire safe until Howard was picked up were the best that could be done. However, he was more concerned about her.

"Do you have to go to rehearsal tomorrow? Frankly, I'm not comfortable about your safety knowing that Jackson is still lurking about."

Helen turned in his arms to face him. She wore a face of determination. "I can't hide in a shell like a turtle because of Mr. Jackson, or anyone else," she replied.

Baderinwa stirred behind them, and he turned to see her rising. "Well, I'll let you two get back to it," she said. "Sorry to have to be the bearer of bad news."

"Thank you, Baderinwa," Helen said.

"You're welcome."

Baderinwa returned inside, leaving them to mull the situation.

"Sgt. Diamond believes that somebody in the family knows who killed Joann and her daughter." Sean said pensively, speaking his thoughts out loud. He picked up his glass of lemonade; the frost had melted off the glass, the once cool drink was tepid.

Helen spun, her hands on the rail behind her. "Do the police think Ray knows? I mean about the murders?"

"It's not farfetched," Sean replied.

Frowning, she shook her head as if with pity. "There was a time when I would swear that was not possible of him. But he's a politician now, and the deaths of his family promise a level of sympathy that enhances his political career. If it comes out that he knew the killers and didn't tell the police, he can kiss his political aspirations goodbye."

"You sound sorry for him."

"Didn't your mama teach you that jealousy is not attractive?" she quipped.

Sean threw back his head with a chuckle. "You're not going to let me forget that, are you?"

"They were your words," she smiled in reply. She crossed the short distance to him, and slid her arms around his waist and laid her face on his chest.

"I'm sure we can find more substantial things to argue about … where to eat, what to do, which movie to see. But I see monogamy included in the parameters of our affair," she added, looking up into his face, her bright eyes gentle and contemplative. "I don't want to see anybody else. Do you feel the same way?"

"Aw, my belle," Sean crooned deeply as he wrapped his arms around her and held her tightly against him. He didn't want her to see the deep longing he felt fill his eyes, for sure she would see he wanted so much more than an affair. "That sounds perfect to me."

Nuzzling her neck, he thought he had the answer from his earlier question: he would take whatever she was willing to give him.

Chapter Thirty

It was a bittersweet weekend … joyful and happy moments stolen between periods of caution and contemplation.

Sean and Helen each had occasion to experience the gamut of both, the latter because the police still sought the whereabouts of Howard Jackson who lurked in the shadows of their minds.

Sean relished his new role as the recipient of female attention that was bestowed him singularly. He never thought of himself as selfish, but he couldn't nor wouldn't deny the enjoyment he felt when he escorted Elaina and her friends to the *Henrietta Marie*. They made him feel like a hero for helping them plan "definitely an A" project for their class next week. They then lunched at Fisherman's Wharf, followed by window-shopping in the numerous shops on the Galveston strip.

Despite the pleasure he drank in like oxygen, he stayed in contact with Helen, who after her rehearsal joined her girlfriends for drinks, dinner, and gossip.

If the days were sunny yellow, the nights were pure purple. The kingly treatment extended Sean by the girls didn't end when Helen returned to him Saturday night. She loved him like he'd never been loved before.

Even though she withheld the words he desperately wanted to hear, she showered him with her kisses, her bold and fearless caresses, her avowed passionate need to know his full possession without benefit of a condom.

On Sunday afternoon, Helen played for him. "A Remark You Made," he learned was the title of the song from the leader of the Advocates, four-piece jazz combo that performed in Herman Park that afternoon. It was a beautiful, haunting ballad he'd never forget.

***

Neither Helen nor Elaina wanted to return to their home Sunday evening. Once there, Helen regretted that Sean had not come with them.

The entire weekend, she had a sense that he was waiting for something. And while she had considered that that something was sinister like Howard Jackson appearing out of the blue, at home, she felt a change of heart.

As she readied for work on Monday, she thought there were things she failed to tell him, things in her heart, some of which she hardly understood. But she knew they were there.

"Mama ... telephone," Elaina yelled from her bedroom.

"Who is it?" she yelled back. *Now's the time* played like a mantra in her head.

Her heart began a crescendo, gradually increasing in tempo which each step she took, hurrying to the phone on her bedside table. *Tell him,* she told herself, stopping to draw a deep breath.

She picked up the receiver, holding it in both hands as she answered, "Hello," sitting on the side of her bed.

***

Lawyers, friends, relatives and the plain old curious waited for the judge and bailiff to return and renew the legal proceedings that began at 8 this Monday morning.

The noisy, crowded courtroom gave an indication of the serious backlog the courts faced, particularly as this was typically a civil court making a determination on bail for criminal defendants. A slew of them had gone by 10 this morning, and another waited to find out their fate before the Judge.

All that aside, Helen was not terribly displeased to be among the crowd, although she wished differently. Not only for her sake, but Claire's as well, she felt her presence necessary.

A call from Sgt. Benson, now teamed with Sgt. Diamond, informed her last evening that Howard Jackson was scheduled for arraignment. She called the prosecutor's office early this morning to ascertain that ADA Steve Moran was assigned the case.

Although Moran was new to the Harris County District Attorney's office, she didn't question his competency one bit. She was even more confident in his skills after she'd spoken with him.

"It's going to be all right," Sean whispered in her ear.

They were standing along the dark paneled wall in the back of the courtroom near the door.

"I guess I am a little nervous," she smiled back at him. Both were casually dressed. She was taking the day off to look for a new car.

"All rise," the Bailiff announced.

The courtroom quieted, all eyes shot to the front as Judge David Clark took the bench. The proceedings resumed with identification of the docket and case number: The State of Texas versus Howard Jackson.

Standing next to his attorney was Howard Jackson in prison orange, and Helen inhaled deeply. The charge was arson to which he pled "Not guilty."

"That lawyer represented Ray Butler," Sean whispered astonished in her ear.

Helen's gaze shot to him questionably, then back up to the front where Moran requested remand for the defendant, sneaking in that Howard Jackson had only recently been arrested for assaulting the attorney whose vehicle he torched. His attorney cried foul, and the judge banged his gavel on the desktop, in a demanding request for order.

Helen focused on the criminal defense attorney. While she didn't recall his name, she knew him by face as he was often in the media as one of the most successful and popular attorneys in the state. She was certain he cost a mint, and it was a mint in the form of a million-dollar bail that the State requested.

As the verbal spar between opposing counsels continued over bail, she wondered if Ray was footing the bill, remembering the superior tone and supreme confidence he exuded when he initially called her, taunting her with the fact that Howard would be out on bail before breakfast. She shivered at the thought that it could happen again.

"Put up or shut up," Judge Clark said as if bored.

The criminal attorney looked behind him, and Helen followed his gaze to a couple seated in the first audience row. The man nodded, and the attorney faced the judge.

"We call, your honor," he said, a smile in his voice.

Helen's heart sank. As if all of the wind had been knocked out of her, she sagged unconsciously against the wall.

"Don't worry, baby," Sean said softly, as he squeezed her hand affectionately.

She stared at him with her mouth open, thinking about Claire's safety. However, she noted the expression on his face suggested that he couldn't take his own advice.

The next case was called. Helen noticed the couple that was putting up Howard Jackson's bail looked to be in their late-sixties, early seventies. She guessed they were his parents, but neither turned so she could see their faces. Only the backs of their heads were visible as they conferred with the lawyer.

They were probably going to mortgage their home, she thought, staring from one, the woman, presumably his mother, to the other, the man, presumably his father as if looking for signs of kinship as they walked up the aisle toward the exit.

"Come on, baby, let's get out of here," Sean said, lightly tugging her hand.

Helen felt rooted to the spot, her gaze riveted on the couple, their heads close together in profile as they conversed on their way out.

At the exit door, the man turned his head incidentally, and his gaze met hers seconds before the pair walked out.

"Helen?" Sean whispered concerned.

Helen was shaking violently.

Chapter Thirty-One

"Do you have a hearing problem? I don't want to learn. I'm not interested in guns, or shooting, or anything like that!"

It was Tuesday night, and it had been a long day, Sean thought. Still, Helen's temper tantrum beat the hell out of her despondent tears, he mused as he laid out four different automatic handguns and revolvers on the island counter in her kitchen. He was undaunted by her drama. He wanted her to be protected and not a slave to fear. While a gun would not ensure both, at least she would be armed if Howard Jackson tried to attack her again.

"Where did you put my bottle of Remy?" she demanded.

Since the Judge remanded bail on Howard Jackson yesterday, Helen had practically depleted the emotional scale of despair. She was so bad off initially that he wanted to take her to the hospital. But like before - - the day Jackson assaulted her - - she recovered enough to function. It was all rote; however, for she could tolerate no new stimuli. The car-shopping trip had been postponed.

He looked down to where she kneeled in front of an island cabinet where she kept a fully stocked bar. He had removed the alcohol this morning.

"Sean?" she snapped, glaring up at him. "Where's the rest of my darn liquor?"

He ignored the question, and instead pointed to the display of guns. "Which one of these would you prefer? These two revolvers are Smith & Wesson J-frames. The grip on this one is removable and it has laser sight, which I recommend.

"This one is the James Bond Walter PPK. And this one, my favorite," he said, stroking the barrel affectionately, "is the Heckler & Koch P 2000. If you want to use this one, that's fine with me," he shrugged.

Helen stood slowly, her hands on her hips. She gave him a look that was more ominous than any active weapon on the market.

"Go home, Sean, and take your foolish toys with you," she rasped, and then she stormed out the kitchen.

Sean recited a litany of curses in his native Creole. Helen was more stubborn than his grandfather's mule, he thought, sighing deeply.

When he left last night after dinner and seeing her and Elaina home, she had seemed okay. Elaina called him around midnight to tell him that her Mama woke up screaming and crying about some monster. She was frightened as well. He came right over.

"Oh, wow!" Elaina gushed excitedly as she wandered into the kitchen to see the display of guns. "Who's going shooting?" she asked, picking up the smallest Smith & Wesson.

"It's not loaded now, but I want you to promise me that you'll be careful," Sean insisted lecture-like. "These are not toys. They are powerful weapons designed and intended to take the life of a flesh-and-blood human being."

"Okay, I got it," Elaina replied in a singsong rhythm, returning the gun carefully to the counter. "You should know that Mama doesn't like guns," she added, crossing to the stove.

"I see," he replied tiredly, recalling that he and Helen talked all night long last night. Or rather, she talked, and he listened.

He absolutely hated she had to put herself back in that place and time of emotional, physical, and sexual abuse in order to find the balance she needs to do more than survive, but live.

He felt murderous just listening, watching the torment that racked her body and tortured her soul.

But he knew it could not be ignored or pushed aside. Helen had suppressed the truth for years, so it stood to reason that her private revelation would entail an equally long process in order for her to heal.

"Anything left?" Elaina asked, lifting pots lids on the stove.

He hoped he was doing the right thing, referring to the guns as he turned his attention to Elaina. "Isn't it a little late for you to be eating?" he said, noting it was 9:30, according to the clock on the wall.

He amused himself thinking that if he swam as many miles as she and her teammates did nightly, he would be eating around the clock.

"I think I ate too fast, that's why I'm hungry again," she replied. "It's a testament to your great cooking," she grinned mischievously.

"How much is that going to cost me?" he laughed in reply.

"A cell phone?" she replied, looking at him hopefully.

"In the refrigerator." He had prepared shrimp fried rice and steamed vegetables for dinner. "We'll see what your Mama says about it." Helen, he learned, couldn't cook a lick.

Before she turned toward the refrigerator, he halted her with his tone, "Elaina, listen up, this is important." Assured he had her full attention, he continued, "The man who attacked your Mama, and we suspect who also torched her car, is out on bail."

Elaina's mouth dropped open and her eyes widened. "Is that why she's been acting all squirrelly again?"

"Yes," he said simply.

"That man," Elaina said cautiously. "Do you think he'll come after me, too?"

She was looking at him with such trepidation in her big brown eyes that Sean couldn't help himself. He rushed to her and pulled her into his embrace.

"Oh, no, baby," he said, holding her protectively. He didn't like the situation that caused it, but he liked that she looked to him as someone who could protect her from harm. He closed his eyes and silently prayed that he would always be what she needed him to be. "You don't have anything to worry about. Okay?" he added, kissing the top of her head.

"Will you teach me how to shoot a gun, too?" she asked, her gaze sliding up to his.

With consideration in his expression, Sean released her. He debated his reply as he cursed Jackson: criminals had no idea the depth or impact of their actions, he thought bitterly. Gun ownership as a hobby or as competition was one thing, but owning one with the mind that it would have to be used was something else. It was not a lesson he wanted to teach his children.

"I'll teach you something better," he said, thinking he would introduce her to the fields of anthropology, using Artifacts Inc. as his classroom.

"What?" she asked suspiciously, her brow cocked.

"It will be a surprise," he promised, smiling down at her.

"I like surprises," she grinned at him.

He tapped her nose. "Good. Don't forget you have kitchen duty tonight."

"I won't," she replied, crossing to the refrigerator.

"I'm going to see what your Mama has gotten into."

Helen might as well get it in her mind that he was part of their lives now, he thought. There was no way in hell that he was going to go away.

***

Soft lips stirred an awakening in Sean.

He knew it was very late. He didn't get to bed until nearly twelve, staying up to do some research; but mostly, just keeping occupied.

Helen who had stayed locked in her office practicing music all evening had apparently stolen up to the bedroom and was fast asleep. He knew she had to have been as tired as he was, but ...

His lids fluttered open, and his dark eyes found her bright ones in the soft light of the room riveted on him. He felt the clamorous flame of arousal and the sensual heat of her naked body. His pulse quickened.

Sean swallowed tightly and asked, "Nightmare?" He lightly stroked her warm body, up and down her sides. He felt her tremble. Slowly, she shook her head in negative fashion; her gaze reflected a wordless want. His manhood sprang to tumultuous life, poking the fabric of his drawstring pajama pants.

He rose on his elbows and called her name tentatively, "Helen," wondering if she were truly awake and knew what she was doing.

"Yes, Sean," she answered, her breath warm and moist against his face as she straddled him and pressed her lips to his, featherlike.

Hearing all he needed to hear, seeing all he needed to see, his arms snaked around her waist, crushing her to him as their mouths met in a kiss like the soldering heat that joins metals.

***

Helen was no longer shocked by her eager response to the touch of his lips that evoked a delicious sensation in her.

Neither questions nor reasons haunted her in his arms: she knew she was the woman he wanted, and he was Sean.

She simply gave herself over to his giving, relishing his man's hands on her body, kneading her flesh that responded as pliable as dough under his touches. Savoring his firm lips on her mouth, drinking the life of her soul. Treasuring this feeling of desire that invaded her senses silly.

Brown skin pressed against brown skin, light and dark shades of bodies intertwined. They rolled from one side of the bed to the other, as hunger rose and flared like savage animals, alternating positions, as domination was a shared thing between them, seeking delight in each other without limits.

Exquisite tension rose slowly, swelled rapidly, and descended again as limbs and lips touched and caressed, like lovemaking in the round.

He nibbled at the underside of her bosom, causing her pulse to skitter; his firm tongue seared a path down her abdomen, striking a vibrant chord in her; planted kisses on her inner thigh that wrought a curious swooping pull at her innards, and tongued her clitoris, bringing her to tears.

She blew hot air in his ear, jangling his insides with excitement; ran her fingers through the airs on his chest, causing his heart to pound an erratic rhythm; and tasted the hard fullness of him in her mouth, provoking an astral promise.

They sang ageless music with notes of passionate sighs, munificent moans, and breathless pants until neither could stand the sweet torture. Surrendering to overheated senses, he tossed her onto the bed on her back, almost violently. Instinctively, her hips lifted in sensuous invitation, and he accepted with a deep penetrating thrust.

She matched the steady rhythm he set driving into her. They were both the possessed, and the possessor, riding the exquisite wave of ecstasy until the earth fell away, and they went together to that place of rapture, utterly consumed.

Lying in the haven of his love, Helen fell asleep.

Chapter Thirty-Two

Even though it was Wednesday night, to Claire it seemed like a Friday after a long week of work and attending to yourself was the only thing looming in your future plans.

Music played from her new entertainment system in her living room with new modern furniture to match her new look.

She felt gay and relaxed and invincible as she piddled around in her new kitchen in a marine blue with new white appliances. All four burners on the stove blazed at a high heat, a huge pot on each. Two held rib slabs, while chicken filled the other two.

Shaking and singing to the music on her favorite radio station, she sprinkled a dash of seasonings in each, and then wiped her hands on the apron over her clothes. They were new, too, she thought, picking up her glass of wine on the counter.

Howard didn't approve of a woman wearing pants, and jeans were definitely out. If he saw her in the cut-offs she had on now, he would be livid.

She took a sip and muttered deliciously, licking her lips with her tongue. It was a merlot that Jules had picked out.

She smiled to herself, thinking of him.

He was another reason she was so happy.

Jules liked her new hairstyle, he liked how she looked in cut-off jeans and tee shirt, and he liked her for being Claire, a woman worthy of his respect. "When your divorce is final, look out, lady," he promised her, and she shuddered anew with joy.

Ms Parker called earlier to inform her that she was meeting with Howard's attorney tomorrow. She nearly pinched herself because she could hardly believe it … soon she would be a free woman.

Her prospects for the future never looked brighter, she laughed out loud.

The doorbell rang. She didn't have to wonder who it was, she thought, her insides jangling with holiday cheer. It was Jules, and she looked around to assure herself that his pipe was still on the coffee table where he left it.

Blushing uncontrollably, she set the wine on the counter, pulled off her apron, tossed it on the chair and then patted her cheeks, on her way to the front door, calling "Coming."

"You thought I was that nigger you been sleeping with, huh?"

It wasn't a question. The gun pointed at her chest meant this wasn't a friendly visit.

Claire backed up. She knew instinctively that her life depended on her reply, but she couldn't speak; hysteria bubbled up her throat instead of words to deny or confirm that she was indeed expecting Jules.

"You and me, we gonna have a little talk," Howard said, closing the apartment door behind him. He sniffed the air. "What's that I smell?

Trembling so that she could hardly stand, Claire thought about the meats she had boiling on the stove. She had been preparing the chicken and ribs for the school project tomorrow.

Dr. King was paying her handsomely for catering the meal; tomorrow, while the meat cooked on the grills at the Cooks Chambers, she would make a potato salad and prepare the beans. Jules volunteered to drive her out to Galveston and set up for the students' picnic lunch.

"You getting stuff ready to barbeque," he guessed, smiling at her.

Claire recognized that smile and knew it wasn't good omen as she stared at the man she had been married to for three years. He wasn't a bad looking man.

Smooth brown skin, the color of her biscuits that Jules liked so much, his thick hair cut close to his long, rectangular head, with thick brows and curling lashes that initially drew her attraction to him.

She should have paid attention to his weak mouth that grinned too easy or constantly shifting eyes, always suspicious that someone was trying to steal from him.

"What are you doing here?" Claire finally managed to get out breathlessly. Her heart was beating so hard in her chest that she thought she would faint.

"You mean how did I get here? Why, Claire, I thought you knew. I'm renting the apartment right above you," he said, laughing his hyena laugh.

"You been following me?" she asked as the idea overwhelmed her.

"Mm," he muttered thoughtfully as he poked his left index finger in his jaw, the gun steady in his right hand. "Moms did that for me. I think Henrietta helped, too."

"Henrietta?" she repeated dumbly. Her heart beat like a runaway train in her bosom.

"Oh, I forgot, you know her as Honey," he chuckled in reply. "Mama can't stand that name."

"Honey?" she echoed with disbelief. She hadn't spoken to Honey in almost a week, refusing to answer all calls from her friend. She had stopped trusting her that night, but she also believed her when she swore that she hadn't betrayed Claire. "No," she said, shaking her head in denial, "I don't believe you."

"Then you don't know my Moms."

Claire frowned. "You told me your mother was dead."

Howard shrugged indifferently.

"Why are you doing this? You don't want me, and I'm not asking for anything in the divorce," she said with pleading in her voice.

"I want to know about your attorney. What is she up to?"

"Huh?"

"You stupid heifer, can't you hear?" he rasped fiercely. He stalked her, forcing her to step back until she couldn't go any further than the couch at the back of her knees. "I said," he emphasized nastily, "tell me about your damn attorney. I want to know when she's taking her little girl to that slave ship."

"Why?"

"I ask the questions," he snapped impatiently. Suddenly, he grinned again. "Then you and me, we gonna have some fun ... like we used to."

"Howard." She closed her eyes. She knew with indiscernible certainty that he intended to kill her. "What about Toni, Howard? Who's going to take care of my daughter if I'm not here?"

"Mm," he muttered, feinting deep thought, and then that evil grin spread across his face again. "She's a little old for my dad's taste, but I'll find some good use of her.

Dear God, please save my baby, Claire prayed, knowing it was too late for her.

Chapter Thirty-Three

"Listen up, baby girl, you know how I feel about guns. A man who can't solve his problems by thinking them out is an idiot," James Parker recited his philosophy about guns and violence that Helen had heard all her life as his daughter.

"Then why are you calling me, Daddy?" Despite her gruff tone, her mind burned with the memory of a wonderful man who showed her what it meant to be loved. Her body was not unaffected either as her nipples hardened, creating the dull ache of desire for him.

James chuckled. *"He said you were in a bad mood."*

Sean had called her father when they had another argument about his insistence that she carry a loaded gun.

"When yawl getting married?"

"I'm not marrying that fool." The laughter in her voice contradicted her reply. She had been remembering the unprotected sex they had, not with worry, but wondrous wonder whether a little King was already growing inside her.

Her father laughed with her. *"Love him that much, huh?"*

More than I ever thought possible, Helen thought, although she had told neither her father nor Sean.

"Helen? Helen?" Miriam replied, snapping her fingers in Helen's face.

Helen looked at her with a jolt. "Sorry, Miriam, I guess I was somewhere else."

"No doubt with that handsome Dr. King," Miriam replied, her eyes alight with a teasing smile.

Helen chuckled. "Something like that." She gave herself a mental shake. After all today was Thursday, and her last day in the office for the week, so she might as well make the most of it. She was driving the rental, but she intended to be out of it after tomorrow. She and Sean were going to pick out a new car, for sure.

"What do you have for me this time?" she asked, looking at her wristwatch. It was 10:55. In the two hours she had been in the office, it had been practically work non-stop.

"Here's the contract Monique faxed over," Miriam replied, handing her several sheets of paper.

Helen nodded as she perused the contract. Monique Robbins-Thomas owned a popular nightclub in town called *T's Place*. She was among the dozen or so small business clients that she handled.

"Perry McDonald called while you were on the phone with Judge Wiggins."

Helen nodded, taking the pink slip Miriam handed her. "Did he sound hopeful?" Perry McDonald was a criminal defense attorney in Dalston, Texas that she had been trying to convince to come to Houston. If they joined their expertise, then each could expand their practice.

"He's willing to discuss it," Miriam replied. "He was on his way to trial, so if you miss him later this afternoon, he wants you to call him at home tonight."

"Perfect," she commented. "Are we about done for the day, Miriam?"

"Attorney Callier confirmed for one o'clock," Miriam replied.

Helen detected just a hint of disgust in Miriam's tone. "Don't kill the messenger," she said as much for herself as Miriam. Lindsay Callier was Howard Jackson's divorce attorney. "I know Lindsay. She's okay."

"Yeah, I know," Miriam said as if unconvinced. "Even the guilty deserves representation. I don't have to like it."

Miriam left Helen alone with her work, ostensibly to mull about the guilty or legal representation, or even her pending appointment. However, nothing pertaining to the justice system was on her mind.

Sean spoiled her this week with his constant, soothing presence and infinite patience, she mused, an unconscious dreamy smile on her face. She loved waking up next to him in the morning, and going to bed with him at night.

Elaina enjoyed him almost as much as she did. In fact, she would venture to say that their relationship bordered deep affection.

Helen picked up the receiver and held it to her bosom, debating whether or not to make this call. Baderinwa needed Sean to sign some papers, so he had to go to his office this morning, and even though she had her own work to do, she missed him already.

She had known it for days now, she told herself, punching out the seven numbers of his cell from memory. Believing that someone like her, meaning a survivor of child abuse, didn't deserve honest emotions like love, trust, or a beautiful man in her life, she had stubbornly - - and possibly stupidly, she conceded, chuckling - - denied the truth her heart spoke.

"Dr. Sean King is not available at this time. Please, leave a message at the sound of the beep," the recording instructed.

Although disappointed that Sean didn't answer, she listened to the mechanical voice and patiently waited for the beep, taking hurried breaths.

The beep sounded, and she replied, "Hi Sean," her voice sweet and lover-like.

"Sorry I missed you, but as I don't want to pass up another opportunity to tell you something, I guess I'll have to tell your stupid machine. You need to change that voice, by the way," she stalled, and then drew a deep breath.

"I love you, Sean King."

"Helen," Miriam's voice called over the intercom, "Miss Elaina is on the phone for you."

"I'm sure you'll want to talk about it later," she said, with joy coursing through her. Ending one call, she picked up the other. "Yeah, Butterscotch, what's up?"

"Sean wants us to meet him at the Henrietta Marie."

Helen frowned surprise. "When did he tell you that? I just called him. Is something wrong?"

"I don't know," Elaina replied. "I just know that Ms. Jackson called the office and left a message for me from Sean."

A skewed expression marred Helen's face. And she shifted uneasily in her chair, not sure how to take this.

Instead of going to her doctor today, Sean said he wanted to take her out to the range. And while she hadn't been looking forward to it, and thanks in part to her Daddy, the Smith & Wesson revolver was in her purse.

"Are you sure, Elaina?"

"Mama, I'm looking at the message right here in my hand," her daughter replied impatiently. "Something may have come up about our project tomorrow. I'm not even going to tell my group members until after I find out what it is. So will you come now, please?"

She did want to see him, Helen thought, leaning toward capitulation. Maybe by the time they got there, he would have listened to her message.

"Mama, are you still there?"

"Yes, Elaina, I'm here, and I'll be there shortly to pick you up."

***

Sean steered his Jag into the Wind Surf Apartments' driveway behind Jules who was driving the Artifacts, Inc. jeep.

According to Jules, Claire was to have arrived hours ago to put the meat on the grill. When she didn't answer any of his calls, he insisted on driving over. Sean came along to be sure that everything was all right. He, too, had a vested interest in Claire's safety.

He parked in the space next to his cousin, hoped out, and met Jules on the walkway to Claire's apartment.

"Did you stop to consider that maybe she just

overslept?" he asked, skipping to keep up with Jules long, hurried strides.

"Claire is not like that," Jules replied seriously. "Here it is," he said, knocking on the door of an apartment at the corner of the section. "She's one of the few women I know who does what she says she will." He knocked harder.

"Want me to run down to the manager's office and get a key?" Sean offered.

"No need," Jules replied, looking through the keys on his ring. He inserted one into the lock, turned the knob, and pushed open the door.

Sean was right behind Jules. He noticed it right away, and an uneasy sensation curled up his spine. Clothes, a woman's clothes - - shorts, panties, and bra - were haphazardly discarded in the otherwise neat living room.

"Wait here," he instructed Jules.

Following the design flow of the apartment, Sean cautiously walked into the dining area that flowed into the kitchen behind a wall. He saw the pots on the stove, but the burners were off. A frown settled between his brows at the bridge of his nose as he looked in each pot.

The meats for the barbeque, he thought, back pedaling his steps. Jules was no longer in the living room, and he hurried to the bedroom section of the apartment. Just as he reached the door, he heard Jules cry like a wounded animal in extreme agony.

"Oh, my God, no! Oh, sweet Jesus, Claire."

"Oh my God!" Sean echoed. Blood was everywhere, and what was left of Claire Jackson was barely recognizable. Someone had beaten her unmercifully in the face and made slashing cuts across her bosom, stomach and thighs.

"Ah, mon Dieu, non! Non! Ah, Jésus doux, Claire." Jules cried as he approached the bed. "Claire! Qu'a-t-il fait à vous? What did he do to you?" Jules cried repeatedly.

Sean raced to grab Jules, wrapping both arms around his cousin. "No, Jules. Let's go." Pulling and dragging an inconsolable Jules, he pleaded, "Allons, homme. Allons."

"Je suis vais le détruis!" Jules screamed, tears streaming down his face, shaking his fists in the air. "Je suis vais le tuer!"

Sean translated the vicious mantra, I'm going to kill him!" which Jules threatened as Sean lead him from the bedroom, into the living room, and out of the apartment. It was only then that he discovered he was crying, too.

"Je vais le tuer de mes propres mains," Jules cried, crumbling to the walkway in front of the apartment. ""Alors aidez-moi Dieu, je vais le tuer."

"And I'm going to help you," Sean promised, flipping open his cell phone to call the police. "With our bare hands, we're going to kill this animal."

Chapter Thirty-Four

Brown straw bodies were pressed against each other and stacked atop one another. People joked about "sardines in a can," but the reality of the Africans transported to the Americas was no laughing matter.

Helen gulped and closed her eyes on the padlock midway the area. It was a master lock, so to speak, that prohibited the Africans that were chained together from moving. The height of depredation they enjoyed was incalculable, from no toilet breaks and limited movement for thousands of miles at a time, only to be discarded and similarly subjugated on auction blocks for sale to people who proclaimed a superior humanity.

She concurred with the decision of those who managed to reach topside the slave ship in search of death with dignity in the depths of the ocean.

"Sean is going to make sure that it's hot in here tomorrow. We want them to get a feel for what it was like for the enslaved Africans."

Elaina was so excited about her group's history project that Helen wondered if her daughter understood the depths of the supreme humiliation the Africans suffered.

"You don't want anybody passing out," she said, trying to suppress the anxiety she felt from her voice. She was ill at ease, especially without Sean. If the cleaning crew had not been on board when they arrived, she doubly doubted she would have allowed Elaina to get her here.

Here was in the belly of the slave ship, the *Henrietta Marie*. Even though the narrow path was illuminated by discreetly placed yellow lights overhead, it was more shaded than light, and the sound quality like the eerie quiet of night shadows. Even though everything - - the polished floor, sparkling walls, clean fabric that held straw - - was made palatable for museum-like viewing, it all felt real to Helen, and she shivered as she followed Elaina.

"Aunt Pauline will be here, too."

Helen was nodding her head. Even though Pauline and Marcellus were technically Elaina's second cousin, because of their age and tradition, she referred to them as aunt and uncle. "Seems you and your group have thought of everything."

"Sean is having a woman for the Shrine of the Black Madonna Bookstore display some books on slavery, too," Elaina continued as animatedly as ever.

"After the presentation, we're going to have a barbeque at the beach. LaToya wanted us to serve here, but Sean said that we shouldn't make our classmates too uncomfortable that they wouldn't want to talk about the exhibit."

"Uh-huh," Helen replied because a reply was required.

"Remember where we went for the Juneteenth party?" Elaina resumed. "Uncle Marcellus is arranging that for us. Ms. Jackson is preparing the food. "

"Are you sure Sean told you to meet him here?" Helen asked. "Where is he?"

"Mama, will you calm down?" Elaina chided humorously, leading them deeper into the belly of the ship.

"I'll calm down when I see Sean," she quipped. "Where is he? I expected him to have met us topside." While they had lessened tremendously and she had grown stronger, he knew of her nightmares, that they still had the power to enslave her, albeit temporarily.

"The cleaning lady I saw said that he was down here."

"Well, I don't think I want to go any further."

"Mama," Elaina cried exasperated, stomping to Helen's side.

Helen refused to be moved by her daughter's tears or pleas, this time. She pulled her cell from her purse, intending to call Sean and turned around to follow the path back topside.

"Put the phone down."

Helen's pulse jetted as she and Elaina simultaneously spun around, facing the stack of fake bodies in the far corner where the middle cot-looking bed ended. It was as tall as her eye level, and there was another body above and below it. She tried to convince herself that it was just her overactive imagination.

"I said put the phone down, damnit," the brassy female voice snapped impatiently. "Can't you hear?"

"It's the cleaning lady," Elaina cried nervously as she backed into Helen.

Out of the shadows emerged a woman of average height, with a dark scarf wrapped around her long head, and while her facial features were still not clear the closer she moved into the light, Helen saw it was one of the cleaning crew ladies, so distinguished by the company uniform, a dark blue jumpsuit.

But instead of a mop, a gun was in her hand, and it was pointed at her and Elaina.

Sean's voice protruded the speaker on the tiny cell in her hand, instinctively raised in surrender. "Helen. ...Helen? ... Helen, is this you?"

Helen was too scared to answer him. She remained shocked frozen in fear.

The woman bared her teeth as she commanded fiercely, "Hang up the damn phone?"

With her hand trembling, Helen obeyed, closing the phone and slipping it into her handbag.

"Don't make me hurt nobody. At least not here. I ain't that kind of cleaning lady," the woman chuckled snidely.

"Who...who are you?" Helen stammered, her arm around her daughter, drawing her closer.

The woman stepped under the yellow, overhead light, and pulled the scarf from her head. "Don't you recognize me, Corinda?"

With terror racing through her, Helen gasped with recognition. She recalled initially thinking that the cinnamon brown complected face was hard, cruel, and pitiless. The beady brown eyes, long slender nose and wide mouth belonged to the woman from court, which she presumed was Howard Jackson's mother. She was as confused as she was afraid.

"You know you caused me a whole heap of trouble. Just like your mama. She stole Calvin from me, and then when she got tired of him, sent him back, twisted and warped in the head. Between you and Joann, I don't know which of you is the worst. … Henrietta, where are you?" Mrs. Jackson called out impatiently.

"I'm here, Mama."

Elaina and Helen both swung toward the noise made by the appearance of a woman that approximated a female welterweight as she stepped out from the opposite corner where she had been hidden in the shadows. She wore a similar outfit, her Afro sticking out from the front of the headscarf like bangs.

There was manliness about the woman called Henrietta, Helen thought, watching as she untwined string from a cylinder board. But it wasn't the most intriguing thought she had as she faced Mrs. Jackson. She had to be sure she understood correctly.

"You …" The thought shook her so badly she could hardly form the question. "You killed your own daughter?" she asked in a rush.

"Yes, I did," Mrs. Jackson admitted readily and unashamed. "Calvin couldn't keep his thing out of Taylor, and Joann found out about it. She was going to ruin everything," she said cruelly, shaking the gun. "I worked my ass off for years and years and years. You think I was go let her ruin everything I worked so hard for? Hell no, I wasn't!"

The woman was crazy if she didn't see that the hand bringing her down was her own, Helen thought, her mouth askew in repugnance. "I still don't understand. What do I have to do with it?"

"My God, you are a dumb heifer, aren't you?" she said with offensive amazement. "Just like your druggie, whore mama," she chortled sarcastically.

Helen wanted to slap her face, curse her for the vile admission, but the truth didn't hurt her as much as the pain and confusion on her child's face. She could only hope that Elaina saw her love of her through the tears streaming continuously down her face.

"She wasn't anything but a druggie. He only stayed with her because she gave him you. Henrietta," she nodded with her chin to the younger woman standing behind Helen, "had gotten too old."

Helen jerked her head toward the other woman as sympathy coursed through her like a leaden blanket. Henrietta ducked her head shamefully, and then looked up at her with defiance in her expression.

"But I wised up."

The pride in Mrs. Jackson's voice seized Helen's attention. She glowered at the embittered woman, aged by hate more than the passing years. And hatred had filled her with a warped resiliency, as well.

"I gave him Joann," Mrs. Jackson continued, her voice soft and dreamy with her ingenuousness. "He loved him some Joann, and then he wanted Taylor, too," she added bitterly. "But Joann never woulda found out if Patricia had minded her own damn business!" her voice rising with rage. "That's when Joann called you. She said she had enough evidence to have him arrested and put in jail." She shook her head. "I couldn't let that happen."

"Why didn't you just leave him? He's the one who's not worth it?"

"Leave him?" Mrs. Jackson replied as if the idea were preposterous. "For what? I invested my whole life in him. Besides, girls ain't worth nothing … nothing but trouble."

Mrs. Jackson, Helen mused, was a spoke in the cycle of abuse. She had probably been violated sexually and emotionally as a child. Because of the violation, she learned to hate herself, blaming her powerlessness on her gender. She found power by mimicking her oppressor, justifying it because no one protected her.

"What about you?" Elaina asked innocently. "You were a girl once."

Mrs. Jackson smacked Elaina on the side of her head. Elaina cried out, and Helen reacted by advancing toward Mrs. Jackson who halted her instantly as she cocked the gun. "Children should be seen, not heard."

"Mama, we need to go before somebody comes," Henrietta said warily.

Mrs. Jackson chuckled. "Ain't nobody coming down here. They scared these straw bodies go materialize into real slaves and rise up and take their revenge."

Her evil laugh vanished as she commanded, "You, little girly, come here," pointing to Elaina. "Henrietta, you know what you supposed to do.

"Mama."

Helen felt utterly helpless to answer her daughter's cry for help with action as Mrs. Jackson jerked Elaina to her side. But motherly instinct caused Helen to twitch and the woman lifted the gun to Elaina's head. The message was clear, and Helen froze.

"Put your hands behind your back," Henrietta instructed Helen.

Helen adjusted the strap of her handbag on her shoulder, and then put her hands behind her back. Henrietta tied them together.

"Where are you taking us?" Elaina asked, tears streaming down her face.

"We're going for a nice boat ride," Mrs. Jackson said, gesturing with the gun. "And Ms. Parker, if you don't do exactly as I say, I'll kill your daughter."

***

It was another typical June summer day, pristine, ever sunny, and hot as hell. Atypical was the carnival of police that dominated the apartment complex parking lot nearest Claire Jackson's apartment.

Blue and whites, and two different black-and-whites styles of police cars arrived like a parade, retarding traffic on the main thoroughfare. A news truck had joined the fold and the number of curious onlookers had grown to a crowd.

A desolate Jules and an anxious Sean were sitting in the backseat of a black-and-white State Police cruiser. They had given statements twice, to two different sets of policemen.

A jurisdictional turf war nearly ensued when HPD homicide investigators Diamond and Benson arrived on the Kemah, Texas property. Not far away, several police officers stood huddled together, trying to straighten the mess out, stalling justice for the death of Claire Jackson.

Sean felt that he had donated more than enough time to them, as he scrolled to "Outgoing Calls" on his cell.

The time indicated was 12:17. It was his call to Helen when he'd gotten no answer, just a garble of voices in the background.

He looked at his wristwatch: 12:19, and then out the back window of the cruiser where the cops were still in conference. The sense of uneasiness he felt did not diminish.

"Jules, I got to go," he said, opening the door.

"Where?" Single syllable words seemed all Jules could manage as he turned red, red eyes on Sean.

Considering that Claire Jackson was dead, no doubt by the hands of Howard Jackson, it wasn't a leap in rationale that Jackson would then go after Helen. "I believe Helen's in trouble."

"Jackson?" Jules perked up.

Sean nodded. His phone was already opened, the number dialing as he walked off toward his car in a maze of police cruisers. He hoped they didn't block him in.

"Hey, where do you think you're going?" a uniform patrolman yelled at him.

Sean ignored, talking on his cell. "Miriam, this is Sean; do you know where Helen went?" he asked in one breath.

"She and Elaina were supposed to meet you on that slave ship," Miriam replied as if he should have known.

"Helen raced out of here, canceling her one 0'clock because Elaina told her that Ms. Jackson called and instructed them to meet you there.

"Sean, is everything all right? They should be there by now. Aren't they there, yet?"

"God, I hope not," Sean replied, his heart pumping fear through his veins as he started running to his car. Jules was only a step behind him.

"Hey, Sean. Hold up!"

Sean realized Sgt. Diamond was calling him. He paused only because he had to open his car door; Jules was already getting in on the passenger side. "Helen's in trouble," he yelled, getting in the car. He started the engine and shifted into reverse. Before he backed out, Sgt. Diamond stood in front at the trunk of his car, talking to someone on his cell through the earpiece connection.

Sean leaned on the horn as he rolled down his window and yelled out, "Get the hell out the way!"

Sgt. Diamond indicated for him to wait. It was only seconds but Sean felt years steal through his body, aging him.

Sgt. Diamond ended his call, and while dashing to his car, yelled, "Jackson's in Texas City. He's got a boat."

Sean gunned his engine, and Sgt. Diamond jumped out of the way. Sean backed up in a jerk, shifted into first gear, and shot off the parking lot.

"Vous ne pouvez pas m'éloigner de toi, salaud." Jules muttered under his breath, alternately rubbing his hands together and then looking at them.

Sean concurred as he drove like a madman through the traffic, running red lights and stop signs, weaving in and out between other drivers.

Texas City was roughly 15 miles away. But they were in Seabrook where they lived, and right across the bridge where yachts and sailboats gleamed and glimmered in the sun at the Kemah marina, he and Jules stored their boat.

They owned a Sunseeker XS2000; it was a speedboat with a horsepower of 700. It was supposed to have been a pleasure toy, but they had had to work hard for its purchase, upkeep, and storage that they hadn't gotten around to the fun part yet.

"Jules, how fast can we go in our boat?" Sean asked, his foot pressing the gas pedal to the floor, zooming past irate drivers who honked their horns after him.

Jules gave him a sly chuckle. "'Bout 200 miles per hour," his Creole French pronounced with thoughts of vengeance.

"Assuming Jackson has a fishing boat," Sean said, pensively, "about how fast can he go?" He knew for certain that they could reach Galveston faster on the water than on the streets.

"On average, if it's just a fishing boat, 'bout 60 miles, maybe 70."

"Call up the marina," Sean instructed, tossing Jules his phone. "Tell 'em to get the Sunseeker out. We're going fishing," he said cryptically, an evil grin on his face.

***

The throttle stalled. The boat rocked gently in the calm currents of Galveston Bay, a few yards out from the Texas City Dike boat ramp.

They were on a fishing boat that had seen its share of the deep sea. About 30 feet long, it was fully equipped for extended use on the water, and had a square cockpit, where Howard Jackson was manning the control under the beam protected from the hot sun, his mother cursing angrily at his side.

Her daughter, Henrietta had been assigned the task of watching the prisoners. She sat on the other side near the bait well, holding a gun on Helen and Elaina.

It was clear to Helen now that Claire was dead. The Jacksons, a dysfunctional family of freaks, used Claire to get to Helen. They understood the quickest way to do that was through Elaina.

Her dear Sean couldn't help her now. If she didn't think of a way to escape, she and her daughter were assured the fate Claire suffered.

There were quite a number of boats on the bay. Although there was little wind, a few sailboats dotted the waters along with shrimp and fishing boats.

Helen let herself hope that Sean was racing to the rescue and would reach them in time.

Mrs. Jackson turned to inspect them. After casting a warning gaze to remain alert and mindful at Henrietta, who nodded in return.

Satisfied that their quarry was secure under her daughter's watchful eyes, she assumed her position next to Howard who was still trying to get the boat started.

Mrs. Jackson was the obvious leader. Helen recognized her biological mother in the feisty, old woman. Her son Howard, who looked in his late 30s, was her most devoted follower. Henrietta, slightly older than Howard, seemed afraid of her.

It was in Henrietta that Helen believed help would most likely come from, having detected a certain vulnerability or reluctance to go along with her mother's deadly plan.

While riding in the truck and even through the transport process from the truck to the boat, Mrs. Jackson had precluded all conversation. She did most of the talking, and even that was reduced to barking out orders and commands.

During the ten minutes ride from Galveston to Texas City Dike, the world's longest manmade fishing pier, she learned the woman believed that Joann had told her the family secret.

She knew that telling the woman that she never spoke to her daughter Joann was useless.

Although it had not been fully divulged, she could discern enough from their coded language and behavior toward one another that the family practiced incest. The subservience of the children to the mother also suggested that domestic violence was an intrinsic component of their lifestyle, as well.

Incest.

When she and Sean were not arguing about guns or making love, they talked about it. She spoke of what she could remember; he provided insight based on his knowledge and research. While incest was more common than most people believed or were willing to admit, Sean went so far as to proclaim it was a universal phenomenon.

Helen didn't care how old or widespread incest was. She simply wanted a law that made it more punishable than a slap on the wrist.

It stole a child's childhood, and in some cases, it killed, completely destroying a life.

Finally, the engines caught, and Howard carefully steered the boat farther away from shore, and then picked up speed. Everything on land got smaller; people and vehicles miniaturized the deeper they delved into the bay.

Helen knew Sean was on land somewhere trying to find her and Elaina by now. But she wouldn't let herself believe he would reach them in time.

"It's a miracle you're as sane as you are," Sean told her one night. *"You have your parents, the Parkers, to thank for that."*

The Parkers had given her more than safety, she mused, taking in their wet surroundings. James and Candace Parker gave her a life, a reason for living. It was **that** courage she wanted to pass on to her child.

Seated next to her daughter, whose hands were now also tied behind her back, she knew what she was thinking was risky. Howard steered the boat toward the longest pier beyond the tip of the dike.

The water was deeper there, the sharks, a certainty. But Elaina could swim, and she had a good, strong kick; hopefully, once she hit the water, she could get her hands in front of her and reach the safety of the shoreline.

That's what she prayed desperately for.

Helen averted her head as if interested in the endless stretch of blue sky and ever-present sun and murmured softly in her daughter's ear, "Get ready to swim."

"What did you say?" Henrietta shouted over the loud din of the engines.

Helen was grateful her daughter seemed to understand without complaining. They shared a loving smile. Though they could very well end up being sharp bait or victims of multiple gunshot wounds, she was sure it was better than the fate awaiting them. They had no choice.

"Help us," she beseeched Henrietta in a soft conspiratorial voice, casting a stealthy glance toward the cockpit.

She saw Henrietta swallow in her throat as her gaze shifted toward her mother and brother, both of them whose backs faced them. She turned sad eyes on them, looking from her to the Elaina. She shook her head vehemently and quietly replied, "I can't."

Helen was disappointed, although she halfway expected it. Henrietta was trapped, a slave to her mother's domination.

But she refused to linger in regrets. Her own daughter's life was at stake, as well as her own, Helen thought squashing her fear.

Stealthily, she began to lift her feet, pressed together, off the boat floor. She felt Elaina move, as well.

Suddenly, the boat swerved violently, and they were tossed to the floor. The boat curved in the opposite direction, and they rolled to the other side of the floor.

It was as if Howard played a cat-and-mouse game on the water with a reckless driver. He was pushing the engines for all they were worth.

Chaos broke out above them, and although she and Elaina couldn't see, they heard guns firing.

Not only from the boat, but also toward the boat.

Helen wondered what was going on as she saw Henrietta trying to hold onto something. The boat swerved again, and Henrietta fell overboard.

"This is the Texas Coast Guard. Stop your engines now!"

Chapter Thirty-Five

It was early evening, a little or so after 7. The sun looked determined to shine all night over the bay. African American Classical Music played, improvisational and melodic notes mingled with the pungent aroma of burning charcoal and hickory, as Sean barbequed on Baderinwa's patio.

"I love you, Sean King."

Helen, reclined in the lounge chair, with a tall drink, turned her head to the side to look at Sean. He stood before the large, stainless steel outdoor cooker, turning the meat over on the pit as he swayed from side to side in tune with the music. The cell was attached to the waistline of his shorts. Back or front, she thought, he was absolutely gorgeous. "Somebody's going to take that from you," she said playfully.

"I dare them," he replied laughingly.

Helen sipped her drink, smiling pleased about her life and the direction it was going. Just hours ago, she was in fear for her future and that of her daughter, who no doubt was hiding out in the bathroom, playing with her new toy.

Since their return from the ordeal and a side, shopping trip, Sean barely let them out of his sight. She and her daughter needed to talk about what happened to them, she thought, recalling her recent attempt to do so.

Her brave Elaina promised, "Later, Mama," simply wanted to put it out of her mind for a while.

The evening news showed the dramatic capture of the fishing boat trying to dodge a speedboat in the Galveston Bay. Her hero to the rescue, she smiled.

The smile faded as she wished someone could have saved Claire, and a touch of melancholy coursed through her. Jules, who she never suspected of such deep emotions, was badly shaken up.

Claiming he needed purpose in his life, he volunteered to drive to Texas A&M to pick up Toni from swim camp. He was going to bring her back here to the compound, until her family in Chicago could be located.

"I love you, Sean King," the recording of her voice on Sean's cell played again seconds before he joined her, dropping into the patio chair next to the recliner.

"You know you really don't have to play that so much," she said, reaching out to take his hand.

"I can't help myself," he grinned in reply. "I just love hearing it."

Helen sat up, put down her drink, and sat on his lap. She took his face between her hands. "I love you, Sean King."

Sean wrapped his arms around her and pressed his head against her bosom. He gave her a quick, affectionate squeeze. "I've never been so scared in my life."

"Then we were thinking along the same lines," she replied, holding him dearly against her. "I feared we would never see you again, and then I remembered what you said the other night, about my parents saving me. When I realized it wasn't just my life they saved, I knew I had to do something. Thanks to you, I believed in myself enough to realize I had the courage to act, that I didn't have to be a victim."

"Where do we go from here, my belle?" he asked, his accent thick and eyes smoldering with adoration and love.

She shuddered under his intense look and chortled amused. "Not one to let grass grow under your feet, are you?" she teased, kissing his lips gently.

"I told you before," he replied, looking up in her face. "When I see something I want, I go after it."

"And you're sure you want to be saddled with a woman and her teenage daughter?"

"Saddled is not the word I would use, but yes. When are we getting married?"

"Okay, you two lovebirds, break it up," Marcellus teased as he and Pauline walked out onto the patio.

"You know, you and Baderinwa have the worst timing than anybody I know," Sean replied laughingly.

Reaching them, he and Helen hugged with deep affection at length. "I'm glad you're okay," he said over her head.

"Me, too," Helen replied, and then shared a hug with Pauline. "You've been here before, I understand," she took them both in her gaze. She knew that before they married, a crazed woman tried to kill Marcellus, and it was Pauline who came to his rescue.

"Being able to walk away makes you a little more appreciative of life," Pauline said. She shared a smile with her husband.

"I know what you mean," Helen replied.

Baderinwa walked out, carrying a tray of meat. "Come on, chef, do your duty," she said to Sean.

With a springy bounce, he hopped right up and went to the grill. As they arranged chickens and slabs of rib on the grill, Helen thought of Claire again.

Sean wouldn't tell her how Claire died, but when she overheard the policeman arrest Howard for her murder, she shivered knowing that her death had been brutal and vicious.

Marcellus poured glasses of lemonade from the pitcher on the table. As he took one to Pauline, who had taken the recliner on the other side of Helen, said, "On the way over, we heard that the husband turned himself in."

"With an attorney in tow," Pauline added, taking a recliner on the other side of Helen. "What a jerk!"

Helen looked at Sean the same instant he looked at her in exchange of knowing. The *Slave Master* would die of old age in jail.

Marcellus sat at the table. "He said his wife killed his daughter, Joann Butler."

"Already, they're turning on each other," Helen said absently.

She remembered that Mrs. Jackson and Howard remained belligerently silent when they were captured. Once Henrietta was pulled from the water, she just looked relieved that it was over.

"Maybe, just maybe, the whole truth will come out," she said, taking a sip of her drink.

Neither Marcellus nor Pauline knew about her past before she was adopted, or that Calvin Jackson was her biological father, in all likelihood. She almost concurred with Pauline: he was worst than a jerk.

"Hear anything about Ray Butler?" Sean asked, as he rejoined them.

"Oh," Baderinwa said, "I forgot to tell you. He's withdrawing from the race and retiring from politics." She poured herself a drink and sat among them.

"What brought that on, I wonder?" Helen asked, exchanging a look with Sean.

"He said that his wife's death has affected him so that he doesn't believe that he's the right person for the people now."

Helen was thinking that Sean was right, even though he didn't come straight out and say it: Ray Butler knew more than he admitted.

"Baderinwa," Elaina called from the kitchen door, "telephone."

As she sauntered inside, Baderinwa said, "If you guys want to play some cards, you know where the table is."

"I got it," Marcellus volunteered to disappear inside.

"Baby, do you need something from inside?" Sean asked Helen. "I need to check my sauce."

"I'm fine, thank you," she replied. She couldn't help smiling, basking in his attention. She wondered how long it would last. "Where're the boys?"

"They're inside with Elaina," Pauline said. "I see she has a new toy."

Helen threw back her head, laughing. "Sean's going to spoil her rotten if I can't reign him in from buying everything she thinks she wants."

"Yeah, he's probably going to affect the TV ratings, too, cause them to lose at least one viewer."

Helen frowned. "What?"

"Let's see," Pauline replied thoughtfully. "There was Malik Yoba; at least, he was a movie star, a lot better than the make believe Richard Davis and Mark Stone, and whatever other names you concocted."

"You mean, I wasn't convincing?' Helen chuckled surprised. She thought she had done a good job, selling her make-believe lovers to her friends and family.

"Girl, please," Pauline replied, joining her in laughter.

***

"Patricia called me last month. She was dying. I drove out to Beaumont to see her. My granddaughter rode with me."

He wasn't nearly as big as he appeared in her dreams, Helen thought dispassionately. Age had softened the muscular arms and torso she remembered, and even shrunken them a little, so that the *Slave Master* resembled a frail old man.

Gray streaked his dark hair and wrinkles lined his leathery brown face. She didn't recognize him when he appeared in court the day Howard was arraigned; she barely recognized him now.

"You sick bastard, you raped your own granddaughter!"

Sgt. Benson had to wrap both his arms around Sgt. Diamond's waist to prevent him from physically assaulting Calvin Jackson who possessed the common sense to shriek away and huddle in self-protection. The interrogation room offered no hiding, and the video camera caught it all.

"I told you I'm sick," Jackson cried. "I need help."

Their roles had been set beforehand, Helen mused, observing the tactic of good cop and bad cop. It was obvious who was whom when Sgt. Benson promised, "We'll get some help for you, Mr. Jackson," courteously. "Go on with your story, please sir."

"He's only going to lie," Sgt. Diamond exclaimed hotly.

Sgt. Diamond contacted Sean this morning about the interview that occurred last night, wanting to know if he'd like a copy. Helen's unwitting and unsuspecting involvement was revealed.

A copy was transferred to a CD and sent over by courier several hours ago, arriving shortly before Ray Butler sent flowers along with an apology.

Her lover had thrown them out, she recalled, impish dimples appearing on her face. She agreed with the measure, as well as his supposition that had Ray spoken up sooner about what he learned of his in-laws, then all of this could have been prevented.

Helen watched the interview in Sean's home office, sitting at his massive ebony desk. The big screen of his computer showed as clear an image as any piece of video equipment.

"Patricia wanted me to contact the daughter we had together," Jackson continued.

"For what?"

"She didn't think she was going to die. She kept talking about how she was going to beat that virus and start her life over. But she needed money. She had learned that our daughter was a lawyer and believed it was Joann. Pat figured she was good for the money."

Helen couldn't remain totally unaffected hearing that the woman who gave her life never felt anything for her but contempt. A sense of despondency crept into her bosom and seeped through her like a poison.

"Who killed your daughter, Joann Butler and her daughter, Taylor, Mr. Jackson?" Sgt. Benson asked.

Even on her dying bed, Helen thought feeling disgust and anger, the woman expressed no remorse or sadness about the poor quality of her mothering.

"Joann found out that I touched Taylor."

"You more than touched her!" Sgt. Diamond shouted.

Calvin Jackson seemed to slacken in his seat, as if willing himself to disappear. "She threatened to call the police," he continued in a small voice. He swallowed. "My wife ... you have to understand," he said, his expression pleading for sympathy from the detective.

"Shirley was sick. Like me. But we had respectability. She didn't want to lose that."

"How convenient blaming your wife," Sgt. Diamond rasped, his expression a mask of rage and disgust.

"It's the truth," Jackson insisted forcefully. "Shirley and Howard did it together."

"Are you sure it wasn't you, Mr. Jackson, who couldn't run the risk of losing your respectability?" Sgt. Benson began in a calm, matter-of-fact tone that quickly evolved into a vicious one as he detailed the police's belief of what happened.

"Your daughter who was married to a politician was pregnant with your child. When she found out that you had raped Taylor -- after promising you wouldn't touch her -- she was going to make sure you didn't harm her next child. And when you learned that she had contacted an attorney. . the woman you and Patricia Daigre gave away, well, you couldn't have that! You had to get rid of her."

"No! I loved Joann!" Jackson cried.

"You picked up the little girl from swim practice," Sgt. Benson continued.

"Seeing her in a bathing suit turned you on, didn't?" Sgt. Diamond taunted, an evil grin on his face.

"You took her someplace, assaulted her, and then killed her," Sgt. Benson said, slamming the table with his fist.

Jackson jumped, but continued to proclaim his innocence. "No, no, it wasn't me, I swear! It was my wife!"

"You sneaked her dead body back into the Butler home and waited for Joann to come home."

"It was Shirley! You have to believe me. Shirley did it. Her and Howard."

Helen knew she had seen enough. She clicked the mouse, and the image froze on the three men in the small green room.

It was unfortunate, she thought, that she would not be the last. The last female who had her childhood taken away from her, the last female victim of rape or some type of abuse, the last female victim of murder.

She closed her eyes on the teardrop that rolled down her cheek. More fell as she quietly cried for Toni whose mother had been stolen from her and all the Claires who suffered a similar fate.

She cried for Joann who had become so entrenched in the sick lifestyle that by the time she decided to take back her freedom, it was too late, costing her and her daughter's lives.

Helen dried her eyes with her hands and determined that there would be no tears for her. She was one of the lucky ones.

Her parents, Candace and James Parker were in town. They arrived this morning to see the man who had claimed her heart. Of course, her blabbermouth cousin Marcellus had something to do with their presence, she chuckled.

But Sean King had done a lot more than that. He challenged her with his frankness and consuming patient interest. He showed her that she was worth loving and how to love herself. He embraced the lost and scared child who lived inside her and nurtured the woman she had become with patience and tenderness and love. She shuddered thrilled, recalling his smoldering passion for life and giving.

Helen ejected the CD from the computer and tossed it in the trash. Rising, she headed for her future. With every step she took toward the door, she felt a sweet buoyancy invade her body.

On her way to the future, she mused, opening the door.

Sean who had been sitting on the floor by the door stood. She heard the lively and boisterous din drifting here from the patio where both their families were celebrating. His black eyes roved her, alight with concern, burning with emotions.

"Are you …?" he asked in a slightly anxious voice.

Helen placed a finger on his lips, shushing him. She kissed him on the mouth gently, and then took his hand. "Let's join the party," she said smiling brightly.

Together, they walked toward family and an affair for forever.

--the beginning—

ACKNOWLEDGEMENTS

A big thanks to the late Mel Fisher whose Society of divers discovered the Henrietta Marie slave ship and realized her value; and authors Ellen Bass & Laura Davis, <u>The Courage to Heal</u>, and Grant Cameron, <u>A Guide for Men Helping Female Partners Deal with Childhood Sexual Abuse.</u>

Gratitude for old friends who have always been present for the journey - - Joy Kamani and Sam Sloan-English; plus loved ones who chipped in with research, godson Che Kamani and son Sherman II, and former anthropology professors, Drs. Susan Rasmussen, Janis Hutchinson, and Dorothy Franzone.

And my most supportive editors, first kudos to an angel who lives in the memories of many, Monica Harris, my first editor; and the dynamic duo of reader/editors Taita (Barbara) Meloncon, and Marcia Johnson.

I own all the errors, which I hope you will forgive. But most of all, I hope you enjoy the read.

ABOUT THE AUTHOR

Margie Walker is one of the original Arabesque writers. She is also the author of ebooks A SLICE OF REPARATIONS, the first in a mystery series featuring Marcia Chenault-McKissack and romantic suspense IN BLOOD ONLY. Write Margie at www.margiewalker.net.

67673825R00261

Made in the USA
Charleston, SC
17 February 2017